MYSTERY AT LAKE NOJIRI

TITUS IVAN MAUNDREI

outskirts press

Mystery at Lake Nojiri

v2.0

This is a work of fiction. Names, characters, businesses, places, events, locales, and incidents are either the products of the author's imagination or used in a fictitious manner. Any resemblance to actual persons, living or dead, or actual events is purely coincidental.

The opinions expressed in this manuscript are solely the opinions of the author and do not represent the opinions or thoughts of the publisher. The author has represented and warranted full ownership and/or legal right to publish all the materials in this book.

Outskirts Press, Inc.
http://www.outskirtspress.com

ISBN: 978-1-9772-2282-4

PRINTED IN THE UNITED STATES OF AMERICA

This book is dedicated to my son, Ken, without whom I would not have had a character for my story.

THANKS AND ACKNOWLEDGEMENTS

Special thanks to my patient wife, Mako Beecken, who checked my use of Japanese and confirmed and/or corrected my accounts of Japanese customs and culture.

Thanks, also, to Allison Elliott for the cover artwork for this book.

And finally, thanks to the group The Verve whose CD "Urban Hymns" I listened to repeatedly while writing and which inspired my writing muse.

TABLE OF CONTENTS

ABOUT THE AUTHOR

Tim Beecken adopted the pen name of Titus Ivan Maundrei because the initials spell out—well, you can see what they spell.

Tim was born in Bethlehem, Pennsylvania in 1949 but grew up in the town of Annaka in Japan, where his parents were missionaries and he was known as a neighborhood terror. He attended Elmhurst College outside of Chicago where he somehow managed to graduate despite too many hours spent in the TV lounge of his dormitory. After four years of wandering from job to job—including taxi driver in Chicago, ditch digger, youth outreach worker, and other menial jobs, Tim moved back to Japan where he taught English for nine years in a women's junior college. While there, in 1979 he married Masako (Mako) who also taught English but was not one of his students.

In 1985 the Beeckens moved to Fort Collins in Colorado where they attended Colorado State University (CSU) and earned Master degrees in Teaching English as a Second Language. This time Tim studied in earnest and achieved a 4.0 average. Mako was hired by CSU where she taught Japanese for 30 years before retiring in 2018.

Tim became a stay-at-home dad once their son, Ken, was born in 1987, teaching Japanese part-time at a local elementary school and occasionally organizing and leading sightseeing tours for Japanese people. He continues to enjoy teaching Japanese to elementary school children and volunteering every morning in various classes at the school where he teaches. He no longer plays kickball in the living room with Ken, but Ken and his wife, Crystal, occasionally join Ken's parents for sessions of mah jong.

Tim hopes that children of many ages—and adults—will enjoy this novel, sharing not only the main character's experiences, but also learning something about Japan.

PROLOGUE

THE BREAK-IN

The cabin was dark and held the musty smell of summers gone by when they broke in. By the light from a flashlight, the older one picked up a rock that was lying nearby and using it as a hammer, smashed a glass pane of the back door.

"Man, that's loud. Somebody's gonna hear us," the younger one whispered nervously.

"Hey, don't sweat it. There's nobody up here this time of year." The older one reached through the now jagged hole in the door and unfastened the lock from the inside.

"Good thing these people don't have a wooden shutter on the door, huh," the younger one said. He dreaded the thought of what they would have had to go through to enter a cabin with a solid wooden storm door on it.

"I know. That's why I picked this one. Come on, get inside," the older one ordered.

The two slipped inside the silent building, shutting the door behind them. The older one ran the beam of his flashlight over the walls of the room in which they were standing.

"It's usually in the kitchen," he said. And then, "Yeah, there it is," as the narrow ray of light found the fuse box. A few quick steps and he was in front of the box. Reaching up he pulled the master switch to the "on" position. Immediately lights blazed on throughout the cabin.

"Aw, come on, man!" protested the other. "Somebody's gonna to see us."

"Relax. RELAX! How many times do I have to tell you, there's nobody else up here this time of year. And besides, all the window shutters are closed. Nobody's gonna see us."

"I still think we shoulda picked a place farther from the road. What if one of the local people goes by?"

"Do you wanna do this or not?" The older one was irritated now, nearly shouting.

"Well, yeah, but..."

"Then shut up with all the complaining." His voice turned softer, forgiving. "Listen. I've been planning this one for months. And I've done this before. There's nothing to worry about. Like I told you, I picked this place 'cause it's near the road so they'll think some locals or some fishermen or somebody like that did it. And this time of night nobody comes by here anyway. I've been coming here for years and I've checked everything out."

"OK. OK. I'm with you man. I'm just a little nervous, OK? It's the first time I've ever done anything like this."

"Hey, no sweat. It's no big deal. Come on, let's get to work."

The white sheets covering the furniture stood like ghostly sentinels. Ignoring them, the two went through the house systematically, room by room, opening drawers, cabinets, closets, dumping the contents on the floor, looking for anything that might be valuable. A half hour later the two stood together in what had once been a cozy, shipshape dining room/living room. Now the floor was littered with empty drawers, books, and clothing. The sheets that had been used as dust covers on the furniture lay crumpled on the floor.

"Didja find any money?" The older one was perspiring now, his face flushed from both the exertion and the excitement of the moment.

"Nah. But I found some CDs. They probably have some teenagers."

"Yeah, they do. She's a freshman at my school."

"You mean you know these people?" asked the younger one.

"Yeah. The girl's a real nerd. What else you got?"

"That's about it. Looks like they took all the good stuff with them when they left. Must have taken the CD player, too. There's that old radio there".

"That's not worth anything. Any booze?"

"No. Just a bottle of cooking wine. Not too much food. Just cooking stuff. Soy sauce, oil—junk like that. How about you? What'd you find?"

"Not a stinking thing. That's the trouble with the people who come up here. Most of them don't have anything valuable here."

"How about the TV?" The younger one nodded toward the old Sony sitting on a table in the corner.

"Nah. Too big to carry. It looks pretty old, anyway."

"Well, let's get outta here, then."

"Uh uh. Not yet. Now comes the fun part."

"What..."

"Check this out, man." The older one picked up a vase that had been sitting on a table.

"You think that's worth something?" asked the younger

one. "Like maybe it's a rare vase or something?"

The older one turned to him with a strange, sinister gleam in his eye. Suddenly, without warning, he heaved the vase across the room with all his might, straight through the screen of the television set which exploded in a flash of shattered glass.

"What're you doing?" shrieked the younger one. His face turned pale.

His partner gave him a sly, sideways glance, then grabbed a glass dish from a cabinet and hurled it across the room. The plate shattered against the wall, splattering jagged shards across the wooden floor. Then he took a delicate, porcelain teacup from the cupboard and placed it in the hand of the younger one.

"You try it," he commanded.

"Aw, man, I didn't plan on this," he choked. "I thought we were just gonna take some stuff."

"Do it!" demanded the older one. His voice was cold but his eyes were fire. "Do it!"

The younger one halfheartedly flung the cup on the floor. It cracked but didn't break.

"Again!" barked the older one, handing over another cup. This one made it to the wall and disintegrated into dozens of tiny pieces.

"Again!" This time there was more power in the throw, and the cup connected with a clock on the wall, splintering the clock's face as well as the cup itself.

The beginning of a smile worked its way into the corners of the younger one's mouth.

"Wow. This is really... I don't know man, it's..."

"Do another." This time it was a large serving dish that smashed into a bookcase, leaving fragments scattered among the few books that remained on the shelves.

"This is really something, man," gasped the younger one, breathlessly. "It's like I really got the power. You know."

"Yeah, I know.

Soon the two were caught up in a frenzy of destruction. Dishes, cups and bowls flew about in a flurry of glass and china. Tables were overturned and chairs were splintered. Pages from ripped books fluttered about the room. Pictures pulled from walls lay trampled amid the clutter.

Coarse laughs mingled with grunts and wild shouts as the rampage continued. The shadows of the two raced back and forth across the walls, like misshapen monsters, as the light hanging from the ceiling swung wildly, buffeted by flying debris. Only when a misdirected book smashed directly into the bare light bulb, dashing the room into darkness, did the fury stop.

The pair stood panting, looking at each other, then at the chaos surrounding them.

"Oh man, what've we done? gasped the younger one.

"Felt pretty good, huh?"

"I don't know. Yeah, I guess so. I, uh, I've never done anything like that. What if we get caught?"

"Hey, it's cool. You're a man now. Come on. Let's get out of here."

Grabbing up the few CDs they had found, the two stepped over the broken pieces of what had been somebody's cabin life and headed for the kitchen. By the doorway connecting the two rooms, where a shaft of light from the kitchen speared its way into the dining room, they stepped over a cracked picture frame. The younger one glanced down to see a photograph of a family—a father, mother, teenage daughter and young boy, smiling happily from the edge of a pier, a sparkling lake behind them. A lump rose briefly in his throat, then was quickly swallowed as the older one turned the electric switch in the fuse box to the "off" position and the house went black.

By flashlight, the two eased out the back door, carefully closing and locking it behind them. The younger one thought this didn't make much sense, considering the shattered pane of glass. But who was he to question the leader? The two made their way around the side of the cabin, then followed the stepping stone path from the front porch a dozen yards or so to the narrow main road.

On the other side of the road they could make out the gray shape of a narrow concrete pier reaching out over the lake. After waiting a few minutes to be certain they were alone, the duo crossed the paved road. As the older one held the flashlight, the younger one picked up a rock about the size of a softball from the roadside. The older one did the same, and the two shuffled silently to the end of the dock, twenty yards away. Far across the lake a string of lights from the village flickered in the night. In the rippling surface of the lake, their reflections sparkled like a string of glistening pearls. Clouds scudded across the sky, occasionally revealing an infinity of twinkling stars.

"You know what to do." The older one was quiet now, composed, methodical. The frenzy of only moments earlier was gone.

"Yeah."

Each one took a sturdy plastic bag from his pocket. They removed work gloves they had been wearing as well as the cloth bags that had been firmly wrapped around their shoes and held in place with rubber bands. Gloves, foot bags and rubber bands were placed in the plastic bags, along with a rock in each bag.

"Make sure you squeeze all the air out of the bag before you tie it," directed the older one.

"Yeah, I know."

Once the bags were tight and tied, the two paused again, standing silently at the end of the dock. From across the lake came the occasional muffled bark of a lone dog. A splash not too far away told them that fish were awake and hunting food. A chorus of crickets chirped from the shore. Sleepy waves gently lapped at the piles of the dock.

"OK," said the older one. He swung his bag back and forth and when the momentum was at its peak he let it sail out across the lake. The younger one did the same. A second later both bags landed with muted kerplunks and quickly sank out of sight.

"No fingerprints, no footprints," chuckled the older one.

"What about DNA and all that stuff?" asked his partner.

"Hey, listen. I don't know if the village even has a police department. And even if they do they probably don't even know how to do fingerprint stuff, let alone any DNA stuff. No way they're gonna bring in anybody from a big city or anything for something like this. Nah, no one's ever caught me yet and they aren't gonna. We're home free, man. Now let's get back home and get some sleep."

The two retraced their steps to the shore, turned left and followed the road along the lake front. Soon their footsteps were swallowed up by the night. All that remained was the chittering of the crickets and an ominous silence.

CHAPTER 1

"GOTCHA!"

"Gotcha!"

"Darn!" Ken Alexander plopped down on the living room floor and began to count. "One. Two. Three. Fourfivesixseveneightnineten."

"No fair!" yelled Andrew from the top of the stairs. "You're supposed to count slowly—ten seconds."

"OK, OK." Ken began counting again. "One. Two. Three. Four..."

Just then a figure came flying out of the kitchen. Dashing past the bottom of the stairs, it unleashed a volley of Nerf darts from a Max Force Manta Ray in the direction of Andrew. All four shots went wide and Andrew retreated back down the upstairs hallway.

"Five. Six. Seveneightnineten. Thanks John!" Ken reloaded his Nerf Crossbow while John plugged four more Nerf darts into his weapon.

"Let's go get 'im," whispered John. The two boys crept up the stairs and down the hall toward Ken's bedroom. Ken was eight, dark haired and tall for his age. John was a year older and had blond, curly hair. Andrew was John's fraternal twin—and at this moment, his mortal enemy. The door at the end of the hall—Ken's room—was shut.

"Ready?" asked John softly.

Ken nodded. He flung the door open and the two allies leapt into the room, weapons ready.

"Where is he?" whispered Ken.

"Here I am!" cried Andrew, rising triumphantly from behind a pile of stuffed animals on the top bunk and letting loose with a barrage of Nerf balls from his Max Force Rapid Fire gun. The two attackers fired back, but not before each had been hit by at least one ball.

"Aaagh!," they screamed, running back down the hall, down the stairs, into the living room, around the corner, through the dining nook, down four more stairs and across the family room, with Andrew in hot pursuit, his Max Force blasting away. Ken and John dove behind the upturned sofa that served as their fort.

"I gotcha each three times," shouted Andrew. "You have to count to thirty."

"We got you, too!" countered Ken.

"Yeah, but that was after I hit you."

"Rats," said John.

"Dang it," said Ken. As Andrew went about looking for stray ammo to reload his gun, Ken and John began to count.

"One. Two. Three. Four..."

"And you have to count right," called Andrew from the living room where a ball had rolled behind a potted plant.

"...Five. Six. Seven..." While counting, the two were reloading their weapons. Andrew, finally with a full load of Nerf balls, stealthily sneaked through the kitchen, past Ken's dad, who was cooking dinner, through the dining nook, and down the stairs into the family room. He crouched at the foot of the stairs, waiting for his opponents to finish counting.

"...Twenty-eight. Twenty-nine. Thirty. Fire!"

Two heads popped up from behind the sofa and a volley of Nerf darts and arrows soared toward Andrew who opened up with his own weapon. Ammunition flew everywhere, bouncing off furniture, the ceiling and the walls. One of Ken's arrows flew astray, and as the three warriors gasped in horror, it sailed clear across the family room, over the railing separating the family room from the dining nook, over the dining table and through the kitchen, where it landed on the stove, a heart-stopping inches from a simmering pan of tofu spaghetti sauce. The chorus of "Uh oh"s had scarcely begun when the fatherly voice thundered through the house.

"OK, guys! That does it! You know the rules. The kitchen is a no-shooting zone."

"But we were shooting in the family room," John protested.

"Doesn't matter. That's enough Nerf war for today." Then the terrible voice softening, Mr. Alexander added, "Why don't you guys play with Legos or something, OK? I've got to get dinner ready. And then I have to go get Mrs. Alexander from work. I'll give you a ride home on the way, if you want."

"OK," said Andrew.

"Let's watch the fat robot cat," John suggested.

"Yeah, that's fine," agreed Ken's dad. He, too, was tall for his age. About six feet and two inches tall and fairly slender for his age, he did 180 sit ups every morning, except for Sunday. His stomach was fairly firm, but the rest of him was turning soft and flabby. Mr. Alexander had blue eyes, a long face with a high nose and brown hair that was usually hanging across his forehead. And there was a growing bald spot on the back of his head. He couldn't see the spot himself unless he used two mirrors, but Ken saw it whenever he stood behind his dad when Mr. Alexander was sitting. And Ken got a frequent view of the hairless wilderness when the two were wrestling.

The three boys paraded into the family room. While John and Andrew sprawled out on piles of cushions like dead fish, Ken fished a video out from the cabinet under the TV and popped it into the VCR. Soon the trio was howling at the antics of Doraemon.

Doraemon was one of Japan's most popular cartoon characters. He was a blue robot cat from the future who had been sent back in time to help a klutzy, fourth-grade Japanese boy with his many problems. Ken's Japanese grandparents, his *Ojiichan* [Grandpa] and *Obaachan* [Grandma], occasionally sent him a video tape on which were several 30-minute episodes of the Doraemon TV program. The dialog was entirely in Japanese, but John and Andrew laughed anyway. Ken occasionally translated the key moments of dialog from Japanese to English for his friends.

"What's he doing now?" asked John. Doraemon was pulling a door out of a huge kangaroo-like pocket across his waist. The variety and size of the items Doraemon could retrieve from his seemingly bottomless pocket were amazing.

"That's his *dokodemo doa,"* replied Ken.

"What's that?"

"It's a door that lets you go anywhere you want. Nobita, the boy, wants to go back in time to see some dinosaurs, so they're going to go through that door."

"Cool. I wish I had something like that," said John. "Then we could go home without going in the rain." A chilling early-May rain was falling outside. The rain was the only thing keeping the trio from their usual outdoor water gun battle. They didn't want to get wet—at least not from the rain. Water gun wetness was another thing.

The cartoon continued and Ken kept on translating. He had dark eyes and a dark complexion inherited from his mother. His mother was from Japan, so Ken had learned Japanese from an early age. His parents kept reminding him frequently how valuable and special it was that he could speak two languages fluently. Ken thought it was pretty cool, too, especially when he and his mom could talk about stuff without anybody else knowing what they were saying. Except for his dad. Mr. Alexander had lived in Japan a long time, so he could speak the language quite well, too. It was like a secret language among the three of them.

"Well, guys, it's time for me to go get Mrs. Alexander," interrupted Ken's dad. "I'll drop you off on the way to the university."

There were protests, but eventually the VCR and TV were turned off. Toys in the family room were picked up and put away. More protests. Furniture needed to be righted. Still more grumbling. The twins gathered their bags and shoes from the front entry where they'd put them when the three boys had walked home from school. They carried their items to the door to the garage where they put on their shoes.

"Our house is Japanese style. You have to take your shoes off when you come in," Ken always told his friends. Most of them didn't mind—even when Ken's dad made them take off their socks, too, if they were especially dirty. The socks, both Ken's and those of his friends, were sometimes a few words beyond "dirty." On such days the boys were quite proud of their socks.

"Ken, do you want to come along?" his dad asked.

"No thanks. I'll stay here."

Soon the twins were bundled into the car, the car pulled out of the garage and the garage door closed with its usual shrieking squeal. (Why didn't his dad do something about that? Ken often wondered.) He settled down to the rest of the Doraemon story. He didn't mind being at home alone, especially since he knew his parents would be back in half an hour or so. That is, unless his mom was busy working in the office when his dad got there. In that case it sometimes took longer because she had to finish up what she was doing while his dad waited. Oh well. More time to watch TV. Ken knew that his limit was 30 minutes of TV and/or computer games each weekday. He usually followed the rule faithfully. But once in awhile he cheated a little when his parents weren't home.

Today he finished the 30-minute video, then went upstairs to work on his latest Lego project—an original three-level transport/fighter spacecraft with a detachable exploration/escape pod. He was quite content to play with his Legos. As he worked on his creation Ken imagined the adventures he could have with a real life spaceship like the one he was constructing. He had no way of knowing that in just a few weeks he would be experiencing a totally different sort of adventure, a real—and frightening—adventure of his own.

CHAPTER 2

"ITADAKIMASU"

"*Tadaima.*" [I'm home.] Ken looked up to see his mother standing in the doorway to his room. The shrieking of the garage door opening and closing a moment earlier had told him his parents were home. She was on her way to her room to change out of her work clothes and had stopped by to see how her favorite—and only—son was doing.

"*Okaerinasai.*" [Welcome home.] Ken was always happy to see his mother at the end of the day. She was about a head shorter than her husband and had long, black, curly hair and dark eyes. She taught Japanese at the university and was extremely busy all the time. Yet she always had time for Ken to help him with his homework, to play with him, and to just talk with him and listen to him talk about his day. She was strict, especially about Ken's school work. She made sure he did his home work and did it well. But Ken didn't mind. He knew she cared about him.

Ken's dad was a stay-at-home dad who took care of the housework. He had a dream of one day writing a novel, but he never got started. He couldn't for the life of him figure out what to write about.

How was school today?" Mrs. Alexander asked Ken in Japanese. The two of them used only Japanese when speaking to each other.

"*Yokatta.*" [It was good.] Ken briefly described his day, then went back to playing with his space craft while his mom disappeared into her room. The Lego exploration pod had just docked with the mother craft after a visit to an unknown planet when his father's voice floated up the stairs.

"Dinner's ready." And then in Japanese, "*Gohan dekita yo.*" [Dinner's ready.]

Ken's dad did most of the cooking. What else he did was a bit of a mystery. Ken knew that Mr. Alexander taught a few before- and after-school classes of Japanese at one of the elementary schools in town. And he volunteered a few hours each week at Ken's school. Other than that, he seemed to have a lot of time on his hands. Mr. Alexander sometimes spoke of wanting to write a novel. But he said he didn't know what to write about and besides, how could someone have the patience to write a long novel. It must take 1000s of hours.

Ken met his mother in the hall and they danced their way downstairs and into the dining nook. The table had been partially set. At the side of each place was a small bowl with lettuce. Ken's lettuce was rolled up with peanut butter inside. This was the only way he would eat lettuce. There were also tomato slices and carrot sticks. Directly in front of each place, demanding attention, was a larger plate of spaghetti covered with tomato sauce with ground up tofu in it instead of hamburger. Ken's dad was a vegetarian.

"I don't think it's right for humans to kill animals," he would say when asked why. This made for some very interesting—and sometimes rather strange—meals. Some of them were pretty decent, though, and Ken liked the spaghetti sauce quite a bit, especially if he was really hungry.

Ken could understand his dad's thoughts about not wanting to harm animals. But on the other hand, when the family ate at a buffet-type restaurant, Ken always headed directly for the meat counter.

When the three were seated, each said "*Itadakimasu*" [(I) will partake.] and began eating. These words are always spoken before drinking or eating anything in Japan, whether it's a stick of gum someone gives you or whether you're about to dig in to a 20-course feast.

After awhile Ken's dad said "Let's have a family meeting."

Ken groaned. His mother said nothing. Family meetings used to be fun, when Ken was younger. It made him feel like a grownup when he could talk about important matters with the adults of the family. But now the meetings seemed sort of silly. Besides, most of his opinions and suggestions were usually turned down. Maybe it had something to do with the fact that every other suggestion he made was to adjourn the meetings.

"The family meeting is called to order," Ken's dad went on. "Is there any old business?"

"I move that the meeting be adjourned," suggested Ken.

"Not yet," replied his dad. "No old business? How about new business?"

"I move that the meeting be adjourned."

"Aarghh," said his dad, rolling his eyes toward the ceiling. He turned to his wife. "Can't you do something about your son?" he pleaded. Mr. Alexander always talked to his wife in Japanese. She just shrugged her shoulders.

"Seriously, though, I have some important news. Our airplane tickets came today, so everything's all set."

Ken was paying attention now. Every year Ken's family saved up money like crazy so that they could go to Japan for the summer. This gave Ken a chance to see all his Japanese relatives and go to a Japanese school for a few weeks.

"When are we going?" asked Ken.

"We leave on Tuesday, the 27th."

"So I'll quit school early again, huh?"

"Yes," replied Mrs. Alexander. You'll miss about a week of school here. But you're OK with that aren't you?"

"Yeah, I don't mind. Can we go to Tokyo Disneyland this year?"

"We'll see," said Mr. Alexander. "We just went to Disney World this past spring, you know, so we might not."

Usually, once a year was all the family could afford to travel. That was the annual trip to Japan. But Ken knew that his dad also had a savings account for other trips. Every time the family saved money by having a low gas or electric or phone bill, his dad put that money into the bank. Ken helped out by almost always turning off lights when he left a room. Once in a great while, somebody was still in the room when he did that. There would be a wild yell for Ken to turn the light back on. But that didn't happen too often.

In two years Ken's family had saved up enough to spend a week in Florida. That had been like a dream, spending day after day at Epcot Center, the Magic Kingdom, and MGM studios. They'd also gone to the Kennedy Space Center and the Atlantic Ocean where they spent an enjoyable and peaceful two hours away from the crowds, playing in the sand and waves. Ken's dad hated crowds so was in paradise on the deserted beach. Ken loved making castles and pools in the sand. And Mrs. Alexander appreciated the soothing rhythm of the lapping waves.

Ken especially enjoyed the day spent in the pools and on the water slides of Typhoon Lagoon. That is, until a huge wave in the wave pool picked him up and deposited him ungracefully, head down on the bottom of the pool. There had been no serious injury, just a minor bump on the head. But the incident had dampened spirits for that day.

"We'll have to let your teachers and the school know that you'll be leaving early again this year." Mrs. Alexander's words brought Ken back from his reminiscences.

"I typed up some notes today to give to your teacher and the office tomorrow," said Mr. Alexander. He was always typing up notes to give to people, making lists of things to do, writing down lists of things to take on trips. He liked to plan ahead. He was efficient. He was predictable. Sometimes he was a real bore, thought Ken.

"Tomorrow I'll take the notes to school when I go to do my volunteer work in the health room," Mr. Alexander said to his wife. Turning to Ken, he switched to English. "We'll have to be sure you finish any projects and stuff that you have to do before we go."

"I know," replied Ken. He was already beginning to get excited by the thought of being in Japan. He had many friends at *Sakura Shohgakkoh* [Cherry Blossom Elementary School]. And Tokyo was an exciting place to be. Plus, his Japanese relatives always gave him money and took him to fancy restaurants and spoiled him in many other ways. He didn't mind that Japanese school continued until the middle of July, or that they had classes every other Saturday morning. No, he always had a great time in Japan.

"Is it OK if we go to Nojiri?" asked Ken.

"Of course. We always spend some time there," answered his dad. This was another one of the highlights of the trip to Japan for Ken.

"Can we go to Annaka first?" asked Ken again.

Ken's American grandfather—his father's father—lived in the small town of Annaka, about 80 miles from Tokyo. This was the town where Ken's dad had grown up. Grandpa Alexander had retired from his job as a missionary a few years ago, but still kept busy teaching English to Japanese children in his home. His second wife, a Japanese woman, took good care of him and helped out by preparing snacks for all the kids who came to the English classes. Grandpa Alexander's first wife, Ken's dad's mother, had died of cancer at the young age of fifty-four, eight years before Ken was born. Ken was sorry to never have known his real American grandmother, but he liked his step-grandmother a great deal.

"That's OK. But I'll have to let my parents know when we'll get to Tokyo," said Ken's mother. Then to Mr. Alexander, "Let me know how long we'll stay in Annaka."

Ken and his family spent most of their time in Japan at his Japanese grandparents' apartment in Tokyo. It was near Sakura Elementary School. And it was free! The Alexanders could never afford to stay in Japan if they didn't have relatives to stay with.

There was one problem, though. The size of Ken's grandparents' entire apartment would easily fit into just the living room, dining room and kitchen area of Ken's American house. In this space were crammed two bedrooms, a dining/living area, a miniature kitchen, the bathroom, and a packed storage room which was converted into a cramped bedroom for Ken's dad. Japan was a crowded country—approximately one third of the population of the United States shoehorned into an area the size of California. Ken's grandparents' apartment was no exception.

The grandparents never complained. They were happy to have their grandson and daughter visit. Ken suspected that his father was not Grandpa Tanaka's favorite person. His Japanese grandfather was old school and preferred that a husband work outside the home and the wife be a stay-at-home mom. Ken's parents were the exact opposite of this ideal arrangement.

Ken's family had figured out years earlier that it made sense to spend their first few days in Annaka with Grandpa Alexander. Houses in the country tended to be larger than big city ones, and Ken's grandfather had a 2-story house with a guest room upstairs. This worked out well, because Ken's family invariably suffered from jet lag.

The first morning in Japan, Ken especially would wake up as early as three in the morning. After all, his body, still running on American time, would think it was twelve noon. Never mind that it was the middle of the night in Japan. Ken's eyes would pop open and he'd be ready for lunch.

In Tokyo, if Ken woke up at that unearthly hour, it would also wake up his mother and grandmother who slept in the same room with him. They would get up with him, fussing over Ken and trying to find some breakfast for him to eat. His grandfather who slept in the neighboring room, separated only by a thin, sliding paper door, would be awakened as well, and would come grumbling into the dining room to see what all the hubbub was about.

In Annaka, Ken could get up, go downstairs, eat a snack, watch videos on TV, play with toys or do whatever he wanted to do without waking up his grandfather and step-grandmother who slept upstairs. This way he also got to spend time with his American grandfather before heading to Tokyo and settling down to school work.

One year Ken's mom had to stay in Tokyo for a seminar and didn't go to Annaka with her son and husband. Since there were only two visitors this time, Ken and his dad slept in the extra upstairs bedroom. Mr. Alexander had the bed and Ken earned the spot on the *futon* on the floor.

That particular year Ken did not sleep at all the entire night of the visit. He was off to a good start, getting to bed by 9 PM, but he was still awake when Mr. Alexander slipped into his bed a half hour later. Mr. Alexander crashed immediately into sleep. There then commenced an infinitely unforgettable night. Every few minutes, it seemed, Mr. Alexander was awakened by a soft voice.

11 PM: "I can't sleep."

"What?"

"I can't sleep."

"Try."

"OK."

11:15: "I still can't sleep."

"Mmmnn. Why don't you go downstairs and read quietly."

"OK."

11:35: "I'm hungry."

"Unghh. OK. I'll come downstairs and get some cereal for you."

11:53: "Papa?"

"Huh?"

"You said you'd get something for me to eat."

"Oh, yeah. OK." Mr. Alexander staggered down the stairs as quietly as one can stagger at 11:53 at night. He found a box of cereal, a bowl, a spoon and milk, set things up for Ken and tottered off back to bed.

1:30 AM: "Papa?"

"Just lie down and try to sleep." Ken tried.

2:00: "I can't sleep."

"Aarghh. Go watch a video or something. Just be quiet. And let me sleep!"

3:30:"The video's finished."

"ZZZZZ."

"Papa!"

A long, low moan. "Now what?"

"I'm bored."

"You wanna do some puzzles?"

"OK." Another slow shuffle down the stairs to find the puzzles and games cabinet.

"These should keep you busy for awhile. Now please, let me sleep."

While his dad trudged off back to bed, Ken worked small jigsaw puzzles of animals, ran little metal balls through mazes and tried to discover the secrets to untangling metal rods that were twisted together.

4:00: Ken looked up to see his father standing in the

doorway, sleepy-eyed and with hair hopelessly messed up looking like a bird's nest.

"Now I can't sleep and I'm hungry," Mr. Alexander muttered and headed into the kitchen in search of breakfast.

Two hours later Grandpa Alexander, a usually early riser, descended the stairs to find his son and grandson draped on chairs in front of the TV watching a Japanese version of Sesame Street. That night had gone down in the abysmal Hall of Fame as an unforgettable, historical and yearly recalled night of nights.

But in recent years Ken had come to sleep longer and later the first few nights in Japan. His father was very, very happy for this!

The present meal continued with eager discussion about the upcoming trip. Amazingly, Ken asked for seconds. Tonight's dinner was actually pretty good, especially with mounds of Parmesan cheese smothering the spaghetti.

"May I be excused, please?" asked Ken when he was finished eating.

"Is there anything else we need to talk about?" asked his father.

"No. May I be excused please?" Ken persisted.

"How about *gochisoh sama,"* Mrs. Alexander reminded him. This was the phrase that was used after eating or drinking anything. It meant "Good treat" or "It was delicious."

"*Gochisoh sama*. Now may I be excused, please?"

"Yeah, but you have to give me a hug," said Mr. Alexander.

Ken rose from his chair, stepped into his father's arms for a good bear hug, then ran up the stairs back to his Legos. The family meeting had been forgotten, left floating up in the air without being properly adjourned. This was how family meetings usually ended in the Alexander household.

Later, when his parents had both finished their meals as well, Ken was called downstairs to clear the table. This was his nightly chore. Then, since it was Tuesday and his turn to wash dishes, Ken set about his next task.

Mr. Alexander went upstairs to prepare the next day's Japanese lesson. Mrs. Alexander began grading papers at the dining nook table. Checking and correcting the Japanese writing of her many students was a time-consuming job.

Written Japanese consists of 46 syllabic letters. Each of these letters, which stands for one sound, can be written two completely different ways, depending on whether the words are native Japanese or words which have come into Japanese from other languages. Ken's last name, for example, was written in the alphabet for foreign words, *katakana,* since "Alexander" was a foreign word. The Japanese word for "radio" was "*rajio,*" which was also written using *katakana* letters because the word came into Japanese from English. On the other hand, the Japanese word for police, "*keisatsu,*" was written in the second alphabet, *hiragana,* since it was an original Japanese word.

In addition, Japanese uses several thousand *kanji,* Chinese characters which have been adapted into Japanese. A person must learn to read nearly two thousand of these *kanji* in order to read a newspaper! Ken could not read a Japanese newspaper, at least not yet. Neither could Mr. Alexander. He'd studied some Japanese in high school. But as often as he claimed that he should/would study Japanese some more, he never got around to it. Mr. Alexander could speak Japanese smoothly.

But when it came to written Japanese he could read only as much as his son—about the level of Doraemon comic books.

Each *kanji* character stands for one meaning. There is a separate character for "tree," "root," "branch," "leaf" and so on. *Keisatsu* is written using two fairly complex *kanji*.

Little did Ken know, as he happily scrubbed the dinner dishes, that he would soon be having a serious discussion with some Japanese *keisatsu*.

CHAPTER 3

"OYASUMI NASAI"

"Hey Pop?" Now that Ken was older he often called his father "Pop" instead of "Papa." His father was in his room sitting on the floor surrounded by a chaotic confusion of papers, books and stuffed animals, preparing a Japanese lesson for the next day. He taught four Japanese classes each week at an elementary school in town. Ken's old stuffed animals and other toys came in very handy during the lessons.

"Yes, Ken?"

"Can we play?"

"Yeah. Just a minute. Let me just finish my lesson for tomorrow. Are you finished washing the dishes?"

"Yeah."

"And you did a good job of scrubbing them and rinsing them—like always?"

"Yep."

"Good. OK. Give me just a couple of minutes."

Ken went downstairs and began preparing for the game. The Alexander household was a little unusual in that there was no furniture in the living room. Nor was there anything in what would ordinarily have been the dining room except for some potted plants scattered about here and there. There were also two small bookcases by the front door where family and guests put their shoes upon entering the house. As a compromise to American culture, the Alexanders allowed visitors to step inside the front door before removing their shoes. This was greatly appreciated by guests, especially when it was cold or blowing snow or the weather was otherwise being unfriendly.

Ken's dad liked to explain the lack of furniture like this: "Well, when we bought the house we were living in a furnished apartment over at University Village. That's the university's family housing apartments. So we didn't have any furniture. By the time we got around to getting all the basic stuff for our house—beds, dining room table, TV stand and so on—we didn't have any more money. And then the living room just kind of became Ken's play area." (Actually, it was just one of Ken's play areas. He played in nearly every room of the house. Only his dad's room was off limits. That was because his dad always had an unbelievable amount of this and that lying all over the room: teaching materials, dirty clothes—and probably more stuffed animals than Noah had animals on his ark.)

The southern wall of the dining room, which was attached to the living room, was where the "jungle" was. Potted plants were everywhere, some reaching nearly to the ceiling, some hanging from the ceiling in macramé netting, all clumped together to present a massive wall of branches, leaves and vines. There was even a stuffed animal dinosaur—a cute little triceratops—lurking somewhere among the greenery.

The living room and dining room made a huge, open "L" shape, with the upright portion being the living room and the bottom horizontal line being the dining room. The kitchen and dining nook were in the crook of the "L," and could be reached from either the living room or the dining room by door-less doorways.

Ken used the entire living room as his play area. It was here that he and his father—and sometimes his mother—engaged in heated contests of football, soccer, kickball—or unusual games of Ken's creation. It was one of these original games that Ken had in mind tonight. He carefully gathered up various Lego pieces, a few remainders of the afternoon's Nerf war and some other toys that lay strewn about the living room floor and placed them in a pile on the stairs leading up from the right corner of the top of the "L." Just then his father emerged from his room and started down the stairs toward Ken.

"OK, I'm ready. Whadaya wanna play? Kickball? Soccer? Or something quiet like chess or checkers?"

"Why don't you come over here and sit down and we'll talk about it," Ken said with a sly grin.

"Where? Here?" replied his dad, circling the living room, carefully keeping Ken at arm's length.

"Here," giggled Ken, patting the carpet in the middle of the room.

"Here?" asked Mr. Alexander, grinning a sneaky smile, still maneuvering to stay away from Ken's reach.

"Here!" shouted Ken, lunging for his father's legs. With a speed remarkable for his age—or at least he liked to think so—Ken's dad jumped out of the way and with a hand on Ken's back, sent his son sprawling on the floor.

"Oh, so you want to play rough," taunted Ken as he dove

for his father's legs again. This time his hands grasped the right leg and Ken quickly tightened his grip. His dad pushed at Ken with both of his hands.

"No fair," Ken protested. "I've got your leg."

"OK, OK," Mr. Alexander said. "You and your rules."

Ken made up all the rules and most favored him. Once he got a hold of one of his father's legs, the older Alexander was no longer allowed to use his hands. Instead, he struggled to walk across the floor, dragging Ken behind him. Ken squealed with delight. He grunted with each jerk of the leg, but he held on for dear life.

Finally, giving up, his father collapsed on the floor. Ken immediately pounced upon him like a panther on its prey.

Heading for the feet, Ken grabbed one of the slippers his father always wore, keeping his other hand wrapped around the lower leg he had snagged. Suddenly Mr. Alexander swung his legs in a huge, violent arc. Ken found himself airborne as the leg he was holding onto pulled him up and dropped him in an awkward pile. The huge legs immediately swung back in the opposite direction and Ken again was yanked off the floor and plopped down a few feet from where he had just been.

But in the split second before he mightily crash-landed, Ken managed to pull the slipper off his father's foot and fling it into a corner of the room. His father began frantically crawling in that direction on hands and knees. Ken released his grasp of the leg and tried to run past his dad to the slipper.

"Oh no, you don't," Mr. Alexander hollered.

Before Ken could take two steps he was brought heavily to the floor as his dad grabbed his right ankle. Mr. Alexander stood up and began dragging Ken across the floor on his stomach, away from the slipper.

"No!" screeched Ken. Twisting his foot frantically, he broke free of his father's hand vise and flung himself at the slipper. He scarcely had scooped up the prize when his father grabbed him by the waist and pulled him to the center of the room. Cradling his son's legs with one arm and his shoulders with the other arm, the father swept up the boy and fell backwards. Ken landed on his father's stomach with a loud, squishy thud, accompanied by an even louder "Uuuaaah" from somewhere deep in his dad's chest.

"Owww. That's not what I wanted to do," grunted Mr. Alexander. Taking advantage of the pause in the action, Ken snatched the remaining slipper from his dad's other foot and raced for the wall. There he quickly stuffed the two slippers under his T-shirt.

"Now you're going to get it," snorted Ken's dad ferociously, jumping to his feet, surprisingly smoothly for someone who had just been acting as though every rib in his body had been broken a split-minute ago. He lurched toward Ken who eluded him with a quick jump to the side and began running around his father in circles. The older Alexander grabbed at Ken and missed. Eventually, though, Ken found himself trapped in a corner. He made a break for freedom but was once again caught up in his father's arms and dumped on the floor. Mr. Alexander dropped down beside him, arms still wrapped around Ken's waist.

"No tickling!" gasped Ken between howls of laughter as his father's fingers probed at his midsection, trying to pry out the slippers from under his shirt. Another of Ken's rules. He could tickle his dad, but not vice versa.

"I'm not tickling you. I'm just trying to get my slippers back," chuckled Mr. Alexander fiendishly. Lying on his back with arms around his son's middle, Mr. Alexander swung from side to side. Ken, flipping back and forth with each swing of his dad's arms, strove to keep his own arms in their protective place over the slippers. But in time his arms were flapping about and his dad quickly pulled the slippers out from under Ken's shirt. Jumping to his feet, Mr. Alexander tried to put the slippers back on, but Ken snatched them from his father's hands.

The game went on like this for quite some time, with grunts, shrieks and many giggles filling the evening air. Finally, Ken's dad, during one of the rare times when he was in possession of the slippers, said,

"Ken, it's time to start getting ready for bed."

"OK," said Ken, grabbing the slippers from his dad's hands once more and tearing up the stairs to his room. His father followed him upstairs, but rather slowly now.

"Ken, I really need my slippers." As hot and perspiring as he was, Ken's dad wasn't too likely to put on his slippers right away. But he always liked to have them back when the battle was over. By the time he reached Ken's room, though, the slippers had been hastily hidden.

"OK, where are they?" asked the father in an exasperated voice.

"Guess," retorted Ken.

Ordinarily the two would have played the "hot/cold" game until Mr. Alexander found the slippers. Tonight, though, Ken's dad was too weary. And it was getting late. Reluctantly, at his dad's insistence, Ken showed where the slippers had been concealed under the mattress of his bed. Then, giving his dad a hot and sweaty hug, Ken headed for the bathroom to take a shower. He didn't much like taking showers at this point in his life, but once the hot water was pouring over him—if they had hot water; sometimes they didn't—and he had a good song going, Ken didn't mind so much.

"How's the water?" called his dad from outside the bathroom door.

"Fine," Ken called back.

"Just leave some hotsywawa for me," yelled Mr. Alexander. "I don't like taking a shower with coolywawa."

Ken chuckled. Sometimes his dad was pretty funny. Sometimes he was a little weird. And sometimes Ken couldn't tell which was which.

Later, after he'd finished his shower, put on his Doraemon pajamas and brushed his teeth, Ken lay in the lower bunk of his bed, his mother sitting on the floor at his side. He liked this part of the day when he got to talk with her about whatever he wanted to. This was the time when he would share about anything that was bothering him, or that he was worried about. His father was always happy to listen to him, too, but sometimes Ken just felt that it was easier to talk with his mom.

"Are you looking forward to going to Japan again?" she was asking.

"*Un.* [Uh huh.] I want to meet my friends again." Ken was put in with the same group of students every year when he went to Sakura Elementary School. He had made some good friends over the years and always looked forward to seeing them again and playing with them during and after school.

While they were talking, Ken's dad came in, his hair still a little wet from his shower. He settled beside his wife on the floor and joined in the conversation briefly. But it was already past Ken's bedtime. And Ken knew that his dad wanted to run downstairs for one of his favorite TV programs which was about to begin.

"Well, Ken..." his dad began his usual bedtime speech, "... sleep well. Tomorrow's going to be another good day. I'll be leaving early to go teach, but I'll see you before I leave. I'll have your lunch ready to go." He began straightening Ken's sheets and tucking them in around him.

"Pop?"

"Yeah," Ken?"

"If I'm still asleep, could you wake me up at 6:58?" Ken liked exact times. Or he liked to be silly. One of the two.

"I'll try. Sometime around then. Don't worry. I won't let you be late for school."

Ken had never been late for school. He was very concerned about being on time for things. Except for getting to bed.

"Pleasant dreams. Don't let the bed bugs bite. If they're really hungry, tell them to come downstairs and I'll feed them a snack. See you in the morning." Sometimes it seemed Mr. Alexander would never stop talking. But it was rather soothing and reassuring to hear his father's words every night. Finally, his dad leaned over and kissed Ken on the forehead.

"Love ya," he said.

"I love you, too," Ken answered. His dad walked to the door, switched off the light, then turned and flashed Ken a friendly, very unmilitary half-salute, half wave.

"Good night, Ken" he said softly, gently.

"Good night." And then he was gone down the hall.

Ken and his mom chatted a little more, mostly about the upcoming trip. Then she made sure he was firmly tucked in, gave him a kiss and stood up to leave.

"*Oyasuminasai*" [Good night.], she said.

"*Oyasyuminasai.*"

Then she, too, was gone. Ken snuggled a little deeper under his covers. The blue glow of his nightlight bathed the walls. The light from the hall flowed in through the open door. Ken liked the light to stay on, at least until he was asleep. He could just make out the animals in the posters on his walls—the wolves, the seal pup, the baby hyena—all watching over him as he closed his eyes. He pulled Merky, the stuffed animal ermine closer to him. Ken felt warm, drowsy—and happy. The Nerf war with Andrew and John had been a blast. He'd had fun playing with his dad, and he'd had a good talk with his mom. And in just a few days he'd be going to Japan. Yes, this was one of those nights when everything in the world seemed just right.

As Ken faded away into a sweet sleep, the final images dancing in his head were of the game he'd played earlier, and the skillful moves he'd made to outfox his dad. He fancied himself something of a ninja warrior, stealthily slipping about in combat, elusive like an eel, cunning like a wolf, fast as a cheetah.

Then he was asleep, safe and sound in his own bed, in his own room, in his own house. His dreams were cheerful ones, full of images of family and friends and fun. Never did he dream that in a month's time he would find himself wishing for all the skills of a ninja in order to save himself.

CHAPTER 4

YELLOW AND PURPLE SOCKS

"Take it Ken—all the way!" The coach was yelling from the sidelines as Ken furiously dribbled the soccer ball down the center of the open field. Out of the corners of his eyes he saw defenders closing in on him from both sides. His breath was coming hard now. Sweat pouring from his forehead nearly blinded him, but he could make out the goal just ahead, and the keeper moving into position to block a kick on goal.

Then, just as he was about to be surrounded by opponents, Ken saw Shawn wide open to his left. With a deft move Ken stopped the ball, spun around to throw one of the defenders off balance and gave the ball a gentle nudge in the direction of his teammate. The ball reached Shawn at the same moment as one of the opponent fullbacks. Shawn had time only to kick the ball back at Ken.

But now Ken was wide open. Settling the ball with his left foot, he looked up to see the goal keeper sliding from left to right to place himself between Ken and the goal. With all his might Ken swung his right foot, hitting the ball head on and driving it past the keeper's outstretched right arm.

Goal!!!

And as Ken raised his arms triumphantly and his teammates gathered around him with high fives and pats on the back, the ref's whistle blew three times. End of game. They'd won by one in the last minute! The last game of the season and they'd finally won a game!!!

Over on the sidelines parents were clapping and cheering. Several were calling out Ken's name. A couple were even jumping up and down, Ken noticed with embarrassment. Fortunately, his own mom and dad were calmly standing there, clapping.

After exchanging low fives with the opponents, Ken and his teammates dashed toward their side of the field. There the "tunnel" was waiting for them. Parents and grandparents stood in two parallel lines, facing each other with outstretched arms arching up and meeting overhead to form a tunnel.

As the boys ran through the tunnel, the moms and dads and grandmas and grandpas hollered and hooted and yelled and generally carried on. But when Ken entered the tunnel, for some reason a pair of arms lowered, catching him as he ran through. Then the arms behind him closed in from behind, trapping him. Soon other arms joined in and Ken found himself struggling in a tangled mass of arms. He twisted one way and another, writhing, trying to free himself.

"Let me go," he shouted. "LET ME GO!"

But the harder he struggled, the more tightly the arms grasped him.

Then suddenly he was in his bed, breathing heavily, wrapped up in a hopeless tangle of sheets and blankets. Ken was relieved to find he'd been dreaming—the tangled arms part, at least. But he was a little sorry that the goal had not been real. His team actually had had a dismal spring season, and Ken, usually playing defense, had not been able to score all season. He wished he could slip back into slumber and relive the glory of his game-winning goal.

Glancing around his room, Ken saw that it was morning. Daylight was trying to sneak into his room through the cracks between and around the curtains. The multi-colored dinosaurs on the curtains were all motionlessly plodding about their merry ways—as always.

Ken rolled out of the lower bunk and shuffled across his room, carefully stepping over and around 100s of Lego blocks, stuffed animals and other toys. He was not exactly known among his friends as the kid with the neatest room. In fact, there was considerable concern—especially among his parents—that Ken would someday disappear in the piles of objects in his room, never to be seen again. But it didn't really bother him, the way the room looked. After all, he knew where everything was. Or at least he told his parents so.

Ken continued out of his room and peeked to his right where his mom was still sleeping on the queen sized *futon* in the master bedroom. She was a fairly sound sleeper, unlike his father who would bounce out of bed, wide awake at the sound of the newspaper landing on the front porch.

Ken proceeded down the hall and down the stairs. His father had apparently finished his morning exercises already and was seated at the table, eating a bowl of raisin bran and reading the morning newspaper.

"Good morning, Ken."

Mumbling a sleepy "Good morning," Ken climbed aboard his dad's lap, as he did every morning, managing to roll himself into a ball that just fit into his father's arms. His dad mentioned something about the weather and this being another nice day. He always said something about the weather. This time of day Ken only paid half attention.

After a few moments of cuddling, Ken slid off Mr. Alexander's lap and found his way to the cabinet to select a cereal for breakfast. There was a good variety, but his parents seldom bought the most fun ones—the cereals with tons of sugar and lots of colors and fun games and pictures on the outside of the box. Ken could understand the idea of eating healthy food for breakfast, but he surely did enjoy those times when his parents let him eat some of the "junky" cereals "for special." As far as he was concerned, there was too much healthy food in his life.

Ken made his choice—a healthy cereal (which didn't actually taste that bad) and shook out a bowlful. He yanked open the refrigerator door and pulled out the milk pitcher. The pitcher was full and heavy, but Ken managed to pour the right amount of milk into his bowl without spelling. Replacing the pitcher in the fridge and grabbing a spoon from a drawer, he sat next to his father at the table. Finding the comics page, he spread it out and began to eat.

"So today's the last day," his dad was saying.

That's right! It was the last day Ken would go to school before leaving for Japan. Usually he just nodded or grunted when his dad said something while he was reading the comics. But today Ken looked up.

"I'm going to do one last load of laundry today, so if there's anything you want me to wash, be sure to put it in the laundry hamper, OK?"

Uh oh, Ken thought. That meant organizing a major search party in his room. But he said "OK." His mind filled with exciting thoughts.

"You're mostly packed, aren't you?" his dad asked for what seemed like the two hundredth time.

"Yeah."

"And you've got stuff to do on the plane?"

"Yeah."

"OK. Good." Mr. Alexander walked over to the sink and rinsed his cereal bowl.

"I'll have to get all this stuff cleaned up before we leave," he said, looking at the pile of dirty dishes in the sink and on the counter. Despite the fact that he was always complaining about people making a mess of the house, Ken's dad always did dinner dishes the following morning—except when it was Ken's turn to wash dishes. Ken thought the house would be neater if his dad washed the dishes in the evening, right after dinner, like Ken did on Tuesdays. But Mr. Alexander always claimed that he was too tired by then to work anymore. And besides, there were his evening TV programs.

"Pop?"

"Yeah, Ken?"

"Are we going out to dinner tonight?"

It was a custom that the Alexanders tried to empty the refrigerator before leaving for Japan each year. The last night before leaving, they would eat out so that there would be no more leftovers or dishes to wash. And usually by the last evening, the fridge was as empty as Ken's toy chest after a good day of play.

"Yep. Where would you like to eat?" There it was. The

choice was his!

"Chuck E. Cheese. Of course!"

"I thought so. Would you like to invite one of your friends to come along?" And there was part two of the treat!

"Can I ask Andrew and John?"

"Yeah, that'd be fine. Why don't you give them a call now so they can ask their parents right away? They can come home with you after school, if you want. As long as you're really ready for the trip."

While Ken made the call, Mr. Alexander started preparing Ken's lunch. Since he worked only part time, Ken's dad had earned the responsibility of making lunches for his full-time working wife and full-time studying (sometimes) son. That's only fair, thought Mrs. Alexander. Ken agreed. Summer vacation had already begun at the university, though, so Ken's mom didn't need a lunch today. She'd been up late working, organizing school materials, cleaning up her desk—all the mysterious things that she did during the night. Now she was enjoying a much-deserved morning of sleeping in.

"They can come," said Ken, hanging up the phone.

"Good. We won't stay too long tonight, of course. We've got an early morning tomorrow."

"I know."

"Yeah, I know you know. Your lunch is ready. Go ahead and brush your teeth and get dressed." But Ken was already on his way upstairs.

Ken dressed in his standard outfit: a T-shirt, shorts and two long soccer socks—of different colors. Other than replacing the T-shirt with a long-sleeved shirt and adding a vest or sweater and a jacket in the winter, this was how he dressed all year long. Even in winter! Winters in the town of Fort Collins, Colorado could get a little nasty at times. And on those really cold days he didn't mind wearing gloves and a warm hat.

This being late May, though, Ken was dressed in his minimal outfit: a T-shirt that said "Essex Soccer Academy" on the front, with a picture of a soccer ball and the words "Don't just play...Become a PLAYER" on the back. A pair of baggy brown shorts. And the trademark thigh-high soccer socks. Today's selection: one deep yellow sock and the other bright purple. Ken was well known for his attire. He received frequent comments about his socks, but never anything negative or unkind. He got along fairly well with most of the kids at his school, and being as tall and athletic as he was, he didn't really have trouble with bullies. In fact, despite his rough play with his dad and his friends sometimes, Ken had never been in a real fight.

Soon Ken was ready to leave for school. He had a few minutes yet, so he started kicking a rubber ball against the living room wall. His dad came in from the kitchen.

"Do you want me to shoot on you?" he asked.

"OK." Ken's dad was also finished with his work for the season. He taught those four Japanese classes at the local elementary school, did some translation work once in awhile and did various other occasional things involving Japanese people who came to Fort Collins. And he often thought about writing a novel, but never got around to it. Today he would probably be doing laundry, packing up for the trip, and maybe mowing the lawn one final time before they left for Japan.

As his father kicked the ball at the wall, Ken played goalie. He repeatedly dove this way and then that way, jumped or slid a foot out to the side to block kicks. He was mostly successful, but occasionally his dad "scored." If the ball hit the ceiling, his dad groaned painfully. Little specks of paint frequently littered the carpet, knocked off the "bubbled" ceiling by high balls. Ken's dad hated it when that happened. And yet he never stopped the playing in the living room.

"Well, I guess you'd better get going," Mr. Alexander said after awhile, looking at the clock hanging on the wall in the dining nook. Ken grabbed his backpack with his lunch already inside, opened the door, set his shoes on the front step, slipped into them and headed down the sidewalk.

"Bye," his dad called after him. "Have fun!"

"OK," Ken called back.

The day was warm already, the bright May sun high in the sky. The world glistened from the previous day's rain. All along the way to school, kids were emerging out of their houses like a scattering of multi-colored butterflies coming out of cocoons, walking or biking their way to Beattie Elementary School. When Ken reached the second corner from his house he saw Andrew and John approaching from the right.

"Thanks for inviting us," Andrew called out as he scurried up to Ken.

"Yeah, thanks, Ken," added John, catching up with his brother. The three walked on together, discussing the games they would play at the pizza restaurant that night. Younger children liked to ride on the moving cars and airplanes and watch the animated musical show. But Ken and his friends preferred the video games, Skeeball and the other games that required skill. In fact, the boys usually ate very little pizza, spending most of their time using up the tokens that came with the pizza.

The day went by amazingly fast. There were final assignments to turn in, books to be returned to the school library, soccer games to be played at recess and a huge stack of papers to take home. Ken had brought along a shopping bag in which to tote home all his items. Still, his father met him at the school to help him carry home everything in the car. And of course there were final goodbyes to be said—at least until the fall.

Dinner at Chuck E. Cheese's was a blast. Ken managed to win over a hundred tickets from many of the games that spit out—or, more accurately, drooled out—tickets. With tickets he had saved from his last visit, Ken was able to purchase a Super Flingy Flying Disk. Andrew and John loaded up with many little prizes, including creepy plastic bugs and some little plastic dinosaurs. And then it was back home to finish packing and off to bed.

Ken was tired and excited as he lay once more in the dark of his room. The night light shone softly on the posters on the wall—the wolves, the seal pup and all the other animals that he loved. The next day, he knew, would bring great adventure. But as he drifted off to a warm, busy dreamland, a greater adventure, an undreamed one that he would have avoided if he could, waited for Ken.

CHAPTER 5:

ENCOUNTER AT NARITA AIRPORT

"A! *Nihon da!*" [Oh! It's Japan!] Ken had the window seat—as always. The gradual descent of the plane had told him and his family that they were nearing Japan. But only now, as the jumbo jet broke below the clouds could he actually see the land. Far below waves in crooked white lines were washing up on the eastern shore of the Bohsoh Peninsula. Soon the sandy beaches faded into lush green hills which were then replaced by scores of tiny rice paddies, many of which were no larger than a typical American back yard.

Lower and lower the plane went, and now between the hills and fields there were highways and houses and soaring hotels. The plane swooped down over a last string of hills and just when it seemed they would crash into some rice paddies, the edge of the runway appeared beneath the huge wings. There was the short screech of tires smacking onto concrete and the plane shook restlessly as it began to brake and slow down.

The day had begun many hours earlier with the gentle voice of Mr. Alexander at the unholy hour of 4 AM.

"Ken, time to get up."

Normally, Ken struggled to wake up in the morning. But on this day he had bounced out of bed immediately. It was as if his mind had been preparing for this moment all night long.

There had been the hour and a half drive to the Denver airport beginning in the dark gray of night. Dawn had caught the family on the expressway, its fingers creeping up from the eastern horizon. Cotton clouds painted the morning sky in glowing pastels.

The first leg of the trip had been a quick two and a half hour flight from Denver to San Francisco on a small plane. Part two of the trip was the ten hours of gradually approaching Japan, painfully slowly. But as they neared Japan, Ken's heart soared as high as the airplane.

Now the huge United Airlines airplane was taxiing past rows of parked aircraft and huge hangars. Far across the airfield, in the center of a gently sloping, shiny green lawn were gigantic letters that read "NARITA." To the left of the sign was an enormous clock that proudly announced to all visitors to Japan that it was 2:14. The clock didn't say "PM," but obviously it was the afternoon. It was 11:14 PM back in Fort Collins, long past Ken's bed time. But here it was the middle of the afternoon. No wonder he felt so groggy. Groggy, but excited at the same time. He was in Japan!

It wasn't long before the plane shook itself to a bumpy stop,

"This is the part I hate," grumbled Ken's dad. People were beginning to stand up throughout the plane, but Mr. Alexander remained seated, staring past his wife and over Ken's shoulder, out the window. A row of buses was lining up outside the plane, and stairs were being wheeled up to the plane.

"It's ridiculous!" Mr. Alexander mumbled on. "One of the world's newest, most modern airports but we have to take a bus from the airplane to get to the terminal. Who ever heard of such a thing?" Ken's dad complained like this every year when they arrived at Narita Airport. Ken and his mom just ignored him.

Shortly the lines of passengers in the aisles began moving forward. The Alexander family pulled their carry-on luggage out from under the seats in front of them, stood up and squeezed their way into the slow stream of people oozing by. A few minutes of shuffling along and they reached the open door. Stepping out onto the top stair, Ken noticed how humid the air seemed. It was cloudy—typical weather when they arrived in Japan—and misting lightly.

The Alexanders followed the other passengers hurrying down the stairs. At the bottom they were directed by a uniformed airport employee towards one of the waiting buses. All the seats were already taken when they climbed aboard. Ken and his family set their luggage down on the floor and hung on tightly to upright poles as the doors closed automatically and the bus lurched forward.

The trip was mercifully short. The bus wove its way around the airport between monstrous airplanes scattered about and smaller baggage carts and other service vehicles which scurried here and there like an army of worker ants.

Ken knew that some airplanes were able to pull up directly to the terminal. Lucky people flying those airlines could disembark directly into the building. Unlucky people flying other airlines—like us, Ken thought—had to take a bus to the terminal. Ken didn't mind, though. Actually, he thought it was pretty exciting—despite his dad's complaining.

From the bus the passengers were guided through huge glass doors. Then came a crazy, fun walk: up stairs, down corridors, down more stairs, down another hallway, up still more stairs with people going fast, fast, fast, trying to be the first in line at the other end. Ken's dad walked fast and Ken and his mom rushed to keep up.

And now—immigration. Here the family had to split up. Ken and his mom had Japanese passports, and were thus allowed to use the short line for Japanese citizens. Mr. Alexander, with only an American passport—after all, he was an American—was required to stand in a line that said "Aliens." Ken always expected to see green-skinned, three-eyed, six-legged creatures in that line. But he saw only his father and people from other countries.

The immigration officer was polite but official. He checked the two passports Ken's mom set on the counter in front of him, asked Mrs. Alexander a couple of questions, stamped the passports and motioned them through. Ken looked across the great room to see his father still standing in line, backed up behind a flustered-looking young woman who was desperately trying to explain something to the immigration official. The officials mostly spoke good English, but many visitors to Japan spoke neither English nor Japanese. Ken knew his dad wouldn't have any trouble because he spoke fluent Japanese and was married to a Japanese citizen. "Spouse of a National" was a good title to have when you came to Japan, even if you did have to stand in the "Alien" line.

Down some more stairs, then on to the baggage claim area. Just about the time the Alexander family's suitcases came rolling around on the carousel, Mr. Alexander caught up with his family.

"Hi, Alien," Ken greeted his dad, surprised and chuckling at his own ability to find humor in his tired state of mind. Mr. Alexander made a face, too—was that supposed to be the expression of an alien, or was he just tired, too?—and struggled through the waiting crowd standing next to the conveyer belt. He yanked the heavy bags from the moving belt, nearly bashing a couple of people in the process. Mr. Alexander had a favorite complaint about baggage carousels, too.

"If everybody would just stand back while they're waiting for their bags, then when their bags came, they could just step up to the belt and get them without being in the way of other people." This complaint of his dad's actually made a lot of sense to Ken. His father wasn't just hot air all the time.

The bags were loaded onto a cart and steered toward the customs counter. When their turn came, the three Alexanders stepped up to the counter and handed over the custom forms they had filled out on the plane. The customs agent asked a few questions in Japanese.

"Are you three together?"

Ken wondered what would happen if he would say something like "She's my mother, but I have no idea who this strange man is." But he guessed that this would not be a good time or place to pull such a stunt. (He was quite correct.)

"Do you have any alcohol?" (No way. Ken's dad never drank alcohol, and he'd certainly not bring it as a gift for anybody. His mom might. Alcohol was a popular present for people in Japan. But the Alexanders didn't have any alcohol on this trip.)

"Do you have any cigarettes?" (Even more "no way!" Nobody hated smoking more than Ken's dad. His having cigarettes in his possession would be like—well, it would be like a 6-year-old boy carrying around a bar of soap in his pocket.)

The customs man motioned the Alexander family through, and they exited the baggage area into the waiting area and into—cigarette smoke.

"Welcome to Japan," Ken's dad grumbled. "Land of cigarette smoke."

Japan had made great improvements in the last 10 years in providing nonsmoking areas in airports and train stations and some restaurants, and all trains now had at least some nonsmoking cars. Still, coming from an American town like Fort Collins where smoking was banned in most public areas, the Alexanders were shocked when they reached Japan.

The arrival area had supposedly become a no-smoking zone a few years earlier. But the area was small and the "smoking area" off to one side was packed with nervous-looking men puffing away on their icky cigarettes. The clouds of putrid smoke they produced clouded the entire building with a foul-smelling blue haze.

Only twenty years earlier, most long distance trains in Japan had not had even a single nonsmoking car. Ken's dad had suffered many miserable trips in smoke-filled trains. But he had fought back, writing letters to newspapers and complaining to railroad officials. In fact, he had been the only foreigner in a group of fourteen people who had sued the Japanese government and national train corporation many years earlier. They had demanded compensation for health problems and misery caused by riding smoke-polluted trains.

They had lost their case, but as a result of the publicity and their efforts, nowadays all trains had nonsmoking cars. Many train stations had even started banning smoking in most areas of the buildings and on platforms. Things were much better indeed. But this didn't prevent Mr. Alexander from griping as they passed through the crowds of people who had come to meet loved ones.

Ken helped push the cart toward a counter marked ABC. His mom went ahead to pick up and start filling out shipping forms. The three big suitcases were going to be checked in for delivery to Ken's Japanese grandparents' home. Ken's dad excused himself to go to the bathroom.

Ken found himself standing at the end of a long line, alone with the cart and the family's pile of bags. The arrival room was crowded and noisy. All around him Ken heard a cacophony of different languages. Mostly he heard Japanese, but here and there were sprinklings of English, Chinese, Korean and various other foreign tongues, all somehow melting together into a jumbled drone of human communication.

Ken felt tired. He longed to stretch out on a soft *futon* and drift off to sleep. But that would not come for several more hours. He'd been up nearly 20 hours already. Back home it was the middle of the night. But here in Tokyo it was only mid-afternoon.

The din around Ken gradually settled into a vague, distant murmur. He wasn't asleep, but his mind was halfway to dreamland. He stood there by himself, his thoughts floating in and out of a strange dazed state of mind.

Suddenly Ken's peaceful reverie was shattered by a commotion behind him. He heard harsh English voices knifing through the thick, heavy air. Turning, he saw two tall Western-looking boys pushing their way through the crowd. One was quite blond, the other had darker hair. They both had blue eyes, which made them stand out from the mass of black-haired, brown-eyed Asians around them. The boys appeared to be of high school age. And they were obnoxious, laughing and talking loudly, bumping into people without apology and swinging lit cigarettes in their hands—even though this was supposed to be a nonsmoking area. The shorter one held a suitcase in his hand..

The larger, blond fellow bumped into one poor little old lady, nearly sending her sprawling. As the boy turned to look back at the woman, a coarse laugh breaking from his mouth, he accidentally plowed into Ken's pile of suitcases.

"Hey, watch it punk!" he glowered at Ken. "Outta my way."

Ken, rudely yanked from his daydream, was surprised, confused. What was happening?

"Wha--?" Ken started to blurt out. But the big teen's face was now inches away from his own.

"Ya lookin' for trouble?" the huge teen growled.

Ken stood silent, helpless, not knowing what to say or do. He sensed a crowd of eyes on him, staring. His face began to turn red in shame and anger. The second boy was right behind his buddy, chuckling meanly.

"Better watch it, kid," the shorter boy snapped at Ken. "This guy'll beat your head in if you get in his way." He blew a cloud of smoke into Ken's astonished face. Ken coughed. He reached in his mind for words, but none came to him.

"Yeah, shrimp." The bigger one went on. "Don't mess with us." And then to his partner, "Come on, Phil."

And then the two were gone, pushing a ripple of waves through the crowd as they dashed out a door, ran across the street and disappeared into a parking lot.

Ken's knees felt weak and his heart pounded frantically. He'd never been in a fight—never hit anyone in his life. The two big boys had terrified him with their actions and threats of beating him.

"Hey, Ken. How's it going?" Suddenly Ken's dad was there, back from the bathroom. Ken started to describe what had just happened. Tears were warm on his cheek now. He wished his dad had been there when the bullies came.

Mr. Alexander put his big arm around Ken and drew him near. Ken let more tears flow freely. He was relieved now, but still scared. What could make people so mean? And why had they picked on him? Who were they? Why were they—just two teenage boys—at the airport?

Then Ken's mom was there, listening to Ken repeat his story, hugging and comforting him.

"I don't know, Ken," his dad was saying. "Some people are just mean and rude. Sometimes American teenagers come to Japan with their families. You know—business people, embassy people—even missionaries. And if their parents are too busy or don't spend enough time with their kids, the kids get kind of wild. They think they're special when they're here because they're different. And they do stuff they wouldn't do back home in America. Or maybe they would. I don't know. Anyway, don't worry about it. There's no way they can hurt you."

Ken was only half listening. The tears had stopped and his heart was nearly back to its normal rhythm. But he still felt scared. And drained. How he wished he were back in his bed in Fort Collins—safe, snug and warm.

The Alexanders were eventually at the front of the line. They checked in their larger suitcases for delivery service to Ken's Japanese grandparents' apartment. Carrying only their carry-on bags, the three walked down more stairs, bought train tickets and headed for the platform. By now Ken had nearly pushed the miserable incident out of his mind. The two bullies were long gone, he reasoned, and surely their paths would never cross again. If Ken had only known how wrong he was.

CHAPTER 6

TOKKYU DENSHA

A ticket puncher standing in a small, waist-high cage-type box took Ken's ticket, slipped the end of it in a handheld puncher, clipped a hole in the edge of the ticket and handed it back. What a boring job that must be, thought Ken. His father often thanked the ticket punchers but most people just ignored the uniformed men as they flashed through on their hurried ways. Imagine standing there all day punching tickets for people without a single "hello" or "thank you." Ken was positive that this was a job he would not want to have some day.

The train the Alexander family was taking from the airport was a limited express, a *tokkyku,* called the Sky Liner, the fastest train run by the Keisei Company. The word came from two other Japanese words, *tokubetsu* [special] and *kyuukoh* [express]. Ken couldn't figure out why the train wasn't called a "special express" in English. Why "limited express?" In fact, he asked his dad.

"Pop?"

"Yeah, Ken."

"How come *tokkyu* isn't called "special express" in English?

"Good question. I've wondered that a lot myself. I think maybe it means that it's an express train but it doesn't stop at as many stations as a regular express. It only stops at a limited number of stations. Or something like that. Does that make any sense?"

"Yeah, I guess so," Ken replied. But he still wasn't sure.

"I used to ask my dad the same question when I was a kid."

"What did he say?"

"He didn't know either."

"Oh."

The special express or limited express—whatever it was called—stopped at only 3 stations between the airport and downtown Tokyo. In that way it was special—and fast. All seats were reserved, so there was no need to rush to a seat. The Alexanders took an escalator down to the platform, boarded the waiting train, found their seats on a nonsmoking car—of course—and settled in.

Ken had noticed the many vending machines on the platform.

"Please give me some money," he begged his mother. She fished some coins out of her purse and handed them to Ken. His parents seldom bought him soft drinks or snacks when they were in the U.S. His father was especially stingy about buying items from vending machines. But in Japan, for some reason, his dad magically loosened up with his money. Just another reason Ken liked coming to Japan.

Ken hopped off the train and walked over to a nearby machine that sold many kinds of drinks. He dropped two 100-yen coins in the slot and was just about to push a button when he felt somebody behind him. He turned to see his dad move in beside him, a couple of coins in his hand.

"Anything good here?" the older Alexander asked.

"Yeah. I'm getting a *miruku tei* [milk tea]," Ken responded, pushing the button. A second later there was a clatter inside the machine and a can of chilled milk tea popped out into the trough at the bottom of the machine. Ken's change clanked into the dispenser. Three brown 10-yen coins and a silver 50-yen coin with a hole in the middle.

"Can I have two of your tens?" asked Ken's dad. Ken handed the coins to his dad who added them to one of his silver 100s and dropped them in the slot. He pushed a button and retrieved his can of orange juice. In the U.S. he would have gotten twice the amount for half the price. But this was Japan!

Time was running out so the two Alexanders returned to their places on the train. Recorded voices were announcing in Japanese and English the train's schedule, stations along the way, and the location of smoking and nonsmoking cars, the telephones and toilets. Out on the platform a bell began ringing and last minute passengers scampered for the doors. A whistle blew, the doors slid silently shut and the train glided smoothly out of the station.

There were a few moments of flashing through a tunnel, a brief stop at another station, and the train pulled out into the gloomy, late afternoon air. Lush, green hillsides spread out on both sides. All level open space between the hills was taken up by tiny rice paddies. Rain was coming down steadily now, occasionally splashing against the window, dancing across the glass in little rivulets pushed back across the glass by the force of the air.

The ride was quiet, gentle. The countryside flashed by

soundlessly. Most trains in Japan were *densha* short for *denki* [electric] and *sha*, a variation of a Japanese word meaning "vehicle." These electric trains glided everywhere across the entire land, silently and cleanly.

Ken and his parents eased their seats back and stretched out. The plane had been cramped, but here they could remove their shoes and place their feet on the facing seats. Ken sat by the window, facing forward. His mom sat next to him, in the aisle seat. Both had their feet on the seat across from them, next to Ken's dad who was sitting by the window facing them. His shoeless feet were jammed between Ken and his mom. Fortunately, Mr. Alexander's feet didn't smell that bad.

There were many empty seats, including the one next to Ken's dad. In a situation like this it was acceptable in Japan to put stocking feet on an empty seat. But never shoed feet. Only foreigners who didn't know their proper manners would put shoe-clad feet on seats. Tsk, tsk, the Japanese would think. Those silly foreigners and their poor manners. But many things that foreigners did were tolerated or even forgiven. It was assumed that people from other countries couldn't possibly understand the delicacies and fine points of Japanese culture. Foreigners were expected to be bumbling, awkward and not understanding. So the poor unsophisticated outsiders had to be excused for their cultural inadequacies. Or something like that.

As the Japanese countryside flashed by, the scenery began to change. Open spaces and greenery were replaced by the gray of concrete. Towns merged into one huge metropolis. Tiny houses in postage stamp yards were mixed in with huge high rise apartment buildings stretching up into the grimy sky. Large signs, in both English and Japanese, advertised everything from electronic goods to food. Many words were familiar: Sony, Honda—even the occasional golden arches of McDonalds.

The train sped through many stations without stopping. Passengers waiting for their own trains stepped back to avoid the rush of air as the *tokkyu* swished by. Some looked up at the passing train. Others continued reading their newspapers, magazines, books or comic books. Japanese people loved to read, and train commuting was a great opportunity to do so. Either that or sleeping. Ken had been amazed at the way Japanese people could sleep on trains, even standing up, it seemed. But of course some trains were so crowded that you could pass out and never fall down. The press of the crowd would hold you up.

Public transportation could be very sardine-like in Japan. This was so on trains, subways or buses. It was amazing how many people could be packed into a single train car or bus. Ken's dad had told the story of how once he had been on a crowded bus carrying a suitcase. After struggling to find a place to set his bag down, Mr. Alexander had given up and just let go of the suitcase. Surprisingly, the suitcase hadn't budged an inch. It was suspended in the air, held up by the mass of people pressed against it.

Ken thought he'd like to try that sometime. But not today. Right now he just wanted to relax and stare out the window. This part of the trip was comfortable. But he knew things would get rougher later on. He breathed a deep sigh, snuggled his head on his mother's shoulder and watched Japan go by.

CHAPTER 7

UENO

Barely an hour after their departure from Narita Airport, the Alexanders' train descended into a dark tunnel deep beneath the city of Tokyo. The train slowed down and eased into the final station of the line, Ueno. Literally, Ueno means "upper field." Near the station were a famous and popular zoo and science museum. Ken had been to both. The zoo was noted for its oh-so-cute panda residents. Today, though, Ueno was just a place to change trains. The family needed to catch another train at another Ueno station run by the Japanese National Railway.

Tokyo is big. Huge, gigantic, sprawling, massive, colossal. None of these words can adequately describe the city unless you've been there. So—Tokyo is big.

The older, central part of the city is ringed by a commuter train line called the Yamanote Line. Trains on this line continue running around in circles all day long, clockwise and counterclockwise. It takes 64 minutes to make one complete loop—if you really want to go around in circles. (Usually, only people who fall asleep on the train or silly tourists do so.) Many of Tokyo's old parks, temples and shrines, as well as the imperial palace, where the emperor lives, are within the circle.

There are 29 stations on the Yamanote Line. The name of each station is also the name of a section of Tokyo. Each area surrounding a station is practically a city of its own. Many stations are surrounded by department stores, office buildings and entertainment areas, not to mention residential areas. One station, Shinjuku, supposedly holds the record for having the largest number of people passing through it of any station in the world. In fact, according to the Guiness Book of World Records, 3.5 million harried travelers pass through the station each day.

Many of the stations on the Yamanote Line also have other train lines that head out into the outlying areas and suburbs like spokes shooting out from the center of a bicycle wheel. Ueno is one such station.

Underneath the city of Tokyo is a huge maze of at least ten subway lines. On maps, the subway system looks like a bowl of colorful squiggly spaghetti, with each line being designated by a different color. In addition, hundreds of bus lines spread out about the city, like cracks on a window that has just had a sad encounter with a baseball. It's no wonder that more than a few foreigners—and Japanese people—have gotten lost in Tokyo's wondrous transportation system. Even Mr. Alexander had been known to be in places in the city where he hadn't planned on being! He was never lost, he said. He just sometimes wound up being someplace where he hadn't planned on being.

When the Sky Liner stopped, Ken's family rode the escalator up from the platform. At the top Ken and his dad went to the men's room while Ken's mom watched their bags. Ken washed his hands and began wiping them on his pants.

"Why don't you use your handkerchief," Mr. Alexander suggested. He reached into his own back pants pocket and pulled out his handkerchief which he used to dry his hands. Most Japanese public restrooms have toilets and sinks for washing hands, but no towels or hand dryers. Every Japanese person carries with him or her a handkerchief to be used for the purpose of drying hands.

"Uh, yeah," Ken replied, finishing drying his hands on his trousers. Mr. Alexander's eyes rolled ceiling-ward.

The two male Alexanders took a turn watching over the bags while Mrs. Alexander visited the ladies room. Crowds of people streamed by, all in a hurry to get somewhere. Ken's dad dug his watch out of his pocket and studied it.

"Almost 5:10," he said, shoving the watch back in his pants. "We've been traveling over twenty-two hours now." He sounded tired. But he also sounded proud of the ordeal the family was enduring.

Ken looked up at the huge clock hanging from the ceiling of the station. It was indeed 5:10 PM. He, too, was tired. But there was the excitement of being in Japan, in Tokyo. He was eager to board the next train.

As soon as Mrs. Alexander emerged from the pinkly decorated women's room, the Alexanders picked up their bags and headed down a flight of stairs to the station exit. (Hadn't they just come up a long escalator from the platform? And now they were going down stairs to exit the station? This didn't make much sense to Ken, but he didn't want to take the time to worry about this oddity.)

The family handed their tickets to another uniformed man

standing in another waist-high cage and entered the human flow of traffic. They crossed the huge, open room, climbed a few stairs and found themselves out on the street. Mercifully, the rain had stopped, so umbrellas were not needed. It was hard enough to navigate the crowded sidewalk with just bags in hand.

Lights glared from signboards everywhere and reflected in puddles of leftover rainwater. The roar of rush hour traffic was everywhere. Theaters and shops blasted out music and advertisements. Shadowy figures along the edge of the sidewalk called out to passersby, holding up cheap telephone cards for sale. Were these actually usable cards? Why were they so cheap? Who would buy them? Ken wondered.

Ken tried to keep his eyes straight in front of him, but they were constantly pulled aside by the sights. Huge souvenir stores were mixed in with small shops specializing in books, purses, bread or cigarettes. Restaurants had glass cases in front containing plastic versions of menu items to help patrons make their choices. Some of the plastic models looked good enough to eat, Ken thought. And there were people, people, people. Everywhere!

Once inside the cavernous station of the Japan National Railway, Mr. Alexander quickly found the shortest ticket line and joined it. Of course, as so often happened, the people in front of him had complicated requests which required a great deal of time. By the time Ken's dad reached the front of the line, he was obviously agitated. Once he got this far he always seemed to be in a big hurry. Nevertheless, he was polite.

"Two adults and one child, regular tickets, to Annaka on the Joetsu Line, please."

The man behind the window seemed unfazed by the fact that a foreigner had just used nearly perfect Japanese to make a purchase. His fingers flashed over computer keys, he pulled out and inserted plugs in a large electrical board and told Mr. Alexander the cost. As Ken's dad placed several thousand-yen bills on the counter, the clerk punched some more keys and three tickets dropped out of the computer. The sale was complete and the Alexander family moved on.

The family passed through the vast room. It couldn't really be called a waiting room because there was nowhere to sit. And besides, nobody seemed to be waiting. Everybody was going somewhere.

Mr. Alexander glanced up at a huge timetable over their heads. He found the particular line they wanted, looked at the listed trains and turned to his family.

"There's a regular at 5:55. We should be able to get seats if we get on it now."

He led the way to the gates where still another man in a different uniform (different train company—different uniform) punched their tickets. It took another few minutes for the Alexanders to make their way to the stairs leading up to one of several dozen platforms where their train was to arrive.

"Darn it! It's already here!" panted Ken's dad as they emerged from the stairs onto the platform. He began rapidly walking along the platform toward the rear of the train, his family struggling to keep up with him. As they progressed farther from the stairs, Ken could see a few vacant seats here and there in the train. Maybe they would be able to sit. Ken knew from past experience that during rush hour you had to hurry to catch a seat. Also, the farther you went from the stairs that fed the platforms, the less crowded the train would be.

Fortunately, the final few cars of the train were not so crowded yet. Dashing through the open doors of the last car, Mr. Alexander plopped down in an open seat. He put his bag down on the seat to his right, claiming it for his family. Ken was right behind and sank into a space on his dad's left. Mrs. Alexander finally caught up and gratefully settled into the seat which had been reserved for her by her husband's bag.

Mr. Alexander stood and after bouncing a couple of hanging straps off his head managed to shove the family's bags onto the overhead storage rack. Once again he sat down.

"*Ah. Yokatta*" [Oh. That was good (lucky)], he smiled at his wife. But the smile was more like an expression of tired agony.

Mrs. Alexander was used to being left behind when her husband's long legs were in a hurry. She just sighed and leaned forward to look at her son.

"Take off your jacket," she advised. Ken was perspiring from the rush to the train and the humidity. When he stood up to remove his jacket his dad slipped over into Ken's seat and motioned for Ken to sit between his parents. Ken did so, happily.

This train was much different than the previous one. It was considered to be a commuter train. At the front of the car was a restroom on one side of the aisle. On the opposite side of the aisle from the restroom were two sets of seats facing each other, jutting out from the side of the train at a 90-degree angle. This was the only place that four people could sit together and look at each other. The remainder of the car had a long bench-like seat on either side, running the length of the car except at the doors. How many people sat in each section of the long bench was determined by the size of the people and how closely they sat to each other. As more passengers began to wander in and sit down, the Alexander family was gradually squeezed together tightly. This was not so bad. At least they were sitting.

There were four sets of double doors on each side of the car. Down the length of the car on each side, just in front of the seats, were two rows of leather straps hanging from metal bars overhead. Attached to the bottom of each strap was a large plastic ring. Metal poles reached from floor to ceiling near the doorways. These trains were not meant for comfort. They were built to carry as many people as possible as efficiently as possible. Few seats but plenty of places for standers to hold on.

Bells, loud announcements and whistles announced the departure of a train. Ken expected their train to start moving soon. Instead, as panicked commuters ran and made last-second leaps through doors, the train across the platform closed its doors. Firm words over the public address system warned someone to pull back—he was holding up the departure. Twisting to look out the window behind him, Ken saw a man dressed in a gray suit standing on the opposite side of the platform—with his arm stuck between two doors of a train. There was a hiss as the doors parted just wide enough for the man to pull his arm back. The doors immediately slammed shut, and the man walked away in embarrassment to the tune of sighs of relief from the people around him. Small red lights on the side of the train flicked off, the platform master waved his green flag and the train departed.

"Some people are in such a hurry," Ken's dad explained.

"And we're not?" asked Ken.

"Well, yeah, but we don't jump on trains when the door's about to close."

"Yeah, sure." Ken glanced at the platform clock. 5:35. Twenty minutes before their train would leave.

Ken remembered a story his dad had told him about his high school days. For four years Mr. Alexander and his brother boarded with different families in Tokyo when they were going to an American high school. On weekends and for holidays and vacations they went home by train to where the rest of their family lived, in the town of Annaka. The small town, about eighty miles from Tokyo, was where Ken's family was headed now.

In those days, trains were pulled by locomotives or diesel-powered engines. Doors were operated manually by the passengers instead of electrically by the conductor. There was one door at each end of a car. These doors led into vestibules between the train cars. From the vestibule you had to open another door to step into the main part of the car where the seats were.

One Saturday morning Mr. Alexander was headed to Annaka by himself. His brother was staying in Tokyo for a boy scouts activity. Trains ran only once every two or three hours during the day time, so if you missed one, there would be quite a long wait. When Mr. Alexander walked onto the platform he saw his train slowly beginning to pull out of the station. Carrying his suitcase in one hand and his guitar case in the other, Mr. Alexander started running along the platform. Startled, people turned and gasped as he went clanking by, heart pounding furiously, pained breath gasping out in English, "Look out, people, I'm running!"

And just as the train began picking up speed, Mr. Alexander launched himself from the platform through the still open door of the last car, collapsing in a nearly sobbing heap, hearing all around him disapproving mutterings of "*abunai*" [dangerous]. Yes, it had been dangerous. And if he hadn't wanted to get home so badly, he would have waited for the next train. Mr. Alexander never tried anything like that again. Nowadays you couldn't do that, of course. All train doors were firmly shut before a train could move. If you tried jumping onto a moving train, well—splat! You'd just run into a closed door.

The train that had just left was headed for the same destination as the train Ken's family was on. Now everybody who wanted to go their way had to board this train. Or they could wait for the next train which would probably be another half hour or so. But many people were eager to get home and preferred taking this train, even if it meant standing for a long time.

Soon the few remaining seats were taken. Later passengers began maneuvering for something to hold onto. There were businessmen in dark rumpled suits looking tired after a long day at the office. Clumps of giggly high school girls, all alike in their school uniforms, staked out areas in which to stand. Packs of high school boys laughed loudly and played cool. The various designs of the high schoolers' uniforms indicated which schools they attended.

College students were clustered here and there in chattering pods. Women, apparently headed home after a day of shopping at Tokyo's finer department stores, clutched shopping bags. And an occasional child grasped a mother's hand.

Amid the din Ken and his parents sat quietly. Nobody appeared to notice them. Nowadays, Japanese people, especially those living in large cities, were becoming sophisticated and internationally-minded. Long gone were most of the stares, pointed fingers and cries of *Gaijin* [foreigner (literally, "outside person")] that Mr. Alexander had endured—and hated—as a child and youth living in Japan. The attention had seldom been negative or hostile in intention, although there had been some of that. The attention was mostly out of curiosity. But having lived in Japan for 25 years, Mr. Alexander resented being singled out as being different or a curiosity. Ken had not experienced anything like that. He felt quite at home in this country. After all, he was half-Japanese—in nationality, language, culture—everything.

Ken was pulled out of his thoughts by the sound of the conductor squawking over the train's public address system. The crackly voice was listing the names of the stops and the time of arrival at each station. He went on to explain how many cars were in the train, which cars had restrooms and that this was an entirely nonsmoking train. During Mr. Alexander's high school days there had been no such thing as a nonsmoking car. Ken's dad had suffered immensely, especially in winter when closed windows turned the trains into moving gas chambers. No wonder his dad still hated smoking so much.

Now the conductor was announcing that it was departure time. The speakers out on the platform confirmed this fact and ringing bells left no doubt that the train was about to leave. A few last-minute arrivals pushed their way onto the crowded train, the conductor's whistle blew and the doors slid shut.

There was a jerk, slight but enough to send standing passengers dancing around trying to regain their balance. Ken was amazed that people not holding on to straps or poles didn't tumble to the floor in human piles. He had seen people bump into each other but never fall down on a train.

The train edged out of the station, then picked up speed. There was much clicking and clacking as the wheels crossed numerous rail junctions. Each time the train crossed a junction it swayed—and so did the standing passengers, like a wave traveling down the length of the car.

Once the train left the station and train yard, it settled down on its own set of tracks and the ride became smoother. Mrs. Alexander had bought a package of donuts at the station kiosk. Ken wasn't sure whether he wanted to sleep or eat. With standing passengers swaying only inches away from his face, though, he decided eating right now would not be practical.

Ken noticed that his mother had closed her eyes. Her tilted head rested against the window behind her. Mr. Alexander was staring straight ahead, red-eyed, at the shopping bag dangling from the arm of a middle-aged woman standing in front of him. The bag said, in English letters, "HAPPY SHOPin FOR LOVELY LIFE."

Ken had long ago given up trying to make sense of the English messages printed on T-shirts, sweatshirts and shopping bags in this country. The Japanese loved to play with English. "Play" was the key word. If the words or phrases looked and sounded exotic—well, that was good. Never mind meaning!

The woman's eyes were closed. Probably she was tired. Or maybe she was embarrassed by the foreigner who was sitting in front of her and didn't know what to do with her eyes. She probably would have been embarrassed if Mr. Alexander had offered the woman her seat. That didn't happen very often in Japan. No danger of that happening tonight Ken guessed. He was sure his dad wouldn't give up his seat, even if someone was dying. Neither would Ken. As kind and helpful as they could be at times, right now they were tired beyond human decency.

Directly in front of Ken stood a short, slender man, probably not much taller than Ken himself. His dark blue suit was wrinkled and his tie was crooked. His jet black hair, undoubtedly neatly combed and slicked down with hair oil that morning, reminded Ken of the unkempt weeds poking out in every direction of some areas of his yard back home. The thick-rimmed glasses balanced on the man's nose were as crooked as his tie.

Occasionally the man muttered to himself. Some words sounded vaguely like English. Several times the man grinned at Ken, showing pearly white but misaligned teeth. At such times it seemed as though the man was about to speak to Ken. Each time Ken quickly averted his eyes. The man was smiling too happily to be your standard, exhausted commuter. Ken guessed he'd had a few something-or-others to drink after work. He just hoped the man would not throw up on him.

It was not unknown for Japanese businessmen to get sick on trains or in stations on their way home from after-work drinking binges. The explanation was that Japanese men worked so hard and had so much stress, they needed to unwind after work. Their relaxation usually took the form of going out for a "few" drinks with the office buddies. In

Japan drunken behavior had traditionally been tolerated as a necessary evil as a result of the pressure cooker of the work place.

Mr. Alexander didn't drink. Ken was glad for that. But then again he didn't see his dad as working all that hard. Mr. Alexander did a lot of housework—when he got around to it. He also taught his four weekly Japanese classes. Ken thought this was admirable, although Mr. Alexander often complained about how stressed out all his teaching made him. (After only four classes a week?!?) Sometimes this caused Ken stress. More often, though, Ken just ignored his dad.

Ken's mom, on the other hand, taught as many as four classes a day. In addition to her teaching, she organized many cultural events at the university and arranged for guest speakers to visit. She often stayed up until past midnight grading and correcting papers. Yet she never complained. What a difference between his parents, Ken often thought.

Mr. Alexander also occasionally led groups of Japanese people on sightseeing tours around the western portion of the United States. But he always seemed to have an abundance of free time. Ken could never figure out what his dad did with all that extra time. Mr. Alexander kept talking about wanting to write a book some day. But Ken never saw him do any writing.

"I don't know what to write about," Ken's dad would say.

As the train flashed through the night, the young man on Mr. Alexander's left fell asleep. Every few seconds his head would nod, sag and come to rest on Ken's dad's shoulder. The man would immediately snort, jerk his head up and then doze off again. This little ritual repeated itself over and over,

Ken closed his own eyes. Images of the past, long day played tag with each other in his mind. The train wheels played a rhythmic *gatan goton, gatan goton* lullaby on the tracks. Ken slept.

CHAPTER 8

ENCOUNTER ON THE TRAIN

Ken's eyes flew open. What was it? What was happening? The train had jerked to a stop. That is what had awakened him. The mass of people had thinned out with every stop and now Ken could actually see out the windows on the opposite side of the train. There was no station here, only the dark night. Turning to look out the window behind him Ken saw only more ebony darkness. A few lonely lights twinkled in the distance. A farm house, maybe?

Most of the remaining passengers were awake now. Many looked up to the ceiling as if some explanation might come from the speakers above. And sure enough, the voice of the conductor crackled from overhead. Ken caught part of the message.

"...please wait for a little while."

"What did he say?" Ken had missed the first part of the conductor's words.

"There's a red light up ahead," his mother explained. "We won't be stopping long."

Ken nodded. He knew that despite the excellence of Japan's rail system things like this did occasionally occur, especially on local train lines. Ken glanced at his mother. She had already closed her eyes again. His dad had taken out a crossword puzzle magazine and was trying to work a large puzzle. He was having great difficulty. His mind was probably halfway in bed already.

The woman with the shopping bag was gone. Ken looked around for the grinny drunk. There he was on the other side of the train, several seats down. He, too, it seemed, had been startled out of a deep sleep. The man's eyes met Ken's and opened slightly wider with delighted recognition. His mouth struggled to form a grin. Halfway through the effort, though, the incomplete smile faded, the eyes closed and the man's head sagged. Ken breathed a sigh of relief. In a way, though, he felt sorry for the man. Must be a rough life, he thought. And the man hadn't seemed dangerous or evil—just drunk. Maybe he knew some English and had wanted to talk with Ken. Maybe he had a son Ken's age.

Ken's eyes traveled over the rest of the car. Very few people were standing now. There were nearly twenty stops between Ueno and Takasaki, the Alexanders' next destination. It took five to ten minutes between each station. At some stations the train they were on was required to wait five minutes or longer for a *tokkyu* or two to pass them by.

The local train would open its doors and people would shuffle off. Then an odd silence would fill the car. A few people might be talking softly here and there. But most passengers read, slept or stared emptily at nothing in particular. The dozens of advertisements lining the upper sides of the car and hanging from overhead clasps had long since been read. There was nothing left to do but wait.

Eventually there'd be an announcement over the train's PA system followed by an urgent warning over the platform loudspeakers. In the distance there would be the shrill horn of a train approaching. Abruptly the night would explode into sound and motion as a limited express train flashed through the station, rumbling like an earthquake, leaving the local train rocking in its wake. And then once again there would be silence.

If you looked fast enough, you could make out the blurred faces in the quick windows of the passing trains. The passengers always seemed happy, content, even smug—enveloped in their warm and cozy streaking cocoon. And why not? Those people would arrive at their destination much sooner than the poor souls in the pokey local. If his dad weren't so stingy, the Alexander family could be on a train like that, thought Ken. But now they were simply waiting for the train ahead of them—probably stopped at the next station—to move on and allow their train into the station. Ken peeked sideways at his dad. Mr. Alexander was staring out the window now. He hadn't filled in a single square in his crossword puzzle.

Mr. Alexander noticed Ken's sneaky peek.

"Think you can sleep some more?" he asked. He was half asleep himself.

"Maybe," Ken answered. He was about to shut his eyes when the train once again began to move. Sincere apologies for the delay flowed from the conductor. It sounded as though the poor man felt personally responsible for holding up the train, Ken thought. But he knew that this was the way of Japan. People took responsibility for things—their own actions as well as for the actions of their employees, their families—even trains.

They were probably two thirds of the way to Takasaki. Ken liked this latter part of the trip. At each stop people had poured out of the train. Ken was reminded of horses at the beginning of a race, when the gates opened and the eager animals stampeded out of their stalls. He imagined the passengers were eager to get home. An open door was an invitation to walk, run, dash. Freedom at last! Freedom from the confines of the sardine can—at least until tomorrow.

At a few of the earlier stops new people had gotten on the train. But now that the train was outside the city limits of Tokyo, there were scarcely any new passengers. There was finally breathing space. At each stop people who had been standing forever gradually sank onto treasured seats when they became vacant. You could sense their relief as weight was finally removed from tired feet.

Once again the clickety-clack melody of the railroad called Ken to sleep. He answered willingly. Stops came and went. The human cargo thinned out until only a handful of passengers remained. Empty seats outnumbered occupied ones. Ken dozed on.

Suddenly Ken was yanked from his sleep by a commotion. Forcing his eyes open, he saw two incredible figures at the end of the car. Unbelievable! It was the two youths from the airport making their way noisily toward him, surrounded by a shroud of smoke from cigarettes dangling from their mouths.

"But this is a nonsmoking train!" was the first thought that crashed into Ken's mind.

And then, "No! How can they be here?!" Even as his hazy mind struggled to understand what was happening, the two were upon Ken, standing in front of him, sneering, menacing.

Ken's head snapped to his right and left. The seats on either side were empty. Where were his parents? Had they gone to the rest room? Not both at the same time. To the dining car? There was no dining car on this train. Had they gotten off at Takasaki and forgotten him? Where were they?

"So we meet again," the one called Phil snarled at Ken.

"We told you to stay out of our way," the other one growled.

Ken's mind was swirling. Terror had slapped him wide awake. He looked to the back of the train, hoping the conductor would see what was happening and come to his rescue. But only the top of the conductor's hat could be seen through the window of his compartment. He was sitting down, not looking this way.

The older boy's hands reached out, grabbing Ken by the front of his shirt and pulling him up out of his seat. The grip was powerful, unshakeable.

"Leave me alone," Ken wanted to scream. But his voice was lost somewhere deep inside. He wanted to strike out at his tormenters, but his legs and arms had turned to jelly.

"Now you're going to get it," Phil snickered.

Ken felt himself being dragged toward the end of the train car. His eyes pleaded with the other passengers for help, but they were all asleep or they turned away. None of this made any sense. Why were the two bullies on this train? Why had they come looking for him? What did they want? Where were his parents?

"Get the door, Phil," the bigger one barked. Phil turned the handle on the door at the end of the car that connected to the next car and slid it open. The older one pulled Ken through the doorway as Phil reached ahead to open the door to the next car. There were only a few feet separating the two doors. The sound of the wheels on the tracks was unmuffled here between the two cars and crashed like thunder through the floor plates that connected the two cars.

This car was completely empty. Ken's terror grew. There was nobody here to help him—or even to see what was happening to him. Tears and sweat were flowing in torrents. From somewhere a faint surge of strength began to flow into Ken's muscles. He started to squirm, twist and roll. But the hands on his shirt were vises.

"OK. Open the door," bellowed the older boy. Looking down into Ken's face, he snickered.

"We're going to throw you off the train."

"Why?" was all Ken wanted to shout, but still there was no voice.

Phil reached over and jerked open a glass panel beside the door. He pulled on the handle inside the emergency box and the train doors swished open. This can't happen, Ken thought. The doors aren't supposed to open when the train's moving.

"OK, Steve. I got it," Phil said to the older fellow.

A few feet below the floor of the train the parallel set of tracks flashed by in two seamless lines of silver, glistening in the glow flowing through the open doors.

"This is where you get off, kid" cackled Steve. He backed Ken toward the gaping hole into the black night, his hands still firmly on Ken's shirt front.

With every ounce of strength that he could muster, Ken struggled to get free. He jerked from side to side, but Steve's grasp was unshakeable. The night was closer, the roar of the tracks louder. Ken reached deep inside himself one last time to find the shriek that was screaming to escape.

"Ken." A distant voice, coming hazily, as through a mist.

"Ken-chan." His mother's voice. "Ken, we're almost there."

The shaking was gentle now, more of a patting on his shoulders. Ken's eyes flew open. His mother was standing over him, holding him by the shoulders. Mr. Alexander, also on his feet, was pulling down bags from the overhead rack.

"The next stop is Takasaki. Get ready to get off," Mrs. Alexander was saying.

Ken was still in his seat, his jacket draped over him. His eyes raced up and down the car. Only a handful of passengers were scattered throughout the car. There was no sign of the two bullies.

"Are you OK?" Mr. Alexander had set all their bags on the floor and was now seated next to Ken. Ken was wet with sweat.

"I'm hot," was all Ken could think to say. He rolled his jacket into a ball and clutched it in both hands.

"We didn't want you to get chilled," his mother explained. "When so many passengers got off, the air conditioner was blowing right on you."

Ken glanced at the ceiling. He could see the long, narrow blowers hidden inside the grill that contained the cooling system. The blowers moved back and forth from one side of the train to the other. Each time they swung in his direction, a blast of icy air hit him in the face and chest. Suddenly he wanted to be wearing the jacket again. Despite the sweat and flushed face, he felt terribly cold.

"Are you OK?" His dad again. "You were making some strange noises and moving a lot when you were sleeping. Were you having a bad dream?"

Ken wanted to tell his parents the entire dream. But would they think he was silly? The dream had seemed so real—so terrifyingly real. But it was ridiculous. They might laugh at him.

"Takasaki. Takasaki." The conductor's voice interrupted Ken's thoughts with the announcement that the train was about to arrive at their next destination. The voice went on to say that the next stop was the last one on the line and that everybody needed to get off. Then there was a list of the various connections to be made and what time the connecting trains would depart and from which platform.

Ken stood up and shouldered his backpack. The three Alexanders, bags in hand, shuffled over to the nearest door. The train slowed, the platform appeared outside the windows and soon the train jerked to a stop. The Alexander family stepped out onto the nearly deserted platform.

"Go ahead and sit down," Mr. Alexander said, motioning to some benches. "I'm pretty sure our next train leaves from this platform."

There was one more train to take. Only three stops this time. But the line was a remote, rural one and trains were few and far between.

Ken and his mother sat on the bench while Mr. Alexander walked a short distance down the platform. In a moment he was back.

"Yeah, this is the right platform. We've gotta wait about 30 minutes."

This was the part Ken hated. They were barely 15 minutes away from the town of Annaka now—by train. Sometimes Grandpa Alexander drove to Takasaki to meet them. That took about 30 minutes. But Grandpa was teaching an adult English class tonight and wouldn't be able to come to Takasaki to meet them. So they'd take this train for three stops and Grandma Alexander would meet them at Annaka station with the car.

Ken asked his mother for some money, found a drink machine and bought himself another *miruku tei.* His dad wandered off to find a pay phone to call the Annaka house to let Grandma Alexander know what time they would arrive in Annaka.

Here Ken could eat freely. Returning to his seat on the platform bench, he helped himself to a couple of the small, plain donuts his mother had bought in Ueno. His hunger was building, but he knew he'd be able to eat when they got to Annaka.

Soon his dad was back.

"Tomoko-san will meet us at the station," he explained. "Grandpa's still at his class. He should be home soon after we get there."

Mr. Alexander's real mom had died many years ago, long before Ken was born. Ken never had a chance to meet his real grandmother. A couple of years after his wife died, Grandpa Alexander had married a Japanese woman.

"I guess he wanted to follow my example," Ken's dad always explained to people.

Ken's parents had gotten married the same year his dad's mom had died. Ken's parents had been married longer than his grandparents. Ken thought this was a little strange. But this was not as strange as when he tried to explain his family to people who made the mistake of asking. He had an American dad who had grown up in Japan, a Japanese mom who was living in the U.S., a Japanese *Ojiichan* [Grandpa] and *Obaachan* [Grandma] living in Tokyo, and an American grandfather and a Japanese step grandmother in Annaka. Ken didn't even want to explain his various aunts and uncles and where they lived.

There was also a bonus family member. When Grandpa Alexander remarried, he inherited a live-in mother-in-law. *Obaachan*, as she was called, was in her mid-90s. She was short—shorter than even Ken, slightly bent over and as wrinkled as a raisin. She was hard of hearing—you had to shout when talking to her—and peered through a huge magnifying glass, like a scientist studying a rare discovery, when reading the newspaper. She was slowing down with age and was forgetful about certain things. And yet everybody envied her good health and sharp memory of things of long ago.

To Ken, she was—he almost didn't want to go through the tangled family tree for this person—a step great grandmother. Which really wasn't that hard to remember. Or was she his great step grandmother? It didn't matter, really. Ken didn't talk with her much—he hated shouting—but she always greeted him with warmth. And as little as Ken had known her, he found that he had a deep sense of affection for the little old lady.

Grandpa Alexander's wife's first name was Tomoko. Ken's parents both referred to her as Tomoko-san most of the time. "San" was a title that was the equivalent of "Mr.," "Mrs.,""Miss" or "Ms." It was an extremely convenient title. But when Mr. Alexander talked to his stepmother he called her *Okaasan* [Mother] to be polite. It was expected that one would call his or her stepmother or mother-in-law "Mother."

In Japanese it is important to call people by the proper

terms, and to be respectful. And it's also very complicated. There are different words to use depending on whether you are talking about your own wife or somebody else's wife. And you must even use different terms for your own wife depending on whether you are talking to a friend or your boss. Ken knew most of this but once in awhile he goofed. So did his dad.

"So, do you want to tell me what was going on back on the train?" Ken's dad had pulled a donut out of the bag himself and was hungrily stuffing it in his mouth.

"It's kinda crazy."

"Did you have a bad dream?" Ken's mom joined in the conversation.

Ken told them about the dream, the two bullies, about nearly being thrown from the train, his fear.

"Those guys must have really scared you at the airport," Mr. Alexander said soothingly.

"*Daijobu.*" [It's OK.] Mrs. Alexander added. "Don't worry about it." She put her arm around her son. This was comforting.

"Yeah, you'll probably never see them again for the rest of your life."

"But what if I do?" Ken wanted to know.

"Well, they probably won't remember you. And if you do see them, ignore them. They're not going to hurt a little kid."

"I should have punched them at the airport," Ken said angrily. "They were mean."

"Do you really think that would have done any good?" Mrs. Alexander asked.

"Unh unh," Ken replied. "But it's frustrating. It was terrible. And I didn't do anything! I didn't fight back."

Bitter tears began to flow again.

"You did all you could do, Ken," said his father. "It's alright. It wasn't your fault. They were just mean people and you survived without getting yourself hurt. That's the important thing."

"*Wakatta?*" [Understand?] Mrs. Alexander's words were firm but gentle.

Ken nodded. The incident at the airport had been unforgettable, intolerable. The psychological wounds were deep. Ordinarily, Ken was lighthearted, easygoing. Bad things were quickly put out of mind. But it would be a long time before this event was forgotten.

The three Alexanders sat quietly waiting for their train. Time ticked by painfully slowly. Ken was certain he could hear the platform clock saying "*Chiku taku, chiku taku,*" as Japanese clocks said.

Trains pulled into parallel platforms, paused briefly to unload a constantly dwindling number of passengers, then hummed off into the night. The station became empty, silent. The train on which they had arrived had long since exited the station for the train yard where it would be prepared for its run to Tokyo the next morning.

Eventually a two-car local train pulled alongside the Alexanders' platform. A handful of night travelers straggled off. The doors closed for cleaning and a few people began lining up in front of the train. In a few minutes the train had been quickly cleaned and all trash picked up by a cleaning crew. Again the doors opened and the few people who had gathered on the platform quickly climbed aboard. The Alexanders followed. No need to rush this time. Seats were plenty. And they would be getting off in three stops.

The train left Takasaki station exactly at the scheduled time. Trains in Japan almost always departed and arrived on time. You could practically set your watch by the arrival and departure times.

Less than twenty minutes later the Alexanders were walking along the platform of Annaka station. The tiny station had only one entrance, and there it was, right ahead. Ken's heart raced with excitement and joy. The trip was almost over!

Ken followed his father out the exit gate, handing his ticket to the station master. His dad was already hugging Grandpa Alexander.

"I got home from my English class just in time to come get you," the elder Alexander explained. Ken accepted his grandfather's hand for a shake.

"How are you, Ken? Tired?" asked Grandpa Alexander.

"Yeah," Ken managed. He liked his grandfather but sometimes had trouble talking to him. He didn't know why. Right now, though, he was so tired he probably wouldn't have had anything to say to even his best friend.

Grandpa Alexander greeted Ken's mom with a hug and then the four piled into Grandpa's gray Subaru for the 5-minute drive to the Alexander house. The rest of the evening was a daze. Busy chit chat in the car, heard from a distance. Some of Grandma Alexander's (Tomoko-san's) great home cooking. Tonight there were chilled soba noodles, tempura vegetables and shrimp and a dish of tomatoes and lettuce picked from the Alexanders' own field. And then bed. Glorious, wonderful relaxing bed.

Ken's parents spread out the *futon* in the downstairs *tatami* [straw mat] guest room while Ken brushed his teeth and washed. This room was used when all three of the Alexanders visited Annaka. Ken slipped underneath the covers, every muscle crying out in delight to feel the softness of the *futon* and the coolness of the sheets. Ken was lost in sleep before his father ever finished his goodnight speech. This time Ken slept in peace. No evil bullies. No nightmares. Only exquisite sleep. Sleep!

CHAPTER 9

THE MYSTERY

"...Anyway, I hope our cabin's OK," Grandpa Alexander was saying. "Keep an eye out when you're up there."

He looked up at Ken standing in the doorway, his hair still tousled from his pillow.

"Well, good morning Ken. Did you sleep well?"

Ken nodded. "Yeah." He walked over to the dining room table and sat down on one of the rickety wooden chairs with light brown plastic-covered seats. These were old chairs that had been around since his father's childhood days. Old and worn, but comfortable, even though there were wires wrapped around the legs to keep them in place.

"Good morning, Ken. How ya doin'?" This came from his father who was seated at the end of the table, English language newspaper spread out in front of him, empty cereal bowl to his left. Grandpa Alexander was in his personal easy chair in a corner of the room. Beside him was a small table—part book rack and part table. On it were crossword puzzle magazines, paperback books, study materials and his candy box—all his special things that he liked to have near him when he was reading, studying, or watching TV.

The entire dining room was not much larger than the breakfast nook of Ken's house back in America. But this was Japan. Space was scarce and rooms were tight and cozy. Space was used cleverly and economically.

"OK," Ken replied. He was still struggling to find complete wakefulness. He'd already been up once that morning, in the wee hours of the night. Jet lag and that familiar pang in his stomach called hunger had popped his eyes open about two in the morning. He had come downstairs, fixed himself a bowl of cereal—Grandma Alexander's awesome homemade granola, read for awhile, played with some of the puzzles which were on the window sill by the dining table waiting for curious children, and gone back to bed about five AM. Now it was after nine. Ken's mother was still asleep. She could sleep amazingly late when she needed to. Or wanted to. And when she had the opportunity to do so.

Grandpa struggled to his feet. He was a tall, thin man, about the same height as Ken's dad. The hairline on his forehead had moved back quite a bit over the years, but the top and sides of his head were covered with silver-gray hair. The glasses he wore gave him a dignified appearance. He was a little round around the middle, and his skin was wrinkled. But mostly he was in good condition for a man of his age. He was 74.

Grandpa Alexander had been in an accident the previous autumn. He'd been crossing a street on his way home from an adult English class taught at the culture center—the same class he'd been teaching the previous night before meeting Ken's family at Annaka station. It had been dusk and a woman driving a van had not seen him. Fortunately, she hadn't been going that fast. If she had been, Grandpa Alexander probably would not be there today. The impact had sent him flying several yards. Luckily, his legs had escaped injury, other than bruises. But in trying to break his fall, he' broken both of his wrists. He'd also cracked one of the bones in his neck.

Grandpa Alexander was mostly back to normal now. But there was still pain in the neck and the right wrist would never work again the way it was supposed to. Typing a letter was a slow, painful process. He could use only one finger, tap, tap, tapping one key at a time. And yet he managed to type a family letter every 10 days or so. The elder Alexander would type out one copy of the letter, make four copies, add personal notes and then send the letters to his four children, all living in the United States, and to his own mother, still going strong at age ninety-four.

"Well, I guess I'll put in a few laps," Grandpa Alexander announced, heading out of the dining room door. After his accident Ken's grandfather had put on some weight. In order to get some exercise and slim down, he'd taken up hiking—in the house. He started in the dining room, walked out the door into the hall, turned right, walked the length of the hall, made a 180-degree turn in front of the downstairs bathroom and retraced his steps. At the end of the dining room, at the door to the mini-living room he again swung around and headed for another lap. It was a short distance for a long hike—like trying to swim laps in a bathtub. But Grandpa Alexander would make twenty-five laps at a time. This added up, he figured, to approximately one half of a kilometer. Done twice a day, this exercise actually did help him to lose weight and keep it off. The advantage, of course, was that this walking could be done no matter what the weather had decided to do outside.

Ken admired his grandfather's determination. He was certain that Grandpa must get bored to death going back and forth, hundreds of times a week, even though he listened to classical music on the radio—turned up full blast—while he walked. The elder Alexander was also deaf in one ear and hard of hearing in the other. Ken had to talk loud to be understood. Sometimes he felt uncomfortable shouting at his grandfather. But he did want to communicate with the old man.

Ken fixed himself another bowl of cereal. This time it was one of those junky, sugar-packed cereals he had brought along from the U.S. Cereal was becoming more popular in Japan, but there were still only a dozen or so varieties available in this country. Nothing like the hundreds of brands and varieties you could find in an American supermarket. And cereal was expensive over here, maybe three times as much as back home. Grandpa Alexander always told Ken to bring a box of his favorite cereal along from the U.S. so that he would have something to eat for breakfast when visiting the Annaka house. Grandpa paid for the cereal, so Ken always chose one of those "special" cereals that his parents hardly ever let him eat. This was another one of the many reasons Ken loved to come to Japan.

"Hey Pop?"

"Yeah?" Mr. Alexander looked up from the newspaper. Grandpa Alexander always got first shot at the paper. After all, this was his house and his newspaper. But he had long since finished reading the paper, along with his breakfast. Now it was Ken's dad's turn.

"What were you and Grandpa talking about?

"You mean about the Nojiri cabin?"

"Yeah, I guess so."

The Nojiri cabin was located in Nagano Prefecture which was next door to Gunma Prefecture which was where the town of Annaka was. Early in the century some American missionaries had discovered the incredible jewel of a mountain lake called Nojiri. They had formed the Nojiri Lake Association, the NLA for short, and bought many hundreds of acres across a hill along one side of the lake. Back then land had been incredibly cheap and American dollars had gone a long way.

Over the decades missionaries to Japan from many countries, as well as Japanese people with ties to Christian churches, had bought parcels of land and built simple, rugged cabins. Today there were about three hundred NLA cabins scattered about the hillside, mostly hidden from view by the dense forest in which they were located. Grandpa had bought one of the cabins many years ago. The lake—remote, peaceful, surrounded by natural, pristine glory—was an ideal place for weary people to spend their summers. And so had the Alexander family done for many years, ever since Ken's dad was a little boy.

On one side of the lake was a small village named, not surprisingly, Nojiri. Over the last few years Japanese people had also discovered the delights of Lake Nojiri. The village of Nojiri had sprouted an assortment of new hotels, lodges, resorts, restaurants and camp grounds. The area had become a major summertime tourist attraction. Most of the year, though, Nojiri remained the sleepy little mountain village of its past.

In the past few years, though, a frightening problem had arisen. Mr. Alexander explained to Ken what Grandpa Alexander had told him.

"Well, the last couple of years somebody's been vandalizing NLA cabins."

"What do you mean?"

"Somebody breaks into cabins when there's nobody there and trashes them. It happens in the off season so there's no one around to hear or see anything. They think it might be people who come from outside the area to fish. Or maybe even local teens."

"What do they do?"

"Grandpa says they break stuff and mess things up and just ruin the cabins. I guess they've done it two or three times in the past few years. There's never ever any evidence—fingerprints or anything. It'd be pretty hard to catch whoever does it, even if they did find fingerprints."

"Why?"

"Well, unless the people are criminals, the police wouldn't have records of their fingerprints. Anyway, Grandpa's worried that they might break into our cabin. They seem to hit mostly cabins near the road that goes by the lake. We're pretty far back from the road. But you never know."

Ken thought seriously for a moment. He knew that his dad was going to be at the lake alone in a few weeks. He felt a twinge of worry.

"Do they ever hurt people?" Ken wondered out loud.

Mr. Alexander saw where his son's thinking was headed.

"I don't think so," Mr. Alexander replied. "I mean, I don't think anybody's ever even seen them."

"So we're OK if we go up there?"

"Oh, sure. These people are probably just kids out for kicks. They're not going to hurt anybody. Stuff like that doesn't happen as much here in Japan as back home. And not way up here in the mountains. Maybe in Tokyo..."

"So we'll be OK?" Ken was earnest, concerned. Subconsciously the incident at the airport had made him feel less safe, even here in Japan.

"Ken, it'll be OK. Besides that stuff only happens off season."

"But we're going up there off season, aren't we?"

Ken's father was silent for a moment. What Ken had said was true. He thought carefully before he answered.

"I've been up there for several days the last few years during off season and I've never heard or seen anything. I've even been up there on weekends. That's when outsiders are most likely to come up there to fish or whatever. If I thought there was real danger, I wouldn't go up there. And I sure wouldn't let you go up there. So don't worry, OK?

"OK," Ken replied. But he was not at all sure. He had a bad feeling. But maybe his dad was right. Maybe nothing bad would happen. Maybe they would just have a good time together at the lake like they'd had in past years. Maybe.

CHAPTER 10

THE TOY STORE

The remainder of the visit in Annaka was pleasant. Ken forced himself to stay up a little later each night. Actually, his parents were the ones who did most of the forcing, urging Ken to hang in there a little longer before going to bed. And he tried to sleep later each morning. This part was a lot easier. This was the way to adjust to Japan time: Later to bed and later to rise. What a crazy motto that was!

"*Nemui*" [Sleepy], Ken would complain after dinner. Or even during dinner. Or before dinner—whenever he felt like complaining about being sleepy. And indeed he was sleepy. No wonder. About the time dinner ended at 6 PM, Ken's body, still thinking it was back in Colorado, was nagging him that it was three in the morning and that he should be sound asleep. Ken had to tell his body, "Sorry, we're in Japan now. It's not 3 AM. It's 6 PM. So quit bugging me."

But Ken's body wouldn't quit bugging him, and Ken would drag himself off to brush teeth and collapse into bed. He had long since outgrown the age at which he had occasionally fallen asleep at the dinner table, planting his face firmly in his bowl of apple sauce or whatever he was eating. Sometimes, though, he felt pretty close to doing that again. He held out each night, though, striving to work up to a normal bedtime.

And each morning Ken had to force himself—this was the easiest part—to sleep a little later. Soon there were no more two-in-the-morning kitchen raids. Within a few days Ken adjusted to a more-or-less normal sleeping schedule. He could do that. He was a kid, and kids adjusted quickly. His mom could do that, too. During the school year she never got a chance to sleep late. Or even sleep enough, for that matter. Here she could, and she took every advantage of the opportunity. She deserved it.

Ken's dad, now—that was a different matter. For days and days he'd wake up at the crack of dawn. Japan had no Daylight Savings Time. Still, the dawn would crack quite early in summertime Japan—about 4 AM.

"Maybe it's the cracking sound that wakes you up," Ken jokingly suggested once. His dad only growled in response. Ken's attempts at humor were met with a variety of reactions from his parents: groans, laughs, growls and/or chuckles. Then there was revenge: a sick joke counter-attacked with a sicker one. A knock-knock joke answered with a pound-pound joke. A bad pun leading to a deadly, several-minutes-long exchange of pun-fire. Fun times with his dad far outnumbered unhappy ones. For this, Ken was grateful.

Annaka days were full of fun. There were walks down to the nearby river. Stones needed to be thrown into the water. There were visits to the neighborhood playground. Swings needed to be swung on, slides to be slid down. Tag needed to be played. It was Ken's job to keep his father in shape.

There were games and puzzles in the Alexander house.

There were card games and board games, old games and new games—and some pretty weird games. Each had to be played at least once. And if each puzzle—little jigsaw puzzles, ball-in-a-maze puzzles, arrange the-pieces-in-a-square puzzles—hadn't been solved at least once, the visit to Annaka could not be considered complete.

And there was the annual visit—or two—or three—to the local toy store! Grandpa Alexander was very generous to his grandchildren. Each summer, on his first visit to Annaka, Ken received a crisp five-thousand-yen bill, worth about fifty dollars, depending on the current exchange rate. Japanese money always seemed crisp and clean. When visiting the U.S. Japanese people were often amazed at how dirty, tattered and marked up American money could be. How could Americans treat their money so disrespectfully?

Ken always had to earn his money, though. This year Grandpa Alexander announced that the money was hidden somewhere in the dining room. Ken spent several minutes looking around the room, eyes darting left and right, up and down. Finally, after a few vague hints, he spied the bill. It was halfway hidden behind a photograph pinned to a picture bulletin board. The board was attached to the wall between the doors to the kitchen and the hall. Ken eagerly grasped the prize from among the photos of his cousins and other relatives. Ken himself was featured in several of the pictures.

"Can we go to the toy store now?" Ken wasted no time in asking. A look that had more meaning than a dictionary was flashed at Ken from his father.

"Thank you," Ken said, quickly remembering his manners. Ken was always very polite with his "Pleases" and "Thank yous." Except for sometimes when he was excited. And right now he was very excited. Five thousand yen was a great deal of money.

"You're welcome, Ken" Grandpa Alexander replied.

"Can we go to the toy store now?" The question shot out again, almost before Grandpa's "You're welcome" had cleared the air.

"That's fine with me," Ken's grandfather said.

"Sure," replied Ken's dad.

"*Itterasshai,*" [literally, "Go and return."], said Ken's mom from the dining room table where she was enjoying a late breakfast. She had finally risen, only moments earlier. She seemed contentedly groggy. The good night's sleep had refreshed her considerably, but she was still waking up. From her seat of comfort she had been watching Ken hunt his treasure.

Itterasshai is usually said to somebody who is leaving the house to go somewhere, especially to school or work. The phrase can also be used when a person leaves any place to go somewhere for a short time. Mr. Alexander loved to play around with language. If someone had to go to the bathroom, he would say "*ittoire.*" "*Toire*" [toilet] was one word used in Japanese for a bathroom or restroom. "*Ittoire*" [Go toilet] was a pun of "*ittoide*, a vernacular way to say "*itterasshai.*" Use of this phrase would give proper Japanese people fits. Ken had picked up some of his father's ways of massacring language usage, much to his mother's dismay. But it was so much fun.

It was obvious from her response that Mrs. Alexander intended to remain behind with the Japanese language newspaper that also came in the morning, toast and a cup of coffee. Grandpa Alexander subscribed to one of the several English language newspapers that were available in Japan. The paper had only a few comics, much to Ken's disappointment. But it had good coverage of American sports news, something Grandpa appreciated.

Grandma Alexander (Tomoko-san) subscribed to a Japanese language newspaper for herself and her mother, *Obaachan* [Grandma]. Mrs. Alexander appreciated being able to read the news in Japanese, something she never got to do back home in Fort Collins. She could read English quite well, but there was something special about reading a paper in her native language.

"*Ittekimasu*," Ken called to his mother as he headed for the front door. [(I'll) go and come back] was the rough translation of this phrase. It was the proper, traditional thing to say when leaving the house.

Ken, his dad and Grandpa Alexander put on their shoes in the *genkan*, the entry way into the house. They walked down stone steps past the car in the car port. A roof kept the rain and what little snow came in the winter off of the car. A garage was not necessary and would have been much too expensive to add to the house when it was built.

The three Alexander men stepped into the narrow road in front of the house. There was no sidewalk here. They turned left and walked the few dozen yards up a hill to the main street. The main street in Annaka was a narrow, two-lane road. A narrow sidewalk on each side was all that separated the road from the many shops and homes that lined it.

Turning right, the Alexanders hugged the sidewalk and walked in the direction of the toy store. It was a Saturday morning, but even so, students in black uniforms were pedaling their bicycles towards one of the town's high schools. A half day of school was held every other Saturday in Japan. In the past every Saturday had been a school day. Only in recent years had Japan started easing up on the study load for students.

Ken paid no attention to the shops they passed—the noodle restaurant, the vegetable shop, the small book store, the bakery shop—even the tiny candy store. There was only one thing on his mind—toys!

And then they were there. The store was small compared with most of the toy stores back home in Fort Collins. But it was the largest one in Annaka. Every square inch of the shop was crammed with toys—everything from jigsaw puzzles to dolls to sports equipment to Legos. Many toys were native to Japan. There were train sets of the *Shinkansen*, Japan's rapid super express, often called the "Bullet Train" by Westerners, and other *tokkyu densha*. Japanese action figures and cartoon characters gazed at Ken as he walked by. And stacks of Japanese vehicles and heroes reached toward the ceiling.

"You know you can buy just one thing today and save the rest of your money for some other time," suggested Ken's dad. He suspected, though, that this was not a very realistic possibility. And in fact, his words had not connected with any part of Ken's brain. Ken walked from aisle to aisle, display to display, excitement running through his entire body.

Grandpa Alexander and Ken's dad followed Ken at first. Later, they gave up trying to keep up with Ken's flitting and stood talking. After thirty minutes or so Grandpa Alexander said he would go on home. Standing around for a long time—especially in a toy shop—got to be too tiring for him.

"Take your time, Ken," he said in parting. "Hope you find something you like." And he slowly trudged off for home.

The problem was that Ken had found too much that he liked. Eventually, though, he settled for a snap-together plastic model of a huge Bomber Man character. There were dozens of Bomber Man characters that appeared in a television program and comic books. The one Ken bought was a large robot figure. The head and other body parts could be detached to form space ships. A tiny Bomber Man fit into the cockpit of the head of the robot. As did many of the Bomber Man characters, this one had a hole in its midsection. A marble could be pushed into this hole. When a button on the back of the figure was pushed, the marble shot out of the "belly." Each of the arms of the larger robot was also a marble launcher. The toy was complicated, required assembly, had moving parts and was usable for action play. It was everything Ken wanted.

There was still some money left over. Ken used some of it on a package of fireworks. The Japanese word for fireworks is *hanabi*. "*Hana*" means "flower" and "*bi*" is a form of "*hi*," which means "fire." "Flower fire." What a delightful and appropriate name for those blooming explosions of colorful fire! Fireworks were illegal back home in Colorado because of the dry conditions. But here in Japan fireworks were not only legal, they were a necessary part of Japanese summertime tradition. Ken loved the custom.

Carefully clasping his treasures—the robot model, the *hanabi* and a small amount of remaining money—Ken finally, reluctantly left the toy store. His mind was eagerly anticipating the joy to come—making and playing with the Bomber Man, doing the fireworks. He nearly forgot that his father was with him.

As the two made their way back along the street, swallows soared up and down the street, sometimes coming within inches of their heads. Many shops along the road had appealed to the swallows for some reason. Little nests had been built, some above doorways, some higher up, under eaves.

At this time of year numerous little beaks could be seen poking above the edges of these nests. Baby swallows peep, peep, peeping for lunch were keeping the parent swallows busily flying about the town looking for tasty, buggy morsels for their offspring.

Shop owners were very tolerant of these winged guests, even when the birds created little messy piles on the sidewalk below their nests. Some humans had arranged little shelves or canopies to catch the little droppings and protect their customers from unfortunate accidents.

Ken had been halfway interested in the little chirpers on the way to the toy store. Now, lost in his own world of toys and fireworks, Ken didn't even know the creatures existed. He barely ducked his head when the black and white dive bombers zoomed mere inches above his head. Ken was happy as a swallow. Or was it happy as a lark? Rather, most likely, Ken was just happy as a boy on his way home from a toy store with a bagful of goodies.

CHAPTER 11

DANGO AND *HANABI*

"Ken."

As soon as he got home he would assemble the Bomber Man model.

"Ken!"

After that he would eat lunch.

"Keeen!"

Then he could play with the robot all afternoon.

"KEN!"

And then tonight they could do the *hanabi.*

"KEN!!!"

Oops! How long had his father been trying to get his attention?

"Oh, sorry. What?" Ken finally responded, pulled out of his day dream.

"Let's stop at that store over there."

Ken glanced at the shop and knew immediately what his father had in mind. *Dango*!

"OK!"

Traffic was light in the mid-morning. Students were off the streets and in school by now. Many years ago a two-lane bypass had been built around the north side of Annaka. All through traffic now missed the center of the town. The only vehicles in town were tiny cars driven by housewives out running errands, trucks making local deliveries and an occasional bus.

Despite the light traffic flow, Mr. Alexander guided Ken to the next crosswalk before the two ventured across the street. The outside of the shop, though clean, was dark and ancient-looking. The wooden outer walls and eaves were black and soot-covered from years of passing traffic. The shop had probably been there unchanged since Mr. Alexander's childhood.

Ken pushed aside the sliding glass door and stepped inside. A bell dangling above the doorway tinkled, announcing to the shop owner that customers had arrived. A *shohji* [paper] sliding door opened and a middle-aged woman stepped down from a *tatami* room into sandals sitting on the concrete floor of the shop. Most likely her family lived in the adjacent room and on the second story of the building.

"*Irasshai*!" [Welcome] she called out cheerfully.

"*Konnichiwa*" [Good afternoon], Mr. Alexander responded. It was mid-morning. Mr. Alexander probably should have said "*Ohayoh gozaimasu*" [Good morning]. But foreigners were easily forgiven for their language and cultural gaffes. (To Mr. Alexander, who had been awake for six hours already, it seemed like afternoon. His error was less a misuse of language and more of a matter of being confused about the time.)

Ken wasn't paying much attention to either of the adults. His eyes were fixated on a glass case filled with many delightful sweets. The lady shuffled in her sandals over to the case.

"What would you like?" she asked Ken.

"Which kind do you want?" Mr. Alexander asked. It was understood that it was the *dango* they were after.

Dango are little dumpling-like snacks made out of sticky rice. They come in the shape of little, white, chewy balls, about the size of a marble. Usually, three or four come in a set skewered together on a stick. The dumplings themselves don't taste like much. It's the sauce they come in that makes them delicious to eat.

Ken looked at the *dango* in the display case for only a moment. He knew which kind he wanted. The ones in the dark-gray sweet bean paste (*anko*) were good. But his favorites were the ones in the sweet sugar/soy sauce paste. They were more than good. They were great! Delicious! Exquisite! Ken's mouth was already starting to water.

Ken pointed to his choice.

"*Sore kudasai*" [Those please], he told the lady.

Mr. Alexander made some quick calculations, then asked the shop keeper for five sticks.

"That'll be enough for everyone to have one stick," he explained to Ken. "And if somebody doesn't want theirs, you can have the extra." This sounded fine to Ken.

In olden days the *dango* would have been wrapped in a bamboo leaf and then some fancy wrapping paper. Today the skewers were placed in a plastic container which was then put in a plastic bag. The lady handed the bag to Mr. Alexander. He fished around in his pocket for the correct amount of money and handed it to the woman.

"*Dohmo arigatoh gozaimashita*" [Thank you very much], said the shop owner, bowing deeply. "Please come again."

"*Arigatoh gozaimashita*," echoed Mr. Alexander, bowing

awkwardly. Turning toward the door, he bowed again, this time to avoid banging his head on the top of the doorway. Japanese doors have a standard height of six feet. Mr. Alexander was six feet, two inches tall. A single math calculation will tell you that this means trouble.

Ken's dad had learned many years earlier to duck when going through Japanese doorways—in homes, older stores—even on trains. He looked as though he was being very polite, bowing his head whenever he got on or off a train. What a strange foreigner, Japanese people must have thought, bowing to a train like that. Actually, Mr. Alexander was simply trying to save his scalp. Still, his head occasionally had unfortunate encounters with low doorways when he forgot to bow. The Japanese word "*itai*" [ouch] was firmly placed in Mr. Alexander's vocabulary.

The walk home was very quick for some reason. The two Alexanders had barely kicked off their shoes in the *genkan* and uttered their "*tadaima*"s [I'm home] when Ken asked,

"Can I have one now?"

Lunch was not quite ready. Mrs. Alexander was in the guest bedroom reading—not sleeping! Grandpa Alexander and *Obaachan* were nowhere to be seen. Grandma Alexander was busy in the kitchen.

Ordinarily the answer would be a firm "no." But this was special. After all, they were in Japan now. Grandma Alexander understood this, too. When Ken's dad asked her if it would be OK if they ate some *dango* now, there was no objection.

"OK, but just one now. And you have to promise to eat all your lunch," said Mr. Alexander.

"I promise."

Mr. Alexander brought two small plates from the kitchen while Ken took the *dango* out of the shopping bag and opened the plastic container. Ken picked up one stick of *dango*, rolled it in the extra, sticky sauce in the bottom of the container and guided it to his mouth. Being careful not to poke the roof of his mouth with the sharp end of the skewer—that would take something away from the joy of eating—he placed the end of the stick in his mouth and pulled off the first little ball with his teeth.

"Mmmm," was all he could murmur. His dad took another skewer and followed Ken's example.

Suddenly the room was filled with people. Ken's mom had come in from her room. Grandpa Alexander thumped his way down the stairs from his upstairs room where he'd been working on a jigsaw puzzle. Obaachan was back from a friend's house. And Grandma Alexander appeared in the doorway to the kitchen, hands full of the first wave of lunch goodies. More dishes were brought out and soon the entire group—except for Grandpa Alexander—was chomping their way through a before-lunch snack of *dango*.

After that the table was quickly set for lunch. Ken really did eat a full lunch, though probably not as much as he would have if he hadn't enjoyed the *dango* first. For dessert he had—another stick of *dango*. Of course! Grandpa Alexander had opted out of *dango*, and Ken was the lucky winner of the extra skewer.

The afternoon went by quickly. Ken's mom and grandfather took naps. Obaachan puttered about in the garden. Grandma Alexander went to a church meeting. And Ken, with a little help from his dad, assembled the Bomber Man robot.

Later, when the nappers awoke, the Alexanders and Grandpa Alexander played games.

Dinner came and went and soon it was time for the next highlight of the day. Ken took a quick shower. No time for a bath tonight. Darkness had fallen and the time was right for that most magical and thrilling of Japanese summer traditions—*hanabi.*

Hanabi had to be done after dinner—and after a bath or shower. Traditionally, savoring a hot, relaxing, purifying bath, Japanese people donned their *yukata*—light, cotton summer *kimonos*. Sometimes *yukata* are compared with the bathrobes of American culture. But the difference is as big as the world. *Yukata* are perfectly acceptable for wear in public. They are more than evening outer wear. They are a symbol of Japanese summer nights, when the heat of the day is softened ever so slightly by gentle breezes playing wind chimes, when crickets sound a mysterious summer chorus, when the night hangs full and heavy. It's the time of day when families escape the heat of their homes for a cold treat at a shaved ice stand. Or when they go for refreshing walks by a riverside. Or they attend one of the countless summer festivals held throughout Japan in which entire communities gather together to dance Japanese folk dances late into the night to the sound of drums and flutes. Or they gather by the thousands on a riverbank to watch one of Japan's many spectacular public fireworks displays.

Or they find a dark park, riverbank or backyard in which to hold their own private fireworks festival. This is what the Alexanders were about to do. It wasn't summer, really—only late May. The hot, humid days properly associated with *hanabi* had not yet arrived. But the Alexanders were going to do their fireworks anyway.

Ken's family and Grandpa Alexander stood together in a small, open part of the back yard. Ken didn't have a *yukata* in Annaka, so his *Doraemon* pajamas were his attire for the ritual. If he'd had a *yukata*, Ken would have been happy to wear it. He loved all things Japanese.

Grandma Alexander kept Obaachan company sitting inside the sliding screen doors of the *tatami* room that also served as a guest bedroom. Obaachan enjoyed watching the fireworks, but because of her age, it was thought to be better if she didn't hold them herself.

The Annaka yard was tiny, about the size of a large American living room. Every available spot was carefully planted with bushes, trees and flowers. Rocks of various sizes, shapes and colors lay about the yard. They served as borders here, decorative points in the landscape there. The air out here always smelled sweet of something blooming. Grandma Alexander and Obaachan spent many hours lovingly caring for the plants—weeding, trimming, pruning. Everything was perfect.

Ken opened the package of fireworks. By his side was a bucket of water. Just in case. A metal basin lay ready on the ground.

Mr. Alexander lit a match and then transferred the flame to a candle. Ken selected his first firework, a mild sparkler. Holding the harder end firmly in his hand, he turned the soft, papered end toward his father and the candle. The tissue-like paper caught fire immediately. As Ken turned the stick away from the candle, the flame reached the packed powder which began to sputter colored flame. Sparks spewed forth in a gentle shower of red, blue, green and yellow firedrops.

"That's good, Ken," said his father. "Hold it away from you like that."

Ken knew exactly what to do, even without being told. He'd done this many times before.

Beside him Ken heard the sizzle of another *hanabi* starting up. He turned to see his mother holding on to the same kind of sparkler he had. There were plenty to go around, and Ken was glad to share.

"Do you want to do one?" Ken asked, nodding generally in the direction of his father and grandfather.

"You go ahead, Ken," replied Grandfather Alexander.

"Yeah, thanks, Ken," said Mr. Alexander. "Maybe I'll try one. But let's get you started on another one first."

Ken's *hanabi* fizzled out. He dipped the tip of it in the bucket of water, then dropped the soggy remains in the basin.

Next Ken chose one of the smallest fireworks. This kind produced only one color of fire. Once the flame faded from the startup paper, golden-orange sparks flew from the end of the short stick. Little baby sparks darted out to explore the night. They shot out no more than two or three inches, as if they didn't want to wander too far from home. A soft, crackling sound accompanied them—the cheerful laughter of infant sparks at play. Slowly, magically, a tiny glowing ball began to grow at the tip of the stick.

"Look. A sun!" exclaimed Ken. And indeed it did look like a miniature sun dangling at the end of the stick, glowing warmly in the night, giving birth to its orange shooting-star babies. And then the globe was gone, falling to the ground, holding its color for a second before fading into black.

"Darn it," Ken said. He knew the glowing ball was supposed to last longer.

"Don't let your hand shake," advised Ken's dad. "You have to hold it firmly."

"I know!" Ken retorted. He felt badly enough that he'd lost his sun. His dad didn't have to rub it in.

"It's OK." Grandpa Alexander's voice was supportive. "There are a lot more."

Ken's frustration washed away. For his next performance he chose one of the largest fireworks in the package. This one was a cylinder, about a foot long. Like the others, it had colorful tissue at one end. This, too, was a handheld firework.

There were no rockets in the package Ken had bought. Someday he wanted to try one of the really big ones, the ones that soared high into the sky. But they were expensive. A big rocket cost about the same as this entire package of sparklers. His father had promised him they could buy some rockets some other time. But not today. The Annaka yard was too confined for rockets. Besides, shooting off rockets in town was dangerous. It was asking for trouble. Maybe at Lake Nojiri.

The paper was lit and the cylinder was turned and pointed away from the group. A second later a stream of sparks blasted out of the end, shooting nearly five feet. First came eye-dazzling white flame. Quickly the white turned to blue. Next came a spurt of crimson fire. Yellow followed, and then another stage of white light. Several more times the sparks changed color. And then, just as rapidly as the explosion of light had begun, the sparkler sputtered out.

For nearly half an hour Ken and his parents lit up the night with their fire sticks. Grandpa Alexander strolled over to the house and opening the screen door, sat down with his wife and mother-in-law. Standing a long time had tired him out. The three older folks enjoyed their vantage view of the fireworks display.

Ken's mom and dad took an occasional turn, but mostly they let Ken have the honors. Finally, there were only three of the medium sized fireworks remaining.

"Let's do them together," suggested Ken. His parents agreed and with some tricky maneuvering, all three managed to nearly simultaneously light their fireworks. Standing in an intimate semicircle, the three held their burning tips together. Flames from the three sparklers fused together in a frenzied cascade of rainbow colors. Sparks hissed and crackled. Clouds of smoke billowed out in blue waves and wafted across the garden. And then it was all over.

"Wow, that was cool!" exclaimed Ken, dipping the stub of his final firework in the water bucket and dumping it in the basin. "Let's do this again."

"Sounds good," responded Mr. Alexander. "Maybe at Nojiri." Then he added,

"You know, this is pretty weird. I mean, I'm always complaining about cigarette smoke. And here I am doing this. How good can this be for our health?"

Wispy smoke was still floating about the yard in a hazy mist before gradually floating skyward.

"Don't worry about it," scolded Mrs. Alexander. "We're having such a good time. Don't spoil it by complaining."

"I'm not complaining," Mr. Alexander replied. "I'm just saying it's interesting. Besides, I tried to keep out of the way of most of the smoke. And it's a special occasion."

Ken wasn't sure what the point of all this was. His parents were at it again, but he was too happy to care. And his parents weren't really arguing. They were both smiling. They'd had a good time, too.

Ken had gotten a little smoke in his face, too. But that was part of doing fireworks. He'd had fun. Now it was time to clean up and go to bed.

Thirty minutes later Ken was in his *futon*. His parents were on either side of him, tucking him in.

"Well, you had a pretty good day, didn't you?" said Mr. Alexander. "What did you like best?"

"Oh, lots of stuff," smiled Ken. He didn't feel like talking any more. He was tired. Dreamland was calling.

Mr. and Mrs. Alexander sensed this and didn't press for any further response.

"Tomorrow should be another fun day. Well, sleep well. I love you." Mr. Alexander finished his bedtime routine with a kiss on the forehead and his usual salute/wave and was gone.

"*Okaasan* [Mother], can we do *hanabi* in Tokyo?"

"We'll see. Ojiichan and Obaachan might like to do it." In a couple of days Ken would be seeing his Japanese grandparents—his mother's parents. They liked traditional Japanese customs, too. Chances were good, he thought, for more *hanabi*. And with that happy thought rattling around in his brain, Ken slipped into a peaceful, restful slumber.

During the rest of his stay in Annaka, Ken did not once worry about the incident at the airport or the problem at Lake Nojiri. This was a good thing. Had he known what was to come, he would have worried—a lot.

CHAPTER 12

TAKASHIMADAIRA'S NASTY PIGEONS

Ken struggled against the sound that was trying to pull him awake. For a moment it seemed as if he would win. He faded back into his dream—a strange dream occupied by stuffed animals that were singing and talking and dancing. He could blame this image on one of his dad's silly bedtime stories from years gone by. Singing stuffed animals indeed!

And then the sound reached deep into Ken's dream again and yanked on his consciousness. What was that noise? A hissing, swishing sound. Ken gave up the battle and became completely awake. Where was he? What was going on? WHAT WAS THAT SOUND?!?

Oh, yeah. The pigeons.

Ken was in *Ojiichan* and *obaachan's* apartment in Tokyo, in the district of Itabashi. Ken reluctantly opened an eye and looked around the room. The other eye soon joined in the effort.

The *Doraemon* clock said 5:12 AM. Ken sighed. That was too early to be awake, even on a week day. But it was the fault of the pigeons. Those darned pigeons.

Ken glanced out the huge sliding windows to the balcony. The sun was already playing peek-a-boo between high apartment buildings over to the east. (The sun rises in the east in Japan, too!) Ken saw his Japanese grandfather crouched out on the balcony in front of netting that surrounded and covered the area. The scene reminded Ken of pictures he'd seen of wartime foxholes, covered with camouflage netting. Pictures of war zones.

Well, this *was* a war zone! And there was *Ojiichan* fighting off the enemy with his weapon of choice—a water gun! The enemy: pigeons.

Somehow the Takashimadaira Division of the Royal Tokyo Pigeons Army had discovered that the Tanaka's seventh floor balcony, on the top floor of the building, was a very cool place to hang out. And these winged marauders loved to visit VERY early in the morning. The ruckus of their coo coos and their messy droppings on the balcony were unacceptable to Ken's Japanese grandfather.

Understandably, Grandpa Tanaka was not too happy with the idea of two-footed invaders waddling around on his balcony. He fought back with a cold, calculated passion. This was war!

The first step was to design a defense system of ropes and nets. *Ojiichan* was good with papers and figures and diagrams and such. He had been an electrical engineer before retirement. Many hours were spent measuring the balcony—side to side, top to bottom, front to back—in meters and centimeters. If nothing else, *Ojiichan* was very thorough.

More hours were spent hunched over the dining room

floor table amid a sea of paper, pencils, rulers, a compass and all the other thinking man's weapons of war.

Finally, ropes and netting were purchased, cut to the appropriate size and hung with care. The balcony became a closed in safety zone. And it worked! After trying in vain to penetrate the perimeter, as a soldier might say, the pagan pigeons went elsewhere.

Ojiichan quietly basked in his glorious success for an entire day. (He was too dignified to dance and shout. Ken's dad might have. But that was Ken's dad.)

Grandma Tanaka was proud of her husband, as well. In her daily phone calls to her sisters, standing on one leg, the other one crossed at the knee like a flamingo, she described in great detail her husband's great accomplishment. There was great pride and joy and rejoicing all around.

But—

The next day the putrid pigeons were back. Not on the Tanaka's' balcony, of course. That battle zone had been conquered. It was impenetrable.

But the next door neighbors had a balcony that was just as cool for the pigeons to hang out on. And the neighbors didn't have netting. So there were the foul fowls, strutting back and forth across their newly acquired territory and cooing in a tone of voice that most definitely had to be pigeonese for "Nanny, nanny, boo boo" and "Nyaahh, nyaahh, nyaahh, nhyaahh, nyaahh."

So there was *Ojiichan* on this bright, early summer morning, crouched on the balcony in his *yukata*, water gun aimed at the pesky pigeons through the grate separating the two apartments, firing away at the enemy, attempting to send them scattering and muttering to himself. Swish, swish. Coo, coo. Grumble, grumble. Swish, swish. Coo, coo. Grumble, grumble. Ken would have thought the sounds to be humorous if *Ojiichan* hadn't been so earnest in his battle.

Ken wished he had brought his Sooper Soaker 2000 with him from the U.S. One shot from that mighty water gun and the pigeons would be blasted all the way into the next prefecture. He wondered what his father, the animal lover, would say about that. Mr. Alexander hated being awakened early, too. He would probably support the water attack as a necessary use of force—as long as there was no loss of pigeon life.

Ken's face lit up. That reminded him—today was the day he and his mother were going to Lake Nojiri. He'd get to see his dad again before nightfall!

After their stay in Annaka, Ken and his mom had come to Tokyo. Mr. Alexander had stayed behind to spend one more day with his own father. Ken had been excited to come to his Japanese grandparents' apartment. But the train trip back to Tokyo was always a little lonelier when his father was not along.

Mr. Alexander had joined his family in Takashimadaira a day later. He went back and forth between Tokyo and Annaka, spending a few days in each place. Ten days earlier he had left for Annaka to spend a few more days with Grandpa Alexander. From there he had gone to Lake Nojiri to spend a week by himself. Today Ken and his mom would join Mr. Alexander at the lake.

Tokyo is a BIG city. This can't be said too often. Well, maybe it can, but anybody visiting the city for the first time could be excused for using that adjective over and over.

Japan consists of four main islands and scores of little ones, ranging in size from so-so islands to little itsy bitsy ones inhabited only by sea gulls. (Distant relatives of the Takashimadaira Division of the Tokyo Royal Pigeons Army, no doubt.) One island, the huge, northernmost one of Hokkaido is a "doh." Ken's father could never adequately explain what a "*doh*" was. He tried once, over dinner, back in Fort Collins. After his explanation, Mrs. Alexander had said that a "*doh*" was like a prefecture or state, only different.

"That's what I was trying to say," grumbled Mr. Alexander.

"You said it was a prefecture," Mrs. Alexander disagreed.

"No I didn't. I said it was *like* a prefecture," Mr. Alexander argued back. He was no longer muttering to himself. This was a battle. His ego had been challenged. Now he was directly confronting his opponent.

"I said Hokkaido was a..." Mr. Alexander turned to Ken. "What did I say it was?"

"You said Hokkaido was a kind of food," Ken answered mischievously.

"I DID NOT!" hollered Mr. Alexander. And the chase was on. Ken fled for his dear life from the dining nook. He was tackled half way across the living room and a ferocious wrestling match followed.

Eventually Ken remembered that he was still hungry. Somehow shaking himself loose from his father's grasp, Ken ran back to the table, followed closely by a now panting Mr. Alexander. Mrs. Alexander was calmly finishing her meal. Ken and his dad slid into their seats, and amid rolls of laughter the dinner was completed.

"See. I told you I was right," Mr. Alexander proclaimed with a pompous air of authority. "What were we talking about?"

Ken and his mother exchanged knowing looks. Everybody knew that Mrs. Alexander was usually right on such occasions.

Meanwhile, back in Japan...

On the three main islands are a total of 47 *ken*, and one *to*. A *ken* is a prefecture, similar to a state in the United States or a province in Canada. Grandpa and Grandma Alexander lived in Gunma-*Ken*. Lake Nojiri was in Nagano-*Ken*. Narita Airport where Ken and his family had arrived in Japan was in Chiba-*Ken*. And so on. Honshu, the largest island, was the locale of the majority of the prefectures.

However, Ken (the boy) was not a prefecture. His name just happened to have the same sound as the Japanese word for "prefecture." It was as if a girl or boy in the United States would be named "State." This child would not actually be a state—though she or he would most certainly have an unusual name. "Ken," however was not an unusual name for Japanese boys.

Ken's name, when properly written in Japanese, consisted of one *kanji* or Chinese character. There are many *kanji* that can be read as "Ken." One character means "sword." Another one is used in words about health. Still another, totally different *kanji* that can be read as "Ken" means "dog." Ken was thankful that his mother had not chosen this particular *kanji* for his name. Then again, it might have been fun to be able to tell American kids,

"Hi. My name is Ken. In Japanese my name means 'dog.' Woof." Or whatever.

Actually, the *kanji* (Chinese character) for Ken's name consisted of two parts. The section on the right meant "both" or "double." This was appropriate because Ken had two nationalities, two languages and two cultures to call his own.

Ken felt very lucky. He could speak two languages. He was a citizen of two countries. And he knew and loved both the American and Japanese cultures—the customs, the food, the holidays. Nothing like getting Christmas presents, American style, and New Year's gift money, Japanese style. Yes, he had it good, and he knew it. (And he even had two mostly tolerable parents.)

Ken's name had not been assigned the *kanji* for "prefecture." But the 47 prefectures had.

Then there is one *to*. Tokyo, the capital of Japan, is the *to*. It is a huge city that is not part of any prefecture, somewhat like Washington, D.C. in the United States. Tokyo *to* is commonly called the Tokyo Metropolis. That's just a fancy way to say "big city."

To make things even more complicated, Tokyo is made up of 23 *ku*. *Ku* are wards or districts. Many wards have a larger population than Ken's hometown of Fort Collins. Fort Collins had more than 100,000 people. Twenty-three Fort Collins's! No wonder Tokyo seemed so—BIG!

Ojiichan and *Obaachan* lived in Itabashi-*Ku*. The train station where Ken's family had first transferred trains when they first arrived in Tokyo—Ueno Station—was located—in Taito-Ward. When they went to Nojiri, Ken and his mom passed through Shinjuku station (the world's busiest station) in, of course, Shinjuku-*ku*. And so on. And there was even a Tokyo Station, located in Ciiyoda-*ku*, which was in turn located in Tokyo-t*o*.

Now, to make matters even more complicated and confusing, each *ku* or ward has within it many little towns or areas. Most of these towns run together so that one cannot tell where one town ends and the next one begins. (Was it mentioned that Tokyo is BIG?!?)

So there Ken was, in his Japanese grandparents' apartment, on the 7th floor of the *Wakaba Mansion* [condominium] building, in Takashimadaira town, in Itabashi-*Ku*, in Tokyo Metropolis, on Honshu island, in the country of Japan, with his Japanese grandfather out on the balcony, in his *yukata*, squirting a water gun at a flock of rowdy pigeons on the next door balcony.

And my friends ask me why I like coming to Japan! Ken thought to himself.

Ignoring the terrible battle sounds in the background—Swish, swish. Coo, coo. Grumble, grumble—Ken allowed his eyes to survey the rest of the room. Beside him was Mrs. Alexander. Her sheet and blanket—it was too hot these days for any more bedding—were scattered here and there. She was somewhere in between, sprawled out in an interesting shape on her *futon*.

Beyond her were two papered sliding doors that led into *Ojiichan's* room. The door was wide open, in the mainly hopeless hope that some breeze might pass through the rooms. Summer in Tokyo was hot (that should probably be HOT) and humid (and that should properly be HUMID). You could take a shower before going to bed, but if that breeze didn't blow through the night, by morning you would be drenched in sweat. You and your pajamas and your sheets and any poor stuffed animals you might have decided to sleep with might be soaked. Ken didn't sleep with stuffed animals often when it got hot. He didn't want to drown them.

Both *Ojiichan's* room and Ken's room opened out onto the

netted balcony through glass sliding doors. This side of the apartment faced south. In the winter the sunlight streaming into these rooms was welcome, warm, cozy. It heated up the *tatami* (straw mats) to a golden, sweet-smelling toastiness. But in summer the sun beat down on the concrete roof and walls of the building. Ken wished that the solar globe playing early morning hide and seek in Tokyo's concrete labyrinth would go hide somewhere else for the rest of the day and leave them alone.

At the foot of Ken's and his mother's *futon* was *Obaachan*. *Ojiichan* liked to have his own room. *Obaachan* was happy to oblige. She was short, even shorter than Ken now. The three of them fit cozily in the tiny bedroom, like three peas in a pod.

On Ken's other side was a piano. Cushions protected him from banging into its hard surface, just in case he should get restless during the night and begin rolling about. Another positive thing about sleeping on *futon*—at least you couldn't fall out of bed—or at least you couldn't fall very far.

On top of the piano were stacks of piano music, small boxes of toys and a glass case containing more tiny dolls and statuettes than there were at Tokyo Disneyland's Small World. Or so it seemed to Ken. There were many curious, old items in this apartment.

Ken forced himself out of bed and stepping carefully over his still sleeping grandmother, walked through the open set of sliding doors that led into the living room/dining room. Walking around the low table at the center of the room, he passed on to the narrow hallway leading to the door of the apartment. To the right was a little room into which Ken popped.

Ages ago, when Ken's mom was a little girl living at home,

this had been a third bedroom. The floor was still made of *tatami*. In later years, though, the room had been converted into a storeroom. But in the last few years, as Ken grew bigger and his father wanted more space and privacy for sleeping, the storeroom had been changed into a spare guest room. But it was still a storeroom.

Three sides of the room were lined from floor to ceiling with cabinets, bookshelves and boxes, leaving only a small space where a tiny window opened out to the north side of the building. Above the window a huge board which served as a shelf stretched from the tops of the cabinets on either side of the room. A huge closet made up the fourth wall. In it were extra *futon*, pillows and other bedding. On the shelf board and atop the cabinets were more boxes, each with its contents clearly written with marker on the outside: dishes, toys, towels, stuffed animals.

The boxes marked "toys" had always intrigued Ken. Once in awhile he could persuade *Ojiichan* to bring down one of the battered cardboard boxes. Ken would find inside treasures of old toy cars and trucks, balls or other long-forgotten stuffed animals. There was much mystery in this room.

Across the room was hung a long bamboo pole. From it hung an assortment of coats, skirts, suits and other articles of apparel. The pole served as a clothing rack.

Every morning Ken came into this room to get his breakfast. A low table just inside the door was heaped with boxes of cereal. Ken loved Japanese food. He really did. But for some reason a breakfast of *miso* soup, rice and fermented soy beans did not appeal to him. It was the same with his father. So every year when they came to Japan the Alexanders packed their suitcases with several boxes of American cereal. They could buy cereal in Japan, of course, but there was much less variety. And the cost of cereal here was enough to make Ken's dad cry. Well, he didn't really cry over the price of cereal. But if he were the type of person to cry at high prices, he most certainly would have.

Normally, when Ken entered this room he'd see his dad stuffed into his *futon* in the canyon between the walls of books, closets and such. The floor space came out to—Mr. Alexander had actually measured it once—four feet wide by six and a half feet long. One of Mrs. Alexander's aunts, upon seeing Mr. Alexander in his cramped room, had once said,

"You look like a prisoner in a jail cell."

But Mr. Alexander never complained about the size of his living space. He talked about it often to his acquaintances and family, even seemed to brag about it. He actually enjoyed the cozy, snug feeling of the tiny space. By the side of his *futon*, on a short bookcase, there was room for his little transistor radio, tissues, cough drops and throat spray, aspirin bottle, crossword puzzle magazine and books. He spent many hours in that comfortable little cubicle, sometimes coming out only to eat or play with Ken after school. And he often lay in his room dreaming and fantasizing. He wondered about what sort of book he could write. He wanted to write a book. He just didn't know what to write about.

The rack of clothes hung across the room somewhere over Mr. Alexander's midsection. The longer items hung to less than three feet over the *futon*. He didn't mind, though. The row of clothes made a useful curtain, keeping the light from the tiny window from shining into his eyes. They were a convenient clothes curtain.

Mr. Alexander was extremely picky about where he slept. He needed a room to be dark and quiet. Not necessarily spacious. Just dark and quiet.

Just like some kind of bug, Ken thought. Come to think of it, when he's sleeping here in this cramped space, all rolled up in his bedding, he does look like a bug—a big bug wrapped up in a giant cocoon.

This reminded Ken of a song his father had written for him when he was little.

"Dougie was a buggy,

"Who lived under a ruggy,

"Where everything was dark

"And very nice and snuggy."

There were several other verses to the song as well. One went

"Augie was a froggy

"Who lived down in a boggy

"Where everything was damp

"And very nice and soggy."

There was even a verse about Jakey the snakey who lived down by the lakey and danced the "Hippy Hippy Shaky."

Yes, his dad was an interesting—dare he say strange?—man, indeed.

There was a small fan attached to the side of one of the book cases near Mr. Alexander's head. Grandpa Tanaka had set it up to help his son-in-law keep cool at night. In addition to being thorough, Grandpa Tanaka was also concerned about the comfort and well-being of his guests. This was a deeply ingrained Japanese tradition.

Mr. Alexander used the fan for other purposes, too. He

kept it spinning constantly when he was in the little room. The drone of the motor was not only soothing, it helped to drown out obnoxious outside noises such as barking dogs and the wild carousing of the Takashimadaira Division of the Royal Tokyo Pigeons Army at the other end of the apartment, not to mention the ugly sounds of battle: Swish, swish. Coo, coo. Grumble, grumble.

For the last few days Ken had felt a touch of loneliness every time he made his morning trek to fetch the cereal. The 4x6.5-foot spot on the floor had been bare, the futon and bedding folded up and stashed away in the closet. Ken liked it when his dad was in town. Each summer Mr. Alexander spent a few weeks in Tokyo while he visited friends, did some shopping and did who knew what else. Ken couldn't quite figure out what his father did all day long. He seemed to spend a lot of time reading and doing crossword puzzles and such, stashed away in his little room.

Once in awhile Mr. Alexander visited Ken's Japanese school to talk about American life and schools. Ken was proud when his father did that. And Ken's classmates always seemed friendlier to him after a visit from Mr. Alexander.

To them, Ken was just another kid. He looked a lot like them, with his dark hair, dark eyes and dark complexion. To be sure, he was a little different, perhaps, because he came from America every summer to attend Sakura Elementary School for a mere six or seven weeks. And Ken was bigger than most of the Japanese boys and girls in his class. But he spoke fluent Japanese. For the most part, he simply fit in comfortably with his classmates.

But Ken's dad was an entirely different story. He was very

tall by Japanese standards and had—"Wow! Look at that!"—blue eyes. He actually looked like a *Gaijin*, a foreigner. Like his son, Mr. Alexander spoke fairly good Japanese. When he came to the school he used his Japanese to talk about America. But he was obviously a visitor from abroad. Perhaps when they realized this, the Japanese children also understood that Ken was unique. He had new and different experiences and ideas to share.

And there was a sense of pride among the Japanese children in knowing Ken. It gave his companions bragging rights. "I'm friends with the kid whose dad talked to the school yesterday," or "You know that man who talked about America? His boy sits next to me in class."

Ken didn't mind this. He enjoyed the attention. And he knew that his best Japanese buddies, the ones he played with, were his true friends. They were the ones who invited Ken to their houses after school to play such traditional Japanese games as hide-and-seek, tag, soccer—and Nintendo. (?!?) They didn't care whether Ken was from Tokyo or the United States or outer space. They simply enjoyed playing with him.

Today Ken didn't mind seeing an empty space on the tiny bedroom floor. No, not at all. Breakfast, a few short train rides and a long train ride later, Ken would be seeing his dad again. His heart did a quick little twinkle toes dance. The cereal tasted especially good this morning. He even accepted some of the baby tomatoes and steamed broccoli offered to him by *Obaachan*, who had gotten up early to prepare her husband's breakfast. Yes, today would be a good day!

CHAPTER 13

LAKE NOJIRI—AT LAST!

Ken was excited. Maybe not as excited as he always was the night before Christmas. Or just before his birthday every year. But this was right up there with the biggest excitements of the year. This was the "In just a few moments I'm going to see my dad whom I haven't seen in ten days!" excitement.

He gazed out the window again. The *tokkyu* train had sped through cluttered cities and across emerald plains covered with green rice paddies during the first two hours of his trip. Then, at the edge of a plain which had gradually shrunk into a mountain-surrounded valley, the train paused longer than at the other stations they had stopped at. They had just passed through the town of Annaka, home to Grandma and Grandpa Alexander, without stopping. Now they were stopped at the town of Yokokawa and vendors were walking up and down the platform calling out "*Obentoh, obentoh. Kamameshi-bentoh.*" Ken's mom handed him three thousand-yen bills and he rushed to the open door at the end of the car.

"Two *obentoh*, please," Ken told the nearest vendor. The man took the money, counted out change, and handed the change to Ken. The vendor carried a tray suspended in front of him by a strap which reached behind the back of his neck and wrapped over his shoulders. From this tray he took two plastic bowls with plastic covers tied on with a string.

"*Arigatoh*," Ken told the man, receiving the bowls and turning to carry his prize back to his seat.

"*Arigatoh gozaimashita*," he heard the vendor call after him as the door to the vestibule closed behind Ken and he scurried down the aisle.

Ken and his mother waited for the train to start, which happened soon enough. First there was a clank and the train shuddered as two old-style diesel engines were attached to the front of the sleek, modern electric *tokkyu*. Then, with a slightly more noticeable jerk than usual, the train pulled out of the station.

The route now took Ken and his mother through a series of seemingly endless tunnels as they climbed from the Kanto Plain up over the Usui Pass. Electric trains just did not have the power to make this climb on their own. If they had feelings, the older diesel engines would have probably been proud that they were needed to help out these fancy newcomers with a little extra pull.

The ceiling lights cast a soft glow over the interior of the train each time the outside went pitch black in a tunnel. Occasionally the train would stream through a splash of sunlight, only to be plunged immediately into the inky world of the next tunnel.

"Can we eat?" Ken asked.

"*Hai. Dohzo*" [Yes. Go ahead.], replied his mom.

Ken easily loosened the string tied in a bow at the top of the *obentoh*. Next he removed the wooden *hashi* [chopsticks], wrapped in their own paper sleeve. Finally, he removed the square paper covering the lid and gingerly lifted off the lid itself. There it was—the treasure. A mound of white rice lay covered with all sorts of goodies. There was the tiny hard-boiled quail egg. Some *teriyaki* chicken grilled in a soy sauce-and-sugar sauce lay on top of another portion of the rice. Next to these two items were some soft mushrooms prepared in the same sort of sauce. And there were the bright red pickled spicy ginger and some spinach.

Ken removed the chopsticks from their wrapper. They were a small strip of wood, actually, split down the middle but attached at one end. Ken pulled the two sticks completely apart, said "*Itadakimasu*" and began to eat. Mrs. Alexander did the same.

These *obentoh*, or box lunches, had been sold like this as a specialty of the town of Yokokawa since who knew when. Even way back—waaay back—when Ken's dad had been a little boy living in nearby Annaka, and smoky steam locomotives had chugged up and down this mountain, they had been a tradition. One simply *had to* buy a *kamameshi-bentoh* in Yokokawa! *Kamameshi* referred to the bowl and rice. Originally, the *kama* bowls had been made out of stone, but these had been modernized and replaced with plastic bowls. *Meshi* referred to the rice. Ken hungrily gulped down his *obentoh*.

Eventually daylight became a permanent fixture as the train cleared the last of the tunnels. There was another delay as the train slowed to a stop in the town of Karuizawa and the diesel engines were disengaged.

"*Arigatoh gozaimashita*," Ken felt like calling to them. The diesels would sit at this station now until a limited express headed in the opposite direction came along and needed their services to slow it down as it descended the long, steep drop to the plain below.

The cloudy, drizzling, yucky weather of the valley below was replaced up here on the high plains with white clouds and a scattering of blue. As they pulled out of Karuizawa station, Ken and his mother were treated to an awesome sight. There, not too many miles away, stood the lordly Mount Asama, rising like a giant standing guard over the high plain. From its peak, a thin trail of smoke drifted off into high clouds.

This active volcano, one of many in Japan, could often be seen smoking. (Ken's dad didn't mind this kind of smoking!). It had erupted several times in recent years, once when Ken's dad was a boy, sending a cloud of ashes all the way to the town of Annaka in the valley below, and covering everything with a blanket of gray soot. Mr. Alexander couldn't remember the event, but he had a newspaper clipping with a photograph showing a tremendous black cloud of smoke rising from the mountain in a sky-high column. He sometimes showed this photo to students in his Japanese class back home when talking about Japan.

On a previous visit to Annaka, Grandpa Alexander had driven them all to a place not far from Annaka called Oni Oshidashi. This could be translated as Ogres' or Demons' Push-out. It was an area where in the 1780s an eruption of Mount Asama had sent a river of lava over a village that had been built too close to the mountain. Many people had died in the cloud of ashes and soot which buried the town before the lava arrived. Altogether, more than 1200 people died, including many in a flood that followed the eruption. Several decades had passed since Mount Asama had caused any harm. But the possibility of another eruption was always present.

Nowadays the Oni Oshidashi area was a sightseeing attraction. Ken had walked among eerily shaped formations of hardened lava thinking that the rocks did indeed look like something that a demon might have pushed out of hell. Of course what Ken remembered best was the souvenir store. But that was another story!

It was another hour later now, and the train was winding painfully slowly through a narrow valley. Other than an occasional farmhouse or village, the view on either side of the tracks was only of dense green—lush and shiny from the rain of the past few days. A mountain stream tumbled by below, its rapids glittering white in the sun.

Somewhere in the background Ken's mother kept commenting on the beautiful, peaceful scenery. But Ken's mind was on the next station—the place where his dad would be waiting for them. Two thoughts fought for control of Ken's attention. It would be good to see his father again! And: Would his dad buy him a toy at the store?

The train rounded a bend and Ken looked back from the first car where they were seated to see the last few cars just entering the curve. Like a long, shiny snake winding its way through the hills, he thought. But a very pretty snake, with its silver skin and blue and yellow stripes running down the length of the body.

And then there it was, the announcement over the public address speakers that the train would soon be stopping at Kurohime station in Shinano Town. Ken was up before his mom, grabbing at his backpack from the baggage rack overhead and hurrying for the door. His mother gathered up their trash and followed Ken down the aisle.

As the train slid into the station and slowed to a stop, Ken could see through the window of the door that the platform was nearly deserted. This was the second to the last stop on the line. It was too early in the afternoon for commuters to be about and the summer tourist season had not yet begun. But wait—there was one person standing on the platform—that familiar, tall man with the ever messed up hair, grinning from ear to ear. The door whooshed open and Ken hopped straight off into his father's huge arms.

"Hi, Ken! How are you?" Mr. Alexander asked, hugging his son tightly.

"Hi. Fine!" Ken managed. It felt good to be in his dad's arms again.

Ken's mom caught up with Ken and received her own hug—and a kiss—from her husband. (I'm glad he doesn't kiss me in public, thought Ken.)

As the three reunited Alexanders walked along the platform, there was the usual jumble of conversation as Ken told about his trip. Three people trying to make up ten days worth of family talk. Ken hardly noticed the nearly empty train silently slip out of the station.

Ken's dad, carrying his wife's bag, led the way up a flight of stairs in the middle of the platform. As they crossed over a covered bridge, Ken noticed dozens of brightly colored posters on the sides of the walkway. Beautiful girls smiled from rugged mountainsides, verandas of modern—yet rustic—hotels and lodges, or hot spring baths. Many Japanese people spent great deals of money to come here during the skiing season or the summer tourist season to get away from it all. Ken was glad that his family had a cabin where they could stay very cheaply—as in for free!

At the other end of the bridge, the family descended more stairs, then followed the other platform to the exit. The station employee had already gone back inside his office, so Ken and his parents left their tickets on the counter of the office and walked out of the tiny station. Things were informal and easy-going here in this remote part of the country and at this time of year.

The first item of business was to walk, bags still in hand, a quarter of a mile or so to the town's only supermarket. The trio passed several shops—a book store, electrical appliance store, alcohol shop and a few souvenir shops. But the supermarket, small as it was by big city standards, had the best selection of any place in town.

"I've got two tomatoes, one block of *tofu*, one package of bread and a cucumber," Ken's dad was saying. This was not the most exciting conversation in the world, Ken thought, especially considering how long it had been since he had had a chance to talk with his father. But he knew that they would have only this one chance to stock up on groceries for the weekend, and his mom needed to know what they should buy.

"Oh, and plenty of snacks," Mr. Alexander added. Ken's ears picked up at the sound of this. Maybe this conversation wasn't so boring after all.

It didn't take long to buy enough food to last the family for three days, including a package of *miso pea*, peanuts covered in a sweet sauce of honey and *miso* (a salty paste made from soy beans), with sesame seeds mixed in. This was one of Mr.

Alexander's favorite Japanese foods. Normally *miso pea* was eaten in small amounts with rice. But Mr. Alexander preferred to eat it plain, by the spoonful. Japanese people thought this was strange. But Ken, too, liked the crunchy, sweet gooey mixture by itself. He guessed he was strange, too. But after all, he was half *Gaijin*.

Groceries were bagged—self service here, as in most Japanese grocery stores. And yes, Ken talked his father into buying him a toy. Not too hard to do considering how glad Mr. Alexander was to see his son again. Actually, it was a very small box of chocolate candies attached to a larger box containing a robot kit. The robot, once assembled, would be much smaller than the one Ken had bought in Annaka. But putting it together would keep him busy—for five minutes? And then he'd have something to play with while at the lake.

The family walked out of the store and gathered in front of a pay phone. Inserting her prepaid card, Mrs. Alexander called the local cab company and soon one of the town's few taxis pulled up in front of the store. As he always did, Ken's dad reached out to open the rear door of the vehicle—just as the door swung open on its own.

"Oops!" he chuckled. "I always forget." This was the only time Mr. Alexander ever rode a taxi in Japan. Usually Grandpa Alexander drove him to Nojiri from Annaka. And every year Ken's dad forgot that Japanese taxi doors are opened and shut automatically by the driver.

The driver, patient and understanding (he'd probably been the same driver they had had the previous year), hopped out of the cab and helped load luggage and groceries into the trunk. The three Alexanders crowded into the back seat.

The driver slammed the trunk, slipped into his seat, pushed the button to close the rear door and turned expectantly to Ken's mom for directions. It was Ken's dad, though, who in excellent Japanese, but with a little trouble remembering the exact name of the place, explained their destination. The taxi started in motion and with his white-gloved left hand, the driver lowered the flag on the meter.

It took but a few minutes for the vehicle to work its way out of the town. The taxi wound its way along a narrow road through alternating deep forest and open clearings planted hill-to-hill with rice paddies and vegetable gardens.

In less than ten minutes they had arrived at their goal. There were extra charges for the bags in the trunk and two extra passengers, but no tip was required. One of the best things about Japan, Ken's dad often remarked, was that tipping was not expected in this country. Bags were unloaded, the driver was paid, the taxi drove off and the family stood surrounded by silence, except for the calls from a myriad of unseen birds and the buzzing of countless insects.

"Do you remember how to get there?" Mr. Alexander asked.

"Sure," replied Ken, leading the way down a narrow dirt road. They walked past deserted tennis courts and an intersection of more narrow, dirt roads. A canopy of tree tops covered the road entirely, shutting out the late afternoon sun. The road narrowed into a sloping path. As the family walked on, they could see cabins here and there, set back from the main trail, some nearly hidden by underbrush.

When Ken reached a series of steep concrete steps dropping off to the right, he quickened his pace.

"Watch out you don't slip," called Mrs. Alexander—uselessly—from a few yards behind. Ken had been down these stairs many times. He wasn't about to slip as he practically hopped from step to step. Now he could catch glimpses of the lake glistening bright blue through the trees. Then he was at the bottom of the stairway, pausing for his parents to catch up. A dirt path continued the descent straight ahead, but off to the right, an even narrower path led to an old, black-brown cabin.

"There it is," Ken exclaimed. Carefully stepping between the dense underbrush on either side and ducking under an occasional low-hanging branch, he and his parents walked toward the building. The path opened up into a clearing that led to the back door of the cabin.

The outdoor toilet—an outhouse with no flushing—was in front of the cabin, off to the right. This was one thing Ken didn't like about Nojiri. You had to come out the back door, put on sandals and walk past the kitchen to go to the toilet. This was obviously no fun, especially when it was night and the outdoors was as dark as the cavern underneath a kid's bed at night. There was no telling what sort of critters were lurking out there in the woods. Not that there were any dangerous creatures at Lake Nojiri. There weren't. But it was the unknown things created in the imagination that were scariest.

Passing the back door, the Alexanders went around the left side of the house to the front porch where they happily plopped down their heavy load of luggage and grocery bags.

"It's beautiful, isn't it?" sighed Ken's mother, gazing at the panoramic view. The cabin was located at the edge of a hill, with a sharp drop off just beyond the porch. Thick forest surrounded the cabin on three sides. In front, where several trees had been cut down over the years to improve the view, there was a breathtaking scene of the lake below and the practically unbroken blanket of green covering the hills on the other side of the lake. A bird of prey of some sort glided searchingly high above the ruffled surface of the waters below.

Ken felt happy and content. Surrounded by this glorious beauty and serenity, who could have ever known—who would have believed—the ugliness and dark menace that were lurking nearby, waiting to drag Ken into an unimaginable nightmare.

CHAPTER 14

STRANGERS ON THE SHORE

"*Mite!*" [Look!] Ken's mother pointed out across the water. A fish had just leapt for a bug snack, leaving fading ripples a short ten yards from where the Alexanders were standing. They were on one of the docks of the Nojiri Lake Association (NLA), exploring the lakefront. Luggage and groceries had been stored safely in the cabin, a quick snack had been devoured, Ken had assembled his new robot toy and now the family was enjoying the serenity of exquisitely beautiful Lake Nojiri.

The late afternoon was calm. A few lonely sailboats dotted the azure water on the far side of the lake like distant butterflies. Lush, green hills rose from the water's edge in nearly every direction. A motorboat's muffled chug wafted across the still afternoon air. Gentle waves licked the concrete posts of the dock.

"*Ii neh*" [Nice, isn't it], sighed Ken's mother. Ken's dad mumbled agreement. Ken looked around for something to toss in the lake, but there were no stones out here on the dock.

"I remember when I used to come here as a kid..." Mr. Alexander was starting. Ken tuned his dad out and looked deep into the water, hoping to catch sight of a fish or two. It wasn't that he didn't care what his father was saying. It was just that he was sure he had heard the story many times before. Right now he just wanted to enjoy the silence.

"*Mite!*" Ken's mom interrupted her husband's ramblings. This time she was pointing at the sky. Soaring above the lake, not too distant from where the Alexanders stood, was a raptor of some sort. The bird was riding an air current, its wings gracefully outstretched. After a moment, with a seemingly effortless waving of its wings, the creature changed direction, climbed a hundred feet or so, then continued its silent glide. Suddenly the bird dove, swooping toward the lake like a streamlined rocket. At the last minute, in a flash of feathers, it leveled off right at water level. There was a great splashing and then the bird streaked skyward, a flapping fish in its talons.

"*Sugoi!*" [Wow! Fantastic!], Ken and his mother both cried out in excitement. Ken's dad chimed in with "Wow! That's cool!"

This was just one of the many wonderful things about Lake Nojiri. There was always plenty of natural activity to make sure visits to the Nojiri were well worthwhile. The three stood watching in silence as the avian fisher flew back to shore and disappeared among the trees. Ken returned to his search for underwater fish.

A movement on the shore caught Ken's eye. Turning, he saw two male figures walking along the lakeside road. From that distance Ken wasn't sure, but it appeared that one had light brown hair and the other definitely had bright, blond hair. A light cloud of smoke appeared to trail behind them.

"Hey, Pop?"

"Yeah, Ken?" Mr. Alexander was still gazing up at the shoreline trees, straining to catch another glimpse of the bird and its dinner.

"I thought we were the only people up here."

"Well, there are lots of Japanese people who live in the village all year long."

"No. I mean *Gaijin*. Aren't we the only foreigners up here now?"

Mr. Alexander turned to look at Ken.

"Well, I think we are. But there could be other people up for the weekend or something. Why?"

"I think I saw a couple of American boys."

"Where?"

"Over there," Ken said, turning and pointing. But the lakeside was deserted.

"Where?" his dad asked again.

"Well, I saw them walking over there a minute ago. But they're gone now."

"Could be. Sometimes families come up here for just a weekend. Or it could be American college students. They finish school early in the U.S. Then they come back to Japan to visit their parents. And then they come up here for awhile."

"Oh." Ken wanted to say more. But he wasn't sure what to say. An icy unease was growing deep down inside. His skin felt uncomfortably cold and prickly. The two boys he'd seen walking along the lake seemed familiar—terrifyingly familiar. He'd seen them only once before, but he could never forget those faces. Could it be? The two bullies from the airport? What were they doing here?

Shadows were growing longer now. The air was still crisp

and delicious—as mountain air so often is. But a slight breeze was stirring trees and a hint of a chill was descending over the lake.

Far off to the left, visible only from the tip of the dock, Mount Miyoko loomed—rugged, majestic—almost unreal in its splendor. Skies had been clear and topaz blue as the Alexanders arrived at the lake. Now a bank of dark clouds was building up behind Mount Miyoko. There was a sense of change in the atmosphere.

"Well, we'd better head back to the cabin," Mr. Alexander said. "Time for dinner."

Ken's mom agreed. Ken could tell that she was happy here. Mrs. Alexander had grown up in Tokyo. She loved the vibrant and exciting big city—not to mention the huge department stores. She was a big city girl at heart. But a few weeks of Tokyo life, living in the cramped apartment with her parents, had grown tiring and stressful. Here life slowed down. Deep breaths of purifying air eased tense nerves and tired muscles.

Mrs. Alexander slipped her arm through her husband's arm and snuggled up closer to him. Ken smiled. It was good to see his parents liking each other. His dad always seemed to become quite mellow after a week alone at the lake. And his mom relaxed much more up here, too.

Ken walked ahead of his parents as they strolled back along the long, narrow L-shaped concrete dock. Wooden posts reached above the water at evenly spaced intervals in a line parallel to the dock. Rings were attached to the side of the dock at the same intervals as the posts. In summer every shape and color of row boats, canoes and sail boats would be tethered between the posts and rings, bouncing and dancing with every wave that washed in. Now, though, only water filled the spaces. The posts, poking their heads above the water, looked like a row of gigantic chopstick tips protruding above the water line.

The Alexanders walked past the boathouse, boarded up for the off season, and onto the right bottom leg of the H-shaped docks which designated the swimming area. The diving boards which usually sat on the upper left and right tips of the H, facing toward each other, were gone for the season. Even the life guard's tower which rose from the middle of the cross bar of the H was missing its wooden floor. The entire mood was one of a place not yet ready for its human users.

The family crossed the narrow paved road that ran alongside the lake. This, and the road which had brought the Alexanders to the top of the hill from the station, were the only paved roads on NLA property. The NLA preferred to keep the area primitive and as natural as possible. This helped to keep the area rustic. But when it rained, the dirt roads turned into seas of mud—lots and lots of mud.

The Alexanders crossed a small, graveled parking lot as they headed toward the base of the hill. On either side of the parking lot, stretching along the paved road, were open, grassy areas. Just once Ken had been here later in the summer, after the season had begun. Then the fields had been covered with people: families enjoying picnics, sunbathers barbecuing themselves in the sun, children running around playing games.

At the edge of the gravel stood a tiny concrete shack. On either side, like the arms of an upside down Y, were short staircases leading upward. Above the hut the two sets of stairs joined to form the stem of the inverted Y. From the base of the building, out of a metal pipe, poured cold, fresh spring water. In olden days many NLA residents had come here to fetch their household water. Many times Ken had heard the story from his father:

"When I was a kid we had to walk all the way down here to get our water. We had to carry two big buckets. Boy, that was hard work."

And many times Ken had listened to the story, thinking to himself,

"Yeah, but you didn't have to listen to your dad telling you how rough it was getting water back when he was a kid. Now *that's* hard work."

Nowadays, running water was available at several locations on the NLA hillside. Mr. Alexander wasn't even sure any more if the spring water was safe to drink. But in olden days—there they were again, those words, "When I was a kid...," the pure spring water had been a refreshing delight for any passerby to drink, straight from the side of the hill.

Another tradition, one Ken remembered from his one late summer stay at Nojiri when it bustled in full season, was for picnickers to place watermelons in the runoff trough directly beneath the pouring spring water. By the time the main meal was finished, the watermelons would have been chilled to perfection.

Ken had vivid memories of three or four perfectly round watermelons (not football shaped like American ones) competing with each other in the short trough.

"Get me!" He could imagine one green sphere calling to the cool water streaming from above.

"No, no! Hit me. Make me coldest," a neighboring watermelon would protest.

A third roly-poly fruit might argue, "Come on you guys. Quit hogging all the water. My humans want a cold dessert, too." And so it would go, the watermelons vying for the chilliest water, their insides waiting juicy red for the slicing to come.

The three Alexanders climbed the short flight of stairs past the spring to another level area. To the right was the auditorium/chapel. Like the boathouse, it was boarded up for the season. Ken was sorry to see this. The building with its ancient wooden stairs, wooden benches and wooden balconies—everything was made of wood—was a mysterious place to explore. He had especially enjoyed sneaking onto the stage with his family that one year, performing a ridiculous song and dance routine to an empty audience. Now the building was silent, lonely. Only ghosts would be performing on the stage now, if there were any. And the only audience would be the dozens—hundreds? millions?!?—of spiders, hoppers and other creepy, crawly things that made the building their home when the humans were away.

The Alexanders continued to walk past the dark, brown building, in single file across the square, concrete stepping stones that led through a sea of uncut weeds. At the edge of the mini-path, a series of wide, concrete stairs led upwards, diagonally, toward the right.

As they climbed toward the cabin, up the ancient concrete steps, cracked and crumbling in places, Ken felt some of the alarm drain out of his body. True, the weeds encroaching on the stairway—and even peeking through cracks in the concrete—gave a sense of gloom and foreboding to the fading afternoon. And seeing those two figures on the shore had startled him. But the quiet, disturbed only by the sweet, occasional chirping of birds high in the green treetops above was soothing. Besides, he was with his parents and everybody was in a good mood. A weekend of fun and excitement lay ahead. What could possibly go wrong?

If Ken had only known.

CHAPTER 15

BENJO MUSHI

Darkness was well on its way by the time the Alexanders climbed onto the porch of the cabin. They could barely see to remove their shoes, step into slippers inside the door and slip into the cabin. Even here at Nojiri they followed the Japanese custom of not wearing shoes indoors.

Ken's dad always cleaned the cabin when he first arrived at Nojiri, vacuuming the floors and wiping them with a damp cloth, in the centuries-old tradition of Japanese housecleaning. (The damp cloth part. Vacuuming was not a centuries-old Japanese tradition.) So the house was fairly clean. Most of the cobwebs, dead bugs, leaves and other mementos of the long winter had been cleared out. Still, if you didn't want your socks to turn black in a few hours, it was advisable to wear slippers indoors. Except when you were sleeping or taking a bath, of course.

The door was closed and locked, lights were turned on, curtains were pulled and the cabin took on an air of bright warmth and coziness.

"Why don't you take your bag upstairs," Ken's mom told him. Ken picked up his backpack from by the door where he had dumped it when they first arrived and headed out the large dining/living room. A steep set of stairs stretched up into the darkness of the second floor. If they had been any steeper, they would have been a ladder.

"Pop, can you turn the light on for me?" Ken called to his dad who had disappeared into the kitchen to the right of the stairs.

"Sure." Mr. Alexander emerged from the kitchen, a tomato in his hand. Reaching above Ken's head, he turned the switch on a light bulb dangling above the staircase. The switch was just out of Ken's reach. Ken started up the stairs, then paused.

"Pop?"

"Yeah, Ken."

"Can you come upstairs with me?"

"Sure, Ken." His dad didn't need to ask why. The upstairs was dark, and—to put it in simple terms—creepy. At least the first time you went up there, and especially in the dark.

The staircase rose directly into a large room, ending in windows which lined the near side of the room. Ken's dad made a 90-degree turn from the last portion of the steps into the room and turned on another light hanging from the ceiling on a long cord. This one had a long string attached to it which you pulled to turn the light on or off. If you were lucky, it worked. Sometimes the string broke. Everything was old in this cabin.

In front of the stairs, covering the floor in the corner of the room were three straw *tatami* mats. Unlike usual mats which are actually the floor of a house, these mats were laid out on top of the wooden floor. Next to the mats were a small table and a stack of plastic storage containers, full of blankets. In the far corner of the room diagonally, five more *tatami* were spread out on the floor. A curtain hung across the middle of the room, separating the two islands of mats. Another row of windows lined the opposite side of the room above the 5-mat island.

A short, stocky bookcase against one wall housed some of the oldest, dustiest books Ken had ever seen. Had he found these books in a European castle, he would have imagined them to be books of magic. But these books were in Japanese and were religious books.

On either side of the big room were sliding doors which led into smaller bedrooms. Each smaller room had two beds. None of the Alexanders ever used these beds. The mattresses were ancient and lumpier than the mashed potatoes Ken's dad occasionally fed his tolerant family. In addition they were damp and musty. (Everything was old in this cabin. Or has that already been mentioned?)

In the bedroom to the right was a locked, tin-lined closet where Ken's Annaka grandparents kept their personal and best-quality supplies. They sometimes rented out the cabin and didn't want the renters to use these items. From here Mr. Alexander had already taken three folding mattresses and placed them on the five-*tatami* portion of the room. Each mattress had a *futon* on it which was in turn covered with sheets and a stack of blankets. Even summer nights at Nojiri could become unpleasantly cold. And there was a pillow at the head of each *futon*.

Ken's dad slept in one of two bedrooms on the first floor when he was alone at Nojiri. The mattress in that room was also lumpy, but at least the lumps matched the bumps and curves of Ken's dad so he could sleep on it without too much discomfort.

Ken enjoyed their sleeping arrangement. It was about the only time when the entire Alexander family slept together. It was almost like camping. Except that the cabin was somewhat drier than a tent. At least when it was raining. And it was warmer and safer. Well, sort of. Good tents kept the bugs out. The walls, floors and doors of the cabin were like a sieve. As a result the cabin was shared with a number of bugs, spiders, moths and many other little critters. But the worst, at least to Mr. Alexander, were "hoppers," a kind of hopping bug with long legs. When he was a kid, Mr. Alexander's family had called them *benjo mushi* [another way to say "toilet", plus "bug"] because they were often found near or in bathrooms. Ken's dad never knew the correct English name for these monsters. He knew only that the bugs were big and brown and spotted and gross. At least he thought they were. Ken didn't mind them so much. But his father sometimes acted quite oddly when the hoppers appeared.

In the old days, apparently, Mr. Alexander's family had merely squished these critters whenever one appeared indoors. But that generally left a disgusting, sloppy mess for someone to clean up. Nowadays, Ken's dad valued all animal life. He had become a vegetarian so that animals wouldn't have to die to feed him. He wouldn't kill anything, if he could help it. Except for mosquitoes. That was self defense, he reasoned.

"They're out to get my blood," he explained. "They might even carry disease. So killing them is self defense. I feel bad about it, but I have to get them before they get me."

"Whatever," Ken would think. But his dad really did try to protect all other life. At home in Colorado Mr. Alexander had a little empty spice can that he used to catch unfortunate spiders that he discovered in the house. He would catch the crawlers in the can and toss them out the front door into nearby bushes. Ken wondered how many of those spiders eventually found their way back into the house, only to be captured and thrown out again. Ken could imagine two spiders having a conversation in one of the bushes in front of the house.

"Hi, George."

"Hey, Mitch. How ya doin?"

"Just fine. And you"

"Oh, I'm OK."

"Got tossed out of the house again, huh?"

"Yup. Third time. How about you?"

"Oh, I've been thrown out at least five times so far this year."

"No kiddin? What a drag, huh?"

"Yeah. That man's pretty weird the way he keeps dumping us out here."

"Yup. I know. At least I made him chase me around for awhile. You should have heard him hollering."

"Yeah, he gets pretty excited sometimes, doesn't he? Know what I like to do sometimes?"

"What?"

"Well, you know how he puts that can on the floor in front of you and then taps his foot behind you so you'll run into it?"

"Yeah. That lousy basil can. He could at least use something softer like a cardboard box. Or something that smells better. I like cinnamon myself."

"Yeah, I hear ya. Anyway, sometimes when he starts tapping his foot I turn around and run right at him."

"I bet that freaks him out."

"Sure does. You should see how far he jumps. Guess we make him just a little nervous."

"I guess we do. Heh, heh. By the way, didja hear about Arnold?"

"No. What happened?"

"Oh, he went into the house next door. Got squished."

"Ooh. Poor guy."

"Yeah, so we don't have it so bad."

"Guess you're right. Well, nice talking to ya, but I gotta go. It's a long way back to the basement. Got some friends waiting for me there."

"OK. See ya later."

Spiders were one thing. Those *benjo mushi*—or whatever they were called—were another. They never cooperated by peacefully crawling into a can. The encounter would usually go something like this:

Ken's dad would look up at the ceiling and notice one of the bugs sitting quietly in a corner. (Once in awhile one of the critters would accidentally come hopping into the dining room from another room. It usually lived to regret that move.)

"Uh oh! There's one of those bugs." Mr. Alexander would grab his weapons of choice—a broom and a paper bag and head into combat. The first strategy was to snatch up the intruder in the bag, hold the opening tightly, take the bag outside and dump the creature in the bushes, far from the cabin. However, things didn't always go according to plan.

Usually, as soon as the bag was about to close around

the hopper, it would—of course—hop—sometimes right onto Ken's dad.

"Aaghh!" he would scream, madly twisting to shake the bug off. "It's on me!" The bug, terrified for its life, of course, would hop frantically toward a dark corner of the room, with Mr. Alexander in determined pursuit. On calmer days, Ken's dad would attempt a second assault with the paper bag. On more hysterical occasions, however, he would resort immediately to plan B. Paper bag was dropped and Mr. Alexander would open the front door, never mind that a fleet of moths of every size was waiting to charge the indoor lights. Tightly clutching broom in hand, he would approach the bug with stealth. Suddenly he would lunge at his adversary, broom held out in front of him like some prized magical weapon, and sweep it out the door. Once in a lucky while this strategy worked perfectly. More often the bug would hop in every direction but toward the open door, Mr. Alexander running after it hollering, broom flailing.

"Come on, get out! Out! Go out the door! No, not that way—the DOOR!" Eventually, a hopper in a stroke of blind luck would flee out the door. Other times, though, one would disappear into some dark corner or crack, never to be seen again—or at least not until the next evening. Ken and his mother greatly enjoyed watching these performances. Mr. Alexander did not enjoy them.

Ken plopped his bag down on the floor of the upstairs bedroom.

"Pop."

"Yeah."

"Could you come over here a minute." Mr. Alexander had

been adjusting the dividing curtain. Ken was standing by the five *tatami* mats. Ken's dad took a couple of steps around the edge of the *tatami*.

"What is it?"

Ken suddenly wrapped his arms around his father's waist and pushed him—right out of his slippers. The two tumbled backwards onto the *tatami* and piles of *futon* and bedding. Mr. Alexander had been expecting this and had wisely placed the remains of his tomato on the table. There would be no cleaning up of mashed tomato from the *tatami* tonight.

The battle was swift and violent. Mr. Alexander was on his feet in a flash. And although Ken's tackling attacks were many and fierce, he found himself being repeatedly flung into an ever messier pile of bedding. With each landing the entire cabin shook and windows rattled. This was a game that was not permitted in the Tokyo apartment—for obvious reasons. *Ojiichan* and *Obaachan* valued their relationship with the families living in the apartments below them. Here at Nojiri this was an acceptable activity.

Finally, Ken succeeded in sending his dad toppling. The house rumbled as though it had been hit by a sonic boom. This brought Mrs. Alexander dashing up the stairs.

"Dohshitano?" [What happened?] she panted. But seeing the two Alexander boys laughing amid the scattered pillows, *futon* and bedding, she relaxed.

"You're going to break the house," she scolded. As much as she loved the cabin, she was concerned—rightly so—that it might someday collapse into a heap of old, rotted timber.

Despite her concern, though, Ken's mom soon found herself drawn into the struggle herself. The three Alexanders tumbled and rumbled and rolled and grunted and groaned—and laughed. And laughed and laughed.

Anybody hearing the racket escaping from the Alexander cabin would have been hard pressed to believe that it was being produced by one child and two middle-aged adults—and not three little children. But then maybe it *was* three little kids who were romping on the *tatami*.

Eventually, Ken's mom, the sanest member of the family, pointed out the late time and the fact that everyone should be hungry by now. Reluctantly, hostilities were ceased, bedding was somewhat restored, upstairs lights were turned out and the family filed downstairs.

Dinner was uneventful. Tired as he was, Ken did not resist when his parents directed him to get ready for bed. As he lay snuggled in his reorganized bedding, warm thoughts floated across Ken' mind. He was happy to be here with his parents. Yes, indeed, this had been a perfect day.

CHAPTER 16

A DOG IN A TREE

"Ken." A distant voice was slipping softly through hazy dreams.

"Huh?"

"Ken, are you still awake?" He had been asleep. Soundly. He had already passed the border zone where wakefulness fades into sleep. But not anymore. Mr. Alexander was standing at the edge of the *tatami* island, peering cautiously around the curtains that divided the room. He was speaking in whispers. He didn't want to wake up his son, just in case Ken was already asleep. Too late.

"I am now," Ken grumbled. "What is it?"

"Sorry. I thought you might still be awake. Do you want to go for a walk?"

Now Ken was wide awake. What was this silliness? It was ink black outside and long past his bedtime. Was his father serious about going for a hike? Now? In the middle of the night? Or was this some kind of unfunny joke? Or maybe just a peculiar dream.

"I hear a sound," explained Ken's father. "I'm going to go see what it is. Do you want to come along?"

This did not sound good. A strange sound in the night and his father was going to walk out there to see what it was? No, this did not sound good at all.

"What is it?" Ken had visions of monsters and creatures and thugs and all sorts of terrible things lurking out there in the forest, waiting to pounce on any person foolish enough to go wandering in the dark.

"I think it's the dog I saw this morning." A dog had come yipping its way across the golf course's fairway towards Ken's dad, stopping only when its owner called it back. This had upset him immensely.

Now this made sense. There were two things that Mr. Alexander hated. One was smoking. He had already done a great deal of protesting so far during the family's visit to Japan about smokers being everywhere.

"They look so stupid," Mr. Alexander would say. "Don't they know how much they're damaging themselves?" But the worst part was having to breathe the smoke put out by smokers. Ken could understand this. He, too, hated being in a place where many people were smoking and not being able to escape the stinky fumes. And his father pointed out that second hand smoke killed thousands of people each year. This was very unfair, Ken thought

The other thing that Mr. Alexander hated was barking dogs. The man who loved animals so much that he would not even kill bugs and would eat no meat would rant and rave when neighborhood dogs barked. Harsh yipping and yapping, threatening growls and hostile barking irritated him to no end.

Ken didn't mind barking dogs. But he could understand what his father said.

"Dog owners should keep their dogs quiet. It's rude and inconsiderate to let them bark and disturb neighbors."

Back home there was an ordinance stating that dogs were not allowed to bark for unreasonable times. Mr. Alexander had actually gone to court several times with neighborhood dog owners. In each case the court had told the dog owners to keep their dogs quiet or they would have to pay fines. This made Mr. Alexander very happy. But there were many dogs in the area and new people kept moving into the neighborhood so the anti-barking struggle was an ongoing battle.

So here was Ken's dad, asking him if he would like to go out in the dark night with him to find a barking dog. Ken was snug and warm in his *futon*. Leaving his bed to go prowling about in the dark did not sound like much fun—or did it?

"It'll be a little adventure," Mr. Alexander was saying.

"Can't Mama go with you?" asked Ken.

"She doesn't want to go out. She's tired."

Smart woman, Ken thought.

"But I thought you might enjoy the adventure. You know, something special that we don't usually get to do."

Well, that was certainly true.

"Do I have to change clothes?" Changing seemed a troublesome obstacle.

"No, you can just put on pants and a jacket over your pajamas. And you can use the special flashlight."

That was the one that had a button that controlled the light beam. You could spread out the light in a wide spray or narrow it down to a thin ray of light. The idea of a late night sojourn began to sound attractive.

"Can I have a snack when we get back?" Time to bargain,

to work for bribes.

"Yeah, I suppose so. For special. But you'll have to brush your teeth again."

"OK." Ken was up in a flash, pulling on his pants. This could be great fun.

Mrs. Alexander gave the two a disgusted look as they put on their shoes.

"Are you really going up there?" she asked, shaking her head. It will be very late for Ken."

But the discussion had already been held. Both parents had decided that if Mr. Alexander really had to go find the dog and complain to its owners, then it would be OK for Ken to accompany him, late though it was. A nighttime hike would be a special treat, and the long weekend would give everybody plenty of time to catch up on sleep later.

"We'll be back soon," Mr. Alexander promised. "Are you sure you don't want to go with us?"

Mrs. Alexander was quite certain.

"*Ittekimasu.*" [(We'll)] go and come back.] called Ken and his dad as they left the cozy cabin.

"*Itterasshai.*" [Go and come back.] Mrs. Alexander's voice followed them out the door.

The two Alexander men headed off into the night. Mr. Alexander led the way across the yard and up the narrow trail to the main path. Ken followed closely behind. Very closely. As the two turned up the stairs towards the top of the hill, the cabin's lights faded from view. Ken was suddenly not so sure that this was a good idea. The forest looked so much spookier and foreboding in the blackness of the night.

Well, of course it's darker at night, he thought. But why is it so spooky? Why is darkness spooky?

Lights which normally lit up the main paths during the season had not yet been turned on. And those houses which could be made out from the path were people-less and unlit. No friendly beacons of light shining out onto the path tonight.

Ken walked next to his dad now, two lights slicing through the night, side by side. Ken had turned his flashlight to the wide beam. Trees and bushes leaped in and out of his world of light as they climbed upwards.

"You doing OK?" Mr. Alexander sensed the touch of nervousness that Ken was feeling.

"Yeah, I guess so. How far is it?

"Not far. This is kind of neat, though, don't you think—walking in the dark." Ken didn't think so, but he said nothing.

"I remember one time you and I went for a hike up here at night long ago. You were about two, I think. You got really scared and wanted to go home right away. You've grown up a lot since then."

Ken had only vague memories of that time. His father's words made him feel a little bigger and braver. Yes, he'd grown up a lot since those days. Still, he could understand why he'd been so scared those many years ago. It was dark out here. DARK!

"There it is again! Hear it?"

Ever since they left the cabin, they had heard that irritating sound, off and on, wafting down from the top of the hill. Strangest barking Ken had ever heard, he thought. What was wrong with that dog? Was it sick?

The stairs ended and merged with the alternate route up the hill, which joined from the right. The graveled path was much wider now. The ominous forest seemed to have pulled back a bit to let them by. Soon the two reached the spot where the taxi had dropped them off earlier that day. Gravel roads wide enough for a car to pass by split off to the left, straight ahead and to the right. Turning right, the two walked past tennis courts on the left and more cabins on the right. The dog, when they could hear it, was much closer now.

"I was up here hiking this morning, before I went to the station to meet you," explained Mr. Alexander. "I wanted to check out the golf course and see if we could play while you guys were here. That's when the dog attacked me."

A short, nine-hole golf course wove its way along the top of the hill. In June the grass on the fairways was uncut and the sandy "greens" were not smoothed out. But it was fun to putter about the deserted golf course anyway. None of the three Alexanders was terribly serious about their scores. The chief goal was to have fun and lose as few balls as possible.

"Can we? I mean, can we play golf?" asked Ken.

"Sure, if the weather's OK. The greens are a mess, but we don't mind, do we?"

"No." Ken hoped he could hit par on at least one hole this year. He usually took two or three times as many swings as par to get the ball in a hole. His dad wasn't much better. Mrs. Alexander had taken golf lessons when she was young and usually managed to embarrass her husband by beating his pathetic scores.

The road now ran between the golf course on the left and cabins on the right.

"It was right about there." Mr. Alexander pointed. "I was walking on that fairway. There was a car parked across the street and some people were standing around."

"Were they *Gaijin*?"

"Yeah, I think they were moving into that cabin, maybe for the weekend. They had a dog with them. When it saw me it started barking and ran across the road and grass towards me. Stupid thing. If I'd had a golf club, I would have been tempted to hit it."

Ken was fairly certain that his dad would never hit a dog. But then he never knew. Sometimes Mr. Alexander became very angry and frustrated at dogs.

"What happened?"

"One of the people called the dog and it went back. I should have gone over to them and complained. People aren't supposed to have barking dogs up here."

"Really? Dogs aren't allowed to bark up here?"

"Yeah, I think it's one of the rules. Anyway, I'm pretty sure that's the dog that I could hear from the cabin. That's really obnoxious, to have to hear a noise like that up here at Nojiri. Now where's that dog?"

"Which house was it where the people were?" asked Ken.

"Over there, I think. It's hard to tell in the dark." But there were no lights in any of the cabins across the street.

"Maybe they all went to bed really early. Or maybe they went out for dinner. Or maybe they didn't even stay here tonight. I don't know. But it looks like nobody's home. But then why is the dog here? And why is it loose on the golf course. Letting a dog loose at night—that's really irresponsible."

The two were walking on the golf course now, flashlights cutting slices of sharp light through the inkiness. The sound was much closer now, a most hideous barking, like neither

Alexander had ever heard before.

"What the--? Mr. Alexander was perplexed.

"Pop?"

"Yeah, I know." The sound was right before them now, coming from the edge of the golf course. From a clump of trees and bushes. Mere yards away.

"It can't be!" exclaimed Mr. Alexander. "That's impossible!" But it was.

"Pop!" Ken's whisper was a hiss. "It's coming from—it's up in that tree."

"What's a dog doing up in a tree?" his dad asked, incredulously. "The dog I saw couldn't climb a tree."

"Pop--?" Ken's voice was strange, a mixture of emotions. "I don't think it's a dog."

The two trained their flashlights on the tree. Branch by branch the shafts of light glided upward. And then, there they were—two gleaming eyes staring back at them—surrounded by a mass of feathers. The feathers suddenly spread out and in a mighty flapping of wings, a dark form soared from the tree, up over their heads and off into the dark sea of the night.

"What was that?" The stronger of Ken's emotions was rising to the surface. He struggled to control it.

"I don't know. Some kind of bird. Maybe an owl. But I don't think there are any owls up here."

An owl? A bird? The dog was a bird? Ken could no longer control himself and burst out in deep laughter.

"Well, I guess it was a bird. I sure thought it was a dog." Mr. Alexander's voice had lost all its anger. There was embarrassment, but something else, too.

"A bird! A crazy bird! Oh, man, that's embarrassing."

"What about barking owls?" Ken said.

At this, both Alexanders erupted into laughter. The mystery of the moment was gone. Flashlights on, silly giggles lighting their way, the two Alexanders returned home.

There were the necessary explanations when they arrived at the cabin, to the accompaniment of Mrs. Alexander's laughter. The promised snack. Brushing teeth. Another visit to the outhouse, not nearly as scary as the one earlier in the evening. And bed.

CHAPTER 17

A TEASPOON OF ANTS

Ken slept well that night. The long train trip and the exercise of the previous day—and night—had worn him out. Combined with the fresh mountain air, everything proved to be an excellent recipe for sleep. He did have a strange sensation at one time in the middle of the night, though, of moving. It was as though the entire *tatami* island his family was sleeping on was sliding across the floor. But he shrugged off the feeling as being part of a restless dream—a dream full of dogs and owls and mysterious figures on a distant shore. Ken slipped back into sleep.

When Ken awoke, light was flowing into the curtains covering the windows. Not the streaking shunshiny-day sort of light, but more of a muted, soggy cloudy-and-rainy-day type of light. He turned and saw his mother by his side, sound asleep, sheets and blankets wrapped around her in an impossible tangle. Rolling over, Ken saw only a scrambled pile of bedding where his father had slept, between him and the wall. Mr. Alexander always was the first one to rise.

And then Ken saw something that perplexed him. When he'd gone to bed, the five *tatami* they'd slept on had been placed tightly against the two corner walls. But now the entire island was several feet out toward the center of the room. Strange! When and how had that happened? And why?

Ken forced himself out of his cocoon into the chilly morning air. Throwing on a sweatshirt and warm socks, he slipped into his slippers placed at the foot of the straw mats. Holding onto the railing, he carefully descended the stairs.

Mr. Alexander looked up from his breakfast of cereal and his crossword puzzle magazine.

"Good morning, Ken," he said as Ken climbed onto his lap. "How are you today?"

"Good," Ken mumbled as he snuggled into his father's cozy arms. Still shaking cobwebs of sleep out of his brain, he muttered, "What happened to the beds?"

"Ants," his dad replied.

"Ants?"

"Yeah. Ants." Remember how I told you an army of ants went walking through the cabin last year when I was here alone?"

"Uh huh." Ken vaguely recalled some bizarre story of a bunch of ants parading through the kitchen. His dad had been horrified that they were after the food—his precious food—in the cabinet and had attacked them with a vacuum cleaner. But the little creatures had kept coming and coming.

Eventually, when Mr. Alexander realized that the ants were not after his food but were just passing through, he left them alone. He emptied the contents of the vacuum cleaner bag in some bushes far from the cabin. He hoped that the ants he had sucked up weren't dead. Hopefully, they would just walk out of the pile of dust and cobwebs, go marching somewhere else and leave him alone. He would never intentionally hurt an ant—unless it was after his food.

"Well, we had another invasion last night."

Ken waited for his father to continue.

"I woke up last night and felt something on my hand."

Ken shuddered. He suddenly had a vivid picture of hundreds—no, thousands!—of ants crawling all over his father's hand.

"I turned on my flashlight and saw a couple of ants on my hand."

Phew, thought Ken. That wasn't so bad.

"Then I turned the flashlight on the floor and there were hundreds of them parading along the floor between the edge of the *tatami* and the wall."

This time Ken had a major league shudder.

"Yuck!" he said.

"Fortunately," his dad went on, "they were mostly on the wall and the floor. My right hand was sticking out of the covers by the wall and I guess a couple of them wandered away from the rest of the group and climbed on me."

Ken imagined a couple of confused ants roaming over his father's hand, climbing over hairs and wondering what sort of odd jungle they had discovered.

"What did you do with them?" asked Ken.

"I just brushed the ants off my hand. I didn't hurt them. Then I pulled one *tatami* away from the wall and Mama woke up. We pulled the rest of the *tatami* out. We watched the ants for awhile, but they didn't seem to want to bother us, so we just let them be."

"Where did they come from? Where did they go?" Ken

had visions of thousands of ants still hiding somewhere in the cabin.

"I don't' know. They came up over there." Mr. Alexander pointed to an upright wooden post set in the wall between two windows. It was a huge pillar which disappeared below the floor. Down below it rested on the concrete foundation of the house. The upper part of the pillar supported a cross beam which in turn supported the ceiling. Walls, ceilings and floors were all bare boards in this cabin.

"They came climbing up from under the house through those cracks around that post. They just kept parading up the wall, through the downstairs ceiling and out on the floor in our bedroom."

"Then what?" Ken wanted to know. He was beginning to wish he'd been awake. It must have been a fascinating sight to see all those ants marching by.

A silly flash of thought lit up Ken's mind.

"Did they have a marching band?"

"What?"

"The ants. You said they were parading through the house. Did they have a marching band?"

Ken's dad made a funny face. Then his mouth turned into a warped smile.

"Yeah, right. The ants had a marching band. Actually, they did. And the best part was the piano section."

"Pianos?! In a marching band?!"

"Well, you know how strong ants are. They were playing some great music. Like 'When the Ants Go Marching In...'"

Ken groaned. Suddenly he was sorry he had brought up the subject of a marching band. He should have known his dad would come back with a sick joke of his own.

"Where did the ants go?" Ken reluctantly returned to serious conversation.

"They walked along the floor by the *tatami* and into a hole in the wall. I looked in the other bedroom, on the other side of the wall, but they didn't come out anywhere."

"Where are they now?" There was a little concern now. What if the ants were all hiding in the wall between the bedrooms. What if they were waiting to come out tonight and attack the family while they were sleeping? What if they were rare Nojiri man-eating ants. What if...

"I don't know. I tried to look inside the wall, but I couldn't see any of them. My guess is that they just kept going inside the wall—up, down—I don't know. But I doubt that they're in the house any more. They were probably just passing through—like last year."

This was a little more reassuring to Ken. But not entirely.

"What kind of ants were they?" Ken wanted to know.

"Oh, normal ones. Real little reddish brown ones. You could probably fit a hundred of them in a teaspoon."

An interesting picture flashed its way into Ken's mind—hundreds of little ants squirming around in a teaspoon.

"A teaspoon of ants," he chuckled.

"What?"

"A teaspoon of ants. Sounds like something in a recipe."

"A recipe?" Mr. Alexander sounded disgusted.

"Yeah. A recipe for a pie for anteaters."

"Oh, I get it. 'Add three teaspoons of ants. Stir well.' Like that?"

"More like, 'Add two cups of ants.' Anteaters need lots of

ants in their pie."

"Right. And maybe, 'Add a dash of termites.'" Ken's dad was catching on now.

"'Sprinkle with caterpillars.'"

"That's gross! Come on, I'm trying to eat breakfast here."

"But you said 'termites...'"

"I know. My mistake. I quit."

"Or, 'Add chopped cockroaches...'"

"That's enough! Stop it! Yuck!!"

"*Dohshitano*?" [What's the matter?] Mrs. Alexander was standing at the bottom of the stairs, staring into the room in sleepy confusion.

"*Ohayoh*," Ken greeted his mother. And he proceeded to tell her about his anteater pie in great detail. His mother acted properly grossed out at the appropriate parts.

After the story was done and his parents had groaned and grunted sufficiently, Ken slid off his dad's lap and giving his mother a hug, shuffled off to the kitchen to find breakfast. It may have been cloudy and dismal outdoors. And yes, there was a slight drizzle. But as far as he was concerned, the day was off to a wonderful start. A teaspoon of ants indeed!

CHAPTER 18

ELEPHANT FOOTPRINTS

"Hey, it's stopped raining." Ken had stepped out to the roofed porch to check the view. There he discovered that all the plipping and plopping on the tin roof of the cabin was merely raindrops dripping off the ends of leaves overhead. Huge trees surrounding the cabin created a sort of leaky umbrella over the house.

"*Hontoh*?" [Really?] Ken's mother was reading a book, nestled into one of the more comfortable chairs in the living room half of the main room. Much of the furniture was ancient, Ken knew, probably older than his dad. That was *really* ancient. But some newer furniture had been added in recent years. Mrs. Alexander was seated in one of those recent additions—a wooden wicker chair with a luxurious seat cushion. It was half of a pair, two seats which—and here was the part Ken loved—swiveled around. How much fun a guy could have on a chair that swiveled 360-degrees!

Mr. Alexander was seated at a second table, a heavy old wooden table that had probably served as the dining table back in prehistoric times—when he was a boy. It was also in the living room portion of the huge room.

Ken's dad was putting the finishing touches on a 1000-piece jigsaw puzzle he had been working on since the previous week. The picture was of a forest scene with aurora borealis—the northern lights—dazzling the nighttime sky. This was a glow-in-the-dark puzzle, and it really worked. Ken had made certain of that the night before. What was really entertaining was to turn out the lights in the room, turn on a flashlight and stand the flashlight on the puzzle for a few minutes, beam down. When Ken picked up the flashlight there would be a brilliantly glowing circle on the part of the puzzle that had been illuminated by the flashlight. This was great fun for Ken, a trick worth repeating many times.

The other table, a newer one—but not that new—was in the dining room half of the main room. Its legs were metal and the surface was some kind of hard plastic or Formica—or some other material. This was the table at which the family ate. Proof of that was in the small oven toaster sitting on one half of the table. And the small piles of bread crumbs here and there which nobody had cleaned up yet.

Each table sat underneath a fluorescent light which dangled from the ceiling. Both lights were on right now, due to the cloudy weather. When it was in use, the oven toaster was plugged into a socket that hung from the same cord that the light was plugged into.

"What do you wanna do?" Mr. Alexander asked. Breakfast had been eaten, dishes had been washed and teeth had been brushed. There had been another wrestling match on the *tatami* upstairs. And Ken had helped his dad with the jigsaw puzzle. Now it was time for something new.

"Can we go on the boat?" asked Ken.

"Yeah, we can try," responded Mr. Alexander.

A number of sightseeing boats toured the lake every day. But they departed from the village of Nojiri, part way around the lake. It was a pleasant walk to the town—if it wasn't raining.

"I doubt the weather's gonna hold, but we can take umbrellas. *Doh*?" [How about it?] Mr. Alexander asked his wife.

"*Sooh ne,*" [OK. (That's good.)] came the reply.

"OK, let's go!" said Mr. Alexander enthusiastically. "But I think we'd better get some water first. Ken would you get another potful for us please?"

"Now?"

"Yeah. Better get it now while it's not raining. Don't know what the weather will be like when we get back

"Oh, OK."

Ken went into the kitchen, removed one of the teakettles from the two-burner stove, slipped out of his slippers at the back door, stepped into sandals that were on the back porch and headed across the yard toward the main path. The sandals were actually for use by people going to the outhouse at the left edge of the slab of concrete that served as the back porch. Ken hoped nobody would need them while he was using them.

As Ken neared the end of the property, the yard narrowed. So did the path. Heavy trees sagged above. Small bushes and underbrush lined the walkway. They seemed to be reaching out to grab Ken as he walked by.

At the end of the private path was a junction of public paths. To the right was a wider path going downhill. Eventually this path led to the lakefront. If you were coming up this path from the lake, you'd be panting pretty heavily by now. That is, unless you were in excellent condition. Coming from this direction, the private path to the Alexander cabin led off to the left.

A sharp right turn would keep you on the main path, which would take you to the top of the hill. There was another sharp zigzag turn up ahead, but the climb was not that terrible.

But that also depended on how old you were and what kind of condition you were in. For Ken, the climb was a cinch. For his dad, who had given up jogging a few years earlier, the climb to the top of the hill was a bit more of a challenge. As for Grandpa Alexander—with his daily hikes in the Annaka house, he would be a formidable competitor for his much younger son. As for Mrs. Alexander... Well, she was a teacher. She did a lot of desk work. She sat at a table for hours grading papers. She could be excused if she didn't lead the pack in a race up the hill. Not that any of them would ever want to race up the hill. Well, maybe Ken would.

Another choice at this junction, if you were coming up the hill from the lake, was to go straight—up a long flight of concrete steps. This was the stairway the Alexanders had descended the previous day. It was a shorter route to the top. But to be kind to your lungs and legs, it was recommended that you take the easier zigzag route.

Ken turned left out of the yard and began to climb the stairs. There was no choice for him. The faucet he needed to reach was this way, about ten steps up.

When Ken's dad had come to Lake Nojiri as a boy, there had been only three or four places in the entire hillside where water was available. One was the spring by the parking lot that the family had passed the previous evening on their way to and from the lake. The most important chore for each household had been to fetch water at one of the natural springs that fed the area. Water for cooking, cleaning, drinking, washing—everything—had to be hauled in kettles, buckets, pots or whatever the family chose. Many a child had grumbled his or her way up and down the hillside toting precious loads of the wet stuff.

Many years later underground pipes were installed and public water service became available. But the water came only to a number of faucets scattered about the NLA property. Each cabin had its own water tank located somewhere near a faucet. The Alexander tank was a huge blue plastic one, about the size of a bathtub, sitting beside the path where one such faucet protruded from the ground.

Once a day or so somebody would need to come up to the tank. A length of hose, which was attached to the tank, would be stretched out and connected to the faucet. The spigot would be opened and twenty minutes or so later, the tank would be full. From the tank, an underground pipe led to the cabin. Back at the cabin, you could get water from one of two faucets—one in the kitchen and one in another room with a bathtub. Technically, you could use this water for everything—even drinking. After all, it was safe, treated water from the public water company.

One time, though, Mr. Alexander had unscrewed the large cap of the blue tank and let Ken look inside. One glance at the various dead bugs, leaves and other things—much of it beyond recognition—floating around in the water was all it took. Ken now understood why his parents might use water from the tank for the bathtub and for washing hands, but wanted water directly from the hillside faucet for drinking, brushing teeth and washing dishes. Besides, water that had been sitting around in a huge blue tank for a day or two probably didn't taste all that great. (Ken had never tried it, but he could guess.) On the other hand, water fresh from the faucet was always chilled and delicious.

You could drink water from one of the outdoor faucets by one of two methods. You could cup it in your two hands. Mr. Alexander discouraged this method, unless hands had been recently washed. This was not too likely if you had been hiking or swimming or playing tennis or golf.

The other technique was to hold your head under the faucet, turn sideways and let a stream of water flow directly into your mouth. This method allowed the greatest amount of water to enter the mouth in the least amount of time. But it required bending over in a grotesque, awkward position. Worse, this position usually allowed a stream of cold water to run across your cheek and—if you weren't quick enough or hadn't quite mastered the necessary skill—around the back of your head. In the worst imaginable case, the water, now feeling like a glacier, would travel over your neck and down your back. At this point you might just as well take a shower under the faucet. Not a bad idea, actually, on some of the hotter midsummer Nojiri days.

Ken removed the lid of the teapot, held the teapot under the faucet and turned the spigot. The force of the water nearly blasted the pot out of his hand. He quickly reduced the pressure then stood quietly while the cold water rapidly filled the empty container.

Left over raindrops released their grips on overhanging leaves, pattering all about. An occasional direct hit on Ken's head or neck sent shivers down his spine. One drop sent a tickle trickle down Ken's back, inside his shirt. Ken wriggled.

The forest was strangely silent today. Maybe the rain had dampened the spirits of the bugs and birds and they didn't feel like singing. There was an occasional call of some kind of bird. But the call came so seldom that it almost seemed out of place. The song was plaintive, haunting. Normally, the stillness of the wilderness was soothing and refreshing. Birdsongs were bright, cheery. Right now, though, everything was just a little too still—a little creepy. At least it wasn't the dark of night.

Soon the job was completed and Ken was on his way back to the security of the cabin. Taking care not to slip on the wet stairs in the sandals, Ken made his way to the back of the cabin. He felt relieved when he saw the kitchen window again, and the figure of his mother moving about inside. His errand was finished. The solo expedition into the unknown wilderness had been completed. He was home safe and sound. Mission accomplished!

"*Tadaima*," Ken called, stepping out of the sandals and slipping through the back door.

"*Okaerinasai. Arigatoh.*" Mrs. Alexander took the kettle from Ken and set it on the stove. She covered the spout with a folded piece of aluminum foil which they used to keep bugs from finding their way into the Alexanders' water supply. This was Mr. Alexander's idea. As unlikely as it was that one of those *benjo mushi* could possibly get inside the teakettle, Ken's dad didn't even want to think about the possibility of finding a drowned bug in his drinking water. But he *did* think about the possibility. Which was why the foil cover was used.

Ken squeezed into his slippers and clomped through the

kitchen into the dining room.

"OK. Let's go," he said to his father. Mr. Alexander rose from his jigsaw puzzle.

"OK. *Iko.*" [Let's go.] he called to his wife.

Mrs. Alexander walked in from the kitchen where she'd been putting away a few final breakfast items.

"*Hai. Ikimashoh.*" [Yes. Let's go. (The politer form.)]

Mr. Alexander pulled his bright blue nylon jacket off the back of a chair and headed toward the front door.

"We'd better take along umbrellas just in case," he said, looking through a wire basket atop the shoe box next to the door. Like just about everything else in the cabin, the umbrellas were old, well-used. Mr. Alexander found a small black one that seemed fairly decent. Not too many holes. At least no big ones. Nothing big enough for a *benjo mushi* to hop through.

Mrs. Alexander and Ken each selected a sturdier umbrella for their use.

"Think that's big enough?" his dad asked.

"You can share my umbrella if yours starts to leak," Ken fired back.

"Thanks," chuckled Mr. Alexander. Hopefully, none of the umbrellas would be needed. But you never knew. This was Nojiri in June. And the sky, though somewhat lighter now, was still hidden from view by several layers of indecisive clouds. It seemed as if the clouds couldn't decide whether they wanted to yield to gorgeous, blue skies, hang around all day in a sullen mood or throw a tantrum and turn into something truly nasty.

The Alexanders put on their shoes out on the front porch. Ken slipped into his yellow, rubber boots. His mother had bought them for him in Tokyo just for this occasion. She knew what the weather could be like at Lake Nojiri.

Ken glanced at the lake below. Gray, choppy waves made the water look uninviting for swimming. Far out in the lake a small fishing boat bounced across the dark waters. The motor could be faintly heard, chugging through the misty morning.

Ken led the way, down the stairs off the porch. The Alexanders circled around the corner of the cabin and walked past the house, past the back door, past the outhouse, across the yard and out to the main path. A right turn on the path took them downward toward the lake. Moments later they reached the stairs descending to the right of the path. These led down past the auditorium, past the spring and on out to the lake front. Mr. Alexander stopped.

"If we keep going straight on this path it'll lead to the main road," he explained. "It's the fastest way."

"OK," said Ken. Fastest sounded good to him. He was eager to get into town and take a boat ride, maybe do a little shopping. He was hoping his dad would still be feeling generous when they walked by the souvenir shops.

But Mrs. Alexander looked at the trail sloping ahead and said, "The mud might be bad. Let's go by the stairs."

"That's right," Mr. Alexander agreed. "The mud might be bad. Let's go by the stairs."

Ken would have preferred to stay on the straight path. Puddles? A muddy path? He could hear them calling to him.

"Come slobber through us!" How could they NOT go that way?

But Ken was outnumbered. The family turned right down the concrete steps to the level below, crossed the stepping stones in front of the auditorium and descended the final few steps past the spring. The gravel-covered parking lot, much wetter than the day before, was the last obstacle before they reached the safe, mud-free paved road.

The NLA hillside was crisscrossed with dozens of paths and stairways. Gently sloping (sometimes) paths zigzagged back and forth across the side of the hill. They were barely wide enough for the miniature pickup trucks that the maintenance workers used. Closer to the opening of the summer season, the ground crews would whack the underbrush that encroached on the paths and stairways. But this being early in the summer, the workers had not yet begun their yearly task. Therefore, the weeds and bushes reached out into the NLA's walkways.

The stairs, on the other hand, generally climbed straight up the hillside, sometimes continuing mercilessly up, up, up for hundreds of feet. If you could make it to the top of one of these stairways without losing your breath or passing out, you were ready for the Olympics.

Staircases tended to be narrower than the paths. On the worst ones, if two people walked side by side, chances were that one of them would become lost in the underbrush and never be seen again.

The Alexanders turned left and followed the one and a half-lane wide road along the edge of the lake. To their right, occasional concrete docks jutted out into the water. Early in the season like this, the water level was high. Throughout the summer water would be drained from the lake to nourish rice paddies at lower elevations. A few months from now the water level would be many feet lower than it was now. Parts of the swimming area, now behind the Alexanders, would become nothing but a sandy beach. But today the lake was full. Windblown waves spilled over the docks.

The lakeside road curved left, taking the trio away from the lake. Then it curved right. A path from the left intersected with the pavement at this second curve.

"This is where we would have come out if we'd stayed on the path," Mr. Alexander pointed out.

"I know," Ken said. His father said the same thing every year when they came on this hike. Mrs. Alexander grunted her acknowledgement. She knew, too. But she didn't say so. Why spoil the silence with unnecessary talking?

The path—which they hadn't taken—was one of the long sides of a triangle. The stairs and stepping stones past the auditorium down to the lake were the short side. The lakeside road was the third side of the triangle. The Alexanders had taken the long way to avoid the muddy path.

Ken wouldn't have minded the mud. But he thought it was a good idea to humor his parents. After all, they were headed for the village, and his parents were the ones with the money.

The going was easy enough. There was absolutely no traffic, and any puddles they came across were small enough to easily skirt. Unless you happened to be wearing boots. In that case it was required that you would walk through the puddles. It was the law.

Eventually the family came upon a round metallic object sunken into the asphalt road—a manhole cover. Very interesting, thought Ken. The shape of an elephant was carved into the steel lid, surrounded by an array of flowers. A long trunk and two sharp tusks pierced the center of the iron disk.

Ken knew from previous visits to Nojiri that many fossils

had been discovered in the area, including those of the huge creatures that had roamed this area so long ago. Actually, these beasts were Nauman's elephants which had lived there 500,000 to 15,000 years earlier. They were relatives of mammoths that had roamed the earth in ancient times. Every year in the winter, when Nojiri Lake waters had been drained for farming, groups of students and scientists worked on the now-exposed bottom of the lake, digging up thousands of fossils and remnants of the ancient humans who had called this area home. The reputation of the Nojiri area as a site for the elephants' remains had been symbolized in its manhole covers. Ken was fascinated by the idea of huge elephants wandering about Nojiri.

And then he had a big thought.

"They should draw elephant footprints on the road"

"What?" asked his dad.

"*Dohshite?*" [Why?] asked his mother.

"Then kids could follow the footprints to see where to go."

"And where would they go?" Mr. Alexander wanted to know.

"To the statues in the park. It would be neat if the footprints went from the street to the statues."

Then Ken had an even larger thought.

"No, it'd be neat if the footprints started from the train station." Kurohime station in Shinano Town where they'd arrived the day before was about five miles away.

"That would be a long trail of footprints," Ken's mother said.

And then a truly enormous thought entered Ken's mind.

"No, the footprints should start in Tokyo!" he exclaimed

excitedly. "And Kyoto. And Osaka. And, and..." Ken struggled to recall the names of other big Japanese cities. He gave up the effort as a vision raced through his brain. He saw thousands of city children, little backpacks on their backs, strung out along Japan's highways, following endless elephant footprints, walking day after day, arriving eventually here in Nojiri. Then they would have a Nauman's Elephant Party. (Ken wasn't clear yet in his own mind as to what a Nauman's Elephant Party would be like.)

"Hmm," mused Mr. Alexander.

"Hmm," said Mrs. Alexander. "*Omoshiroi.*" [Amusing/interesting.]

But Ken wasn't done. Another jumbo thought was shaping itself in Ken's head. A thought so big that it was—mammoth. Ken chuckled.

"*Nani*?" [What?] Mrs. Alexander wanted to know.

"The footprints should start from all the big cities in the world." Mr. Alexander's mouth opened, words ready to emerge. But Ken was way ahead of his dad.

"There would be footprints on the bottom of the ocean. Kids could wear diving suits and follow them across the ocean."

Ken's image grew to include countless, tiny figures, each bundled up in a huge snowman-like diving suit, plodding along the sea bottom, trails of shimmering bubbles rising from each one toward the surface far overhead, fishes dancing all about. Ken was proud of his ideas. As they walked along the tree-lined road, Ken shared his visions with his parents. They listened attentively, with eager interest. Mr. and Mrs. Alexander were supportive of Ken's imagination. Their questions and comments were food that kept Ken's creativity growing and thriving.

The road T-ed with a larger one. The new road was wide enough that two cars could pass each other without slowing down. And it even had a name: International Friendship Highway—although it wasn't quite a highway. There was no sidewalk. The left branch of the road curved around the far side of the NLA hill on its way to circle the entire lake. The taxi had driven on part of this road on its way to the top of the NLA hill. The right branch led into Nojiri village.

Now there was occasional traffic. On more than one occasion Ken was certain that they would be splattered by a speeding car hitting a puddle that the Alexanders were passing. But in each case, the passing car swerved at the last moment, sparing the Alexanders an unwanted shower.

Before long the road left the shelter of the forest to lead between rice fields and scattered farm houses. Between the road and the lake front were a growing smattering of lodges and campgrounds. They were entering tourist territory. But the lodges were silent and the campgrounds were tent-less. They had entered tourist territory, but they had not yet entered tourist season.

As the Alexanders passed one rice field, a motion in the water caught Ken's attention. Looking closely, he saw a small snake swimming its way between the baby rice plants.

"*Hebi da*!" [A snake!] Ken exclaimed, leaving the road and carefully stepping down the bank toward the edge of the rice paddy. His parents joined him, one on each side.

Ken knew his father had had an unfortunate childhood encounter or two with snakes. One had occurred—Ken had heard this story more times than he ever wished to—when Mr.

Alexander was a small child.

Timmy, as he had been called then—no one dared call him that any more—had been riding a tricycle in his well-gardened yard when he was about two years old. His family had been living in Kyoto at the time, another Japanese city, for just one year. The yard was old and traditional, full of well-manicured bushes and all sorts of plants (as far as Mr. Alexander could remember). As Timmy rounded a corner on his hotrod tricycle, he saw dead ahead of him, slithering across the narrow path from one side to the other, what certainly must have seemed to him, to be the world's largest snake.

The choices were obvious: Run over the snake with the tricycle—or run screaming back to the house. Needless to say, Timmy opted for the second alternative. Sadly, his parents were away at language school at the time, and only the house maid was there to comfort the hysteric little boy. Since that time, Mr. Alexander had had a deep, personal feeling toward snakes which was as far from love as a feeling can be.

But Mr. Alexander, kind, loving and concerned father that he was, didn't want his son to grow up with the same sort of less-than-loving feeling towards snakes that he had. Therefore, whenever he saw a snake, Mr. Alexander would say, as calmly as possible,

"Oh, look—a snake," in a most adult and interested manner. This was amusing to Ken who never really had any feeling regarding snakes, one way or the other. He knew that even as his father was serenely uttering these words on the outside, deep down inside he was streaking down the road, arms flapping wildly in the wind, screaming at the top of his lungs,

"HELP! A SNAKE!!"

The snake S-ed its way among the stalks of rice, oblivious to the three humans watching in fascination. The Alexanders exchanged appropriate comments of appreciation. Mrs. Alexander took a photo or two. And Mr. Alexander took two or three quick steps backward when the snake changed directions and headed his way.

However, the snake then turned and swam in the opposite direction, averting panic. It was eventually lost from view among the weeds crowding the banks of the paddy. The Alexanders resumed their trek and were soon in the village of Nojiri.

CHAPTER 19

THE HELICOPTER BOAT

It seemed that half of the buildings in the village were souvenir shops or restaurants. Vending machines lined the narrow streets, selling cigarettes and every imaginable sort of drink. Mini game arcades and bike rentals beckoned with flashing lights and tantalizing electronic sounds. Ken ducked into one of the souvenir shops while his parents checked out the departure times for the huge tour boats that looped around the lake. By the time his mom and dad returned from the boat office across the narrow street and found Ken in the toy section of the store, he had a mental list of seven items he wanted to buy.

"Let's go on a boat first, before we buy anything," suggested Mr. Alexander.

"Does that mean that I can get something?" Ken asked.

"Yeah, I suppose so. For special."

It was those "for specials" that Ken loved here at Nojiri. Success! He was going to get something. But which one? He knew he dare not press his luck by asking for seven items.

There were three separate tour boats docked at the wharves. Each could probably carry a few hundred passengers. More, if a group consisted of small school children.

One boat, the newest and coolest looking one, did not have permission to sail on the lake. Something about being too big or too noisy or too polluting. From what Ken understood of the situation, which was what his parents understood of the situation—which wasn't much, really—some big shot businessman had bought the boat somewhere else. He'd had it shipped to Nojiri and then assembled here, only to find that he couldn't get a permit to operate it on the lake.

"That was silly," Ken thought. His parents agreed.

The second boat had a huge neck and head of a swan attached to its top. If you saw the boat from a distance, you would think a gigantic—mammoth?—swan was swimming about on the lake. This was the one Ken wanted to ride. But the next departure wasn't for forty-five minutes. Ken didn't want to wait that long. Souvenirs were waiting to be bought.

The third vessel was a plain, ferry-type boat. It would depart in fifteen minutes. But it was so boring.

"Can we go on a small boat?" asked Ken. There were many rowboats and paddle boats that could be rented.

"Sure," answered Mr. Alexander. "Would you rather go on one of them?"

"Yeah. Can we go on one of the helicopters?" The paddle boats were shaped on top either like miniature swans—or were they geese?—or helicopters. A huge advantage on a day like today was that unlike the rowboats, the paddle boats had roofs.

Mrs. Alexander made the rental arrangements. (Sometimes Mr. Alexander was shy about using his Japanese, especially when his wife was available to handle language chores.)

Ticket in hand, Mr. Alexander led the family toward the end of a dock.

An elderly, unshaven attendant took the ticket and hauled in a boat by its mooring rope. He was scruffy-looking and darker than any Japanese person Ken had ever seen. The man must have spent his entire life under the sun, helping people get in and out of boats. But there was no sun today. The attendant wiped off the seats of the boat with a towel. Even though the boat was roofed, the sides were open. Earlier rains had left behind puddles on the seats and floor of the craft.

While the attendant held the boat tight against the dock, the Alexanders took turns climbing over the side and settled onto the small damp seats. Mr. Alexander went first, followed by Ken and finally Mrs. Alexander. Umbrellas were laid on the floor in back of the seats.

The old sun-man untied the mooring ropes from the dock, tossed the loose ends on top of the bow and rear of the boat and gave the vessel a mighty heave toward open water. Mr. and Mrs. Alexander, whose seats put them in the pedaling positions began turning the pedals on the floor in front of their seats. The craft began to move, slowly at first, then faster, as the two Alexanders fell into a rhythm. Ken, by virtue of sitting in the middle, earned the responsibility of steering.

Spinning the wheel in a most enthusiastic fashion, Ken proceeded to guide the boat directly into the path of an oncoming fisherman's motorboat.

"Turn right!" Mrs. Alexander shouted.

"Turn left!" hollered Mr. Alexander.

Ken did neither.

Mr. Alexander began frantically pedaling backwards to

stop the progress of the boat. Mrs. Alexander continued pedaling forward. Since the two sets of pedals were attached to each other, the opposing efforts of the two Alexanders cancelled each other out. The craft slowed to a complete stop.

"Pedal backward!" shouted Mr. Alexander.

No, pedal forward!" shouted Mrs. Alexander.

"Stop shouting!" shouted Ken.

Far from the Alexander chaos, the motorboat veered ever so slightly and skimming across the waves, sped toward the shore. It came nowhere near the helicopter boat.

"Phew, that was close," sighed Mr. Alexander.

"Aw, that boat didn't even come close to us," said Ken.

"But here come the waves," said Mrs. Alexander.

"Sure enough, even as the motorboat cut its engines and glided toward a dock, the trailing wake came bouncing toward the Alexanders.

"Turn into the waves," Mr. Alexander ordered and began pedaling furiously—forward this time. Mrs. Alexander also pedaled forward while Ken turned the steering wheel. Slowly the tiny boat swung around just as the first of the waves arrived. As wave after wave lifted, then dropped the bow of the boat, the three passengers bounced up and down in their seats. The boat continued to bob until finally the motorboat's wake faded away.

"That was fun!" exclaimed Ken. "Let's do it again."

"I feel sick," said his mother.

"I got wet," said his father. Indeed, a sizeable amount of lake had splashed through the side openings of the boat, dousing Mr. Alexander's left arm. Mrs. Alexander had squeezed inward toward Ken and avoided most of the spray.

"That was fun!" repeated Ken. He could do this all day. But unfortunately there was a time limit on the boat rental. His mom had arranged a thirty-minute rental. Just long enough to pedal away from the shore, nearly get run over by a motorboat, get wet, shake up his parents and head back.

If his parents weren't so cheap, they could have taken the boat for an hour or longer. They could have gone all the way around the lake—but who could pedal that far? Or they could have gone to the island.

"The Island," as it was cleverly called by members of the NLA was only a fifteen-minute pedal from Nojiri village. There was actually a Japanese name for the island—Benten Island. But it was commonly referred to only as "The Island." It was a tiny island, as islands go. An adult could walk around the entire thing in ten minutes or so. A boy, eager to get back to the souvenir shop at the entrance to the island could probably run the route in less than 5 minutes.

The two large tour boats stopped here on their way around the lake. A long wooden dock stretched out into the lake. There was ample space along the dock for the huge sightseeing boats, as well as for many smaller rowboats and paddle boats.

At the end of the dock an enormous, bright red *torii* towered over a path leading to the center of the island. A *torii* is a traditional fixture which marks the entrance to a *Shinto* shrine. A torii separates the divine, sacred area where gods are enshrined from the outside world. This one looked like a jumbo hitching post where Paul Bunyan might have tied up Babe, his famous blue ox. But there was an extra cross bar on top. Originally the *torii* was supposedly a place where a bird would roost. The top part of the *torii* symbolized the bird, according to Ken's mother.

But the year before, when Ken's family had visited the island, via one of the tour boats, the top of the *torii* had not looked at all like a bird to Ken. In fact, he hadn't even looked at the *torii* as his family passed underneath. He had been looking for the path that led off to the right, the one that circled the island. And there it had been! Ken was ready for the five-minutes-or-less dash around the island to get to the souvenir shop. And he was off.

"Watch out that you don't slip in the mud." Mrs. Alexander's words had vaguely trailed after him. But Ken was gone.

He knew his parents would remain on the straight path. They would then climb the stairs to the shrine sitting atop the hill in the center of the island. This was the course taken by most visitors to the island. It there was time left over, some tourists would leisurely stroll along the trail that hugged the circumference of the island.

But not Ken. Down below he chugged on, as fast as his booted feet could take him. Never mind that his parents had the money. When he got to the souvenir store he could at least look. And when he got there he looked. And looked and looked. When his parents returned from the shrine and finally caught up with Ken, he had had a mental Christmastime sized wish list of things he wanted. But his parents hadn't bought him anything on the island.

"Things are much more expensive on the island," they had explained. So, all of Ken's running had been in vain.

Ken remembered this as the helicopter boat bobbed around halfway between the lake shore and the island.

"Can we go to the island?" he asked hopefully.

"Not this year," said his father, dousing the hopeful flame that had burned in Ken's eager heart. "We don't have enough time. Besides, the weather's getting worse. I think we'd better head back."

Indeed, the cloud cover had slowly changed to a darker shade of gray. And the air seemed to be heavier and wetter now—and not just because of splashing waves.

"*Soh ne.* [That's right.] Let's head back," agreed Mrs. Alexander. She worried more about the weather than the rest of the family. She was afraid they would get caught out on the lake in a downpour. The boat would fill with water and sink. The family would be lost at sea—or lost at lake. After all, these things were known to happen.

So reluctantly Ken turned the boat around to face the shore—but only after guiding the craft in two complete circles first. Circles were fun!

Partway home Ken and his mother switched positions. This was always a tricky maneuver. It required one person to stand up in a crouched position—you couldn't stand up straight unless you wanted your head to bump against the roof of the helicopter or swan—while the other person slid from the middle seat to the side seat. It was especially hard if both people stood up at the same time—which is what happened at first. Finding their ways blocked, both Ken and his mom sat down again.

"No, I'll stand up," declared Ken, savoring the challenge of trying to balance himself on the wobbling boat.

"*Hai. Doozo.*" [Yes. Go ahead.] Mrs. Alexander replied. She had no desire to test her sense of balance any more.

Ken placed one hand on top of his father's head ("Hey,

I'm not a handrail," Mr. Alexander protested) and rose awkwardly. His mother slid underneath him. A slight bump in the boat—had Mr. Alexander mischievously caused it?—nearly dumped Ken in his mother's lap. But he held his balance. Carefully he sidled over to the side seat vacated by his mom. Just as he was about to settle into his new position, the boat rocked again. This time Ken was certain his dad was playing tricks. Ken plopped down, half on the seat, half on his mother.

"Ow!" Ken complained.

"*Itai*" [Ow!] agreed his mother. As Ken slid fully into his seat, Mrs. Alexander turned to her husband.

"*Kora*!" she scolded. Mr. Alexander was trying unsuccessfully to hide a suspicious grin.

"*Nani*?" [What?] he asked.

"Ken could have fallen into the lake," she sputtered.

"The fish would have thrown him back," Mr. Alexander replied, chuckling.

Mrs. Alexander didn't find this amusing, but Ken did. He knew he had never been in any real danger. At any rate, his mother's anger—if real—didn't last long, and soon the boat was once again plodding its way back to safety. Twice on the way to shore, Mrs. Alexander steered the boat into motorboat wakes and the family had a shaking good time. Ken pedaled hard to keep up with his dad. Once, when the boat had seemed especially heavy to propel, he noticed that his dad had removed his feet from the pedal and was sitting back enjoying the free ride.

"Hey. You're supposed to help," Ken told his father.

"Oops. Well, you're doing so well I figured you could get us back all by yourself."

"Of course I can. But you need your exercise."

"Oh yeah? Well take this!" Mr. Alexander began to pedal furiously. Ken's legs could barely keep up with the rapidly rotating pedals. After a few seconds of trying, he removed his feet from the pedals and let his dad paddle to his heart's content. It didn't take long for Mr. Alexander to realize he was working alone.

"OK, I give up. Let's pedal together," he conceded. And so they did. And necessarily so.

The playful breeze had matured into a full-grown wind, raising waves which began pushing the suddenly very small boat away from the dock. Only with a great deal of effort and much yelling of orders to each other did the Alexander family finally manage to slam their boat into the side of the dock from which they had set sail.

The old man was there to pull them in and secure the boat lines to the dock. A look of obvious relief crossed his sun-browned face as the three explorers staggered out of the boat onto the safety of the dock, umbrellas in hand.

"Two minutes left," sighed Mr. Alexander peeking at his watch. "Made it back just in time."

Phooey, thought Ken. We could have gone around in one more circle.

But Ken and his mom both agreed that it was a good time to be back. Raindrops were being blown about now. Raising their umbrellas as best they could, the three Alexanders scrambled off the dock for the refuge of the shore. A quick decision was made to skip the tour on the sightseeing boat, due to the weather. What was next? Ken wondered.

CHAPTER 20

BUGS IN THE LUNCH

"*Onaka ga suita.*" [I'm hungry. (Literally, "Stomach is empty.")], said Ken as his family huddled in a souvenir shop.

"*Watashi mo,*" [Me, too], said his mother. Mr. Alexander was just about to suggest lunch when Ken suddenly changed modes.

"I want to buy something," he stated. Even as he declared his hunger, his eyes had been surveying the surrounding wares in the store.

"Let's do this," said Mr. Alexander.

This was his take-control voice, the fatherly "Here's the perfect solution to the situation" voice. The "I'm going to make an important statement now" tone of voice. Sometimes his following words were heeded with awe. Well, maybe that had happened once or twice. More often, what came next was drowned out in a chaos of Alexander voices. This, however, was one of those rare occasions on which silence followed Mr. Alexander's words. Mrs. Alexander was too tired and cold to object. And Ken preferred to wait quietly for his father's words of wisdom. He was sure the words would have something to do with buying a souvenir.

Mr. Alexander seemed stunned by the unexpected attention from his family. He looked at his wife and son. Then he looked at his wife and son again. Having convinced himself that they were both not only awake and present, but were actually listening to him, Mr. Alexander proceeded.

"Why don't we go to that restaurant over there." He pointed to a huge, white block of a building off a ways from where they stood. On the second floor was a restaurant. The first floor was—joy of joys—a large souvenir shop. The third story was who knew what. Large letters on the side of the roof of the building proclaimed it to be the "NOJIRIKO TERMINAL."

"We can eat lunch there, then go downstairs and buy you something special," Ken's dad suggested.

"Can I get anything I want?" Ken wanted to know.

"We'll see."

"Ken hated "We'll see." But that was better than a flat "No."

"OK," said Ken.

"*Ii ne.*" [That's good.] agreed Mrs. Alexander. Mr. Alexander seemed proud of himself. He had actually come up with a suggestion that the entire family agreed to.

To tell the truth, Ken greatly respected his father and many of his father's decisions. But jokingly arguing with each other's decisions or suggestions was a common, playful part of the family's way of doing things. Ken knew that in any kind of emergency or serious situation there would be no arguing with his father—or his mother. His parents also knew that. And so they could debate such semi-serious matters as where to eat lunch and what souvenirs to buy. (Or maybe that second issue really was a life—or—death matter. Ken wondered. Naw.

Probably not. Maybe not.)

The Alexanders skirted a small park that lay between the white building and the parking lot by the souvenir shop in which they had just sought shelter. A series of round stepping stones led through the park. On each stone was painted a large footprint of an elephant. The stepping stones continued through the tree-shaded park to a slight hill. At the top of the rise were two life-sized, dark brown and very realistic fiberglass elephants, a baby tagging along behind its mother. These were models of the Nauman's elephants for which the area was famous. Life-sized meant that Ken's head barely reached the top of the mother's front legs. Ken had posed for pictures sitting astride the back of the baby elephant. No one could reach the mother's back without the use of a ladder. The two statues had been built based on actual fossils found in the Lake Nojiri area from up to 500,000 years earlier. A *long* time ago, thought Ken.

Because of the rain today they skipped the park and the mammoth elephants. A quick dash through some truly harsh rain brought the Alexanders to a covered indentation in the corner of the restaurant building. Swinging doors off to the left led into the souvenir shop. Ken hopefully peered through the open doorway of the shop.

On the left side of the shelter was a large glass case. Inside it were plastic models of the entire menu. It took only a quick look for the three to determine what they wanted to order. They had been here the previous year. And the year before. Many times in the past, in fact. No need to try something new which might turn out to be a disappointment.

A flight of stairs directly ahead led to a U-turn in the steps and then a second flight of stairs to another door which led into the restaurant. The Alexanders were greeted by a loud, almost embarrassing chorus of "*Irasshaimase*" [Welcome] from the handful of staff scattered about the huge room.

Mr. Alexander selected a table for four by a floor-to-ceiling window. This way he could open a window to let in fresh air, in case the place should become smoky. He need not have worried. At two in the afternoon on an offseason Saturday—a rainy one at that—there were no other customers in the restaurant.

This eatery—as was the case with most restaurants in Japan—did not have a nonsmoking area. Mr. Alexander hated eating in most Japanese restaurants. Back home in Fort Collins, every restaurant either had a large nonsmoking section or was completely smoke-free. Ken's dad mostly frequented the latter type of restaurant. He enjoyed eating out in Fort Collins. But he frequently complained—often to the managers of Japanese restaurants—about the lack of nonsmoking areas in this country.

On rare occasions, Ken's family had discovered restaurants with a "no-smoking" table or two. These were a joke. A single table—or two—would have a "no-smoking" sign on it. But the poor souls who sat at these tables would be overwhelmed with stinky fumes drifting over from every table around them. A lot of good that did. Mrs. Alexander was sure that the owners of those restaurants meant well. But that didn't stop her husband from grumbling in a most unpleasant way.

However, in recent years some restaurants had begun offering entire, separate sections which were smoke free. Often they were called "Kiddie Corners," and were intended for mothers who didn't want their little children to suffocate while eating. Mr. Alexander was only too happy to join the little kiddies in these clean air zones. If only there were more!

The Alexanders leaned their wet umbrellas against the window and draped their wet jackets over the backs of their chairs without sitting down. As soon as Ken and his parents had entered the restaurant, the staff had been intently motioning for them to approach a counter on the far side of the room. Mr. Alexander had nodded knowingly and called out,

"*Hai.*" [Yes.] He'd been here before. He knew what to do.

But the staff saw only a foreigner—a poor ignorant foreigner, probably—who could not possibly understand the Japanese way of doing things. Mr. Alexander sometimes resented this. He had lived in Japan for a total of twenty-five years, both as a child and as an English teacher in later years. He had lived in this country longer than that young waitress over there, for Pete's sake. How dare she assume he was a dumb *Gaijin*. Sometimes Mr. Alexander's feathers became exceedingly ruffled.

Today, however, he was in a good mood—despite being hungry. This was rare. Being hungry usually equaled being cranky, as far as Ken's dad was concerned. Mrs. Alexander sometimes compared his behavior to that of a young child. But not when her husband was hungry—at least not so that he could hear.

Smiling pleasantly at the restaurant staff—he knew that they thought he didn't know what to do—but he was one up on them, Ken's dad strolled toward the counter in a leisurely but purposeful fashion. Ken and Mrs. Alexander tagged along behind.

"What would you like?" asked a middle-aged man behind

the counter. He was businesslike and efficient. He was probably in charge.

Ken ordered the kid's plate—a combination of a pancake, a mound of Spanish rice, a sausage, a dish of salad greens and an ice cream cone for dessert. He also requested a cream soda to drink.

Mrs. Alexander asked for beef curry and a beer.

And Mr. Alexander ordered a mountain-vegetable *soba* (buckwheat) bowl. Soba were thin noodles in a steamy soy sauce-flavored broth. Mr. Alexander's *soba* and his wife's spicy curry would be excellent warmers on a chilly day such as this. But why Ken wanted items that included ice cream—ice cream with the meal, as well as a scoop of the white stuff in his soda—was beyond his parents. The answer was quite simple: Ken was a kid, and for a kid, it was never too cold for ice cream.

Actually, Mr. Alexander's warm *soba*, or an alternative of chilled noodles, were the only meatless dishes offered at this restaurant. His selection was a matter of limited selections, not unadventurous dining.

The serious man behind the counter tallied up the items. The total was reasonable for a Japanese resort area. During peak season scores of people arrived on large sightseeing buses. Orders were served quickly, the tourists ate rapidly and then they were gone. By serving huge numbers of people quickly, the restaurant could afford to keep their prices low.

Mr. Alexander picked up tickets for the ordered items and paid for the lunch. The family returned to the table and sat down. Ken grabbed a window seat on one side of the table.

Mr. Alexander sat across from him. Mrs. Alexander sat next to Ken.

No sooner had Mr. Alexander placed the tickets on the table than the young waitress slid up to the table and snatched them up. Repeating the order, she deftly snapped the tickets in half with just her right hand and then disappeared into the kitchen. A moment later the waitress reemerged, umbrella in hand.

"I think she's going to hit you with the umbrella," Ken warned his dad.

Mr. Alexander reached over to the window and grasped the handle of his umbrella.

"She better not. I'm armed. I have an umbrella, too, and I know how to use it," he chuckled fiendishly.

But the young woman had no intention of hitting anybody with anything, of course—at least not today. She walked to the door and disappeared down the stairs.

"Wonder where she's going," mused Mr. Alexander.

"You scared her and she's running away," suggested Ken.

"Of course not," shot back Mr. Alexander. "She thinks I'm really handsome, but she can tell that I'm married. So she's leaving before she falls in love with me."

"*Soh da ne.*" [That's so.] chimed in Mrs. Alexander.

Ken snickered.

"What?! You don't believe that?" demanded Mr. Alexander.

Ken couldn't answer. He was choking with laughter.

The three Alexanders craned their necks toward the window and soon caught sight of the waitress, umbrella now raised, emerging from the door below.

"Look! She's running for her life!" exclaimed Ken. His dad

made a motion as if to bop Ken over the head with an imaginary rolled up newspaper—or something.

In truth, the girl took a few hurried steps across the parking lot in front of the building. She paused at a bush and appeared to be looking for something. Quickly reaching out, she plucked something off the bush—once, twice, three times. Then turning around, she retraced her steps to the building.

"Oh, yuck," said Ken. "I bet she caught some bugs for your *soba*."

"No way. I ordered vegetable soba."

"But you scared her. She's going to get even by sneaking bugs into your soba."

A moment later the waitress appeared at the top of the stairs, slightly out of breath. She smiled sweetly at the Alexander table as she passed by on her way back to the kitchen.

"I told you," said Ken. "She's going to poison you."

"No. If she got any bugs, they're probably for you. She's probably going to make a bug face on your pancake. Two little bugs for the eyes and one big one for the nose."

Mrs. Alexander had been trying to ignore the ongoing conversation. But now she couldn't tolerate it anymore.

"That's disgusting. How am I supposed to eat after I hear this conversation?"

Ken suddenly remembered the morning's chat with his dad.

"Anteater pie!" he recalled.

His mother grimaced.

"*Shikata ga nai ne.*" [Hopeless, aren't you.] she groaned.

The discussion of bugs and food and other delightful matters hadn't progressed too terribly long (except in the opinion of Mrs. Alexander who wished the conversation had died long ago) when the waitress, now accompanied by the dour man from the counter, arrived at the table, trays balanced on outstretched arms. The restaurant duo set dishes on the table, the waitress daintily and the man in a businesslike and efficient manner.

Ken's pancake did indeed have a face on it. No bugs, though. The eyes were raisins, the nose was a ripe red cherry, the mouth was a slice of cantaloupe and the hair was scraggly lines of chocolate syrup. A whipped cream hat topped the chocolaty hairdo. A toothpick flagpole flying a tiny paper Japanese flag emerged from the mountain of red rice.

Mrs. Alexander's curry came in a silver bowl, looking hot in both temperature and flavor. A plate of steaming rice was set next to the bowl. A few slices of bright red pickled ginger adorned the side of the plate. Mrs. Alexander began dishing the golden brown curry, full of chunks of potatoes, carrots and beef, onto her rice.

Mr. Alexander pretended to look deep and hard through the steam billowing upward from his bowl for any signs of bugs.

"No living creatures here," he concluded, to Ken's disappointment.

The gray noodles were nearly concealed by *nori* (seaweed) slices and a heap of mountain vegetables of various sorts. Strategically placed at the top of the veggies were three delicate, unidentifiable leaves which looked suspiciously like the leaves on the bush where the waitress had lingered outside. The leaves had been dipped in *tempura* batter and fried in deep fat. They turned out to be crisp but tasteless. But they *were* mountain vegetables.

Mr. Alexander ate using a pair of wooden chopsticks from a black imitation lacquer box at the end of the table. Also at the end of the table was a laminated menu. No pictures here. If you couldn't read Japanese you had to guide one of the employees downstairs and point out what you wanted in the display case. There were also bottles of soy sauce and Worcestershire sauce, two little cans, one with white pepper and the other containing "Seven-flavor spices" and a napkin holder. Next to all these necessary items was a mysterious looking white dome set on a round, flat black base. On the side in curly, blue English letters was written "Secret Bell."

"What's that?" Ken wanted to know.

"A horoscope dispenser," replied his mother. "Point the arrows on the top to your birth year and month, put a hundred yen coin in the slot and pull the two handles together and your fortune will come out."

"I want to try it," said Ken.

"It's just a waste of money," his father cut in.

Ken and his mother dug into their meals with fork, spoon—and relish. They were hungry and the food was good.

Mr. Alexander did his best to appropriately slurp his noodles. Making noise while eating noodles is the polite way to eat in Japan. It indicates appreciation of the food. But having been raised in an American home, even though living in Japan, he had been very strongly discouraged as a child from making any sort of eating noise. It was rather pathetic to watch Mr. Alexander trying to slurp. The noise just did not come naturally to the man.

"I could teach you a thing or two about slurping," thought

Ken. But he was too busy eating to say anything.

By the time the meal had been totally devoured and the final dab of whipped cream had been scraped off Ken's plate, the rain had stopped.

"Let's head home," said Mr. Alexander, wiping his mouth one last time with a paper napkin and rising.

"Aren't you forgetting something?" asked Ken.

"Oh, yeah—my umbrella. Thanks," said Mr. Alexander. He reached over and picked up his still soggy umbrella from where it leaned against the window.

"No. Something else!"

"*Nan deshoh ka*?" [(I wonder) what it is?] Mrs. Alexander played along.

"A tip? No, we don't have to leave a tip in Japan," continued Mr. Alexander.

Ken was getting frantic now.

"NO! You're forgetting something else!"

"What else could that possibly be?" wondered Mr. Alexander, putting on a look of seemingly genuine puzzlement. But Ken knew his dad well.

"The souvenir shop!"

"Oh, no thank you," replied Ken's dad. "We don't need to buy any gifts for anyone." He turned to his wife. "Do we?"

"No, I don't think so," she said thoughtfully.

"I'm going down to the souvenir store," declared Ken as he headed toward the door of the restaurant.

"OK," said his father. "We'll join you down there."

Play time was over. Now it was time for some serious shopping. The highlight of the day! YES!!

CHAPTER 21

OMIYAGE

Japanese people have somehow never developed that horrible evil known as tipping. However, there is an equally awkward custom lurking in the depths of Japanese culture. It is known as gift giving. How bad can that be? Well, it depends on one's point of view.

Giving gifts in Japan is an art form. There are, of course, occasions for Japanese gift giving which are familiar to Americans: weddings, graduations and so on. But there are also uniquely Japanese gift giving situations.

Twice a year, during summer and at the end of the year near Christmastime, gifts are given to relatives, bosses, teachers, neighbors, business associates—people that you were indebted to or had close contact with. Kids' don't have to worry about these times. These are gift giving situations for big people.

New Year's Time is the biggy for kids. What Christmas is to American children (a time to get, get, get), New Year's is to Japanese youngsters. At this time Japanese children receive little, ornately decorated envelopes from parents, aunts and uncles, grandparents and sometimes even neighbors or family friends. The tiny size of the envelopes is made up for by what is inside—MONEY! It is not unknown for a lucky Japanese child to rake in hundreds of dollars worth of yen on this special day. No wonder Japanese kids like New Year's so much!

Another occasion for gift giving is travel. When Japanese people travel—overseas, cross country or even to the next prefecture on a school excursion—they are expected to return with *omiyage*. There should be something in the returnees' suitcases or backpacks for family members, friends, teachers at school and sometimes even neighbors.

To assist travelers and tourists in carrying out their present-buying duties, helpful concessioners have built souvenir shops and gift shops in every conceivable corner of Japan. These stores sell all sorts of local food products, snacks, knickknacks, trinkets, thingamajigs, doodads, ornaments and good luck charms—and toys. The crowded collection of dolls and other mementos in the glass case on top of the piano in the Itabashi apartment had come from many such souvenir shops.

Ken walked past the tables loaded with food items. There were rice crackers about the size of a large pizza. Jars of locally produced jams and jellies lined shelves, individually or in boxed sets. There were Western style cookies, biscuits and wafers. Several tables featured exotic—or at least exotic to a Westerner—foods: dried seaweed of various colors and texture, an assortment of pickled vegetables and fruit, dried fish and dried squid. And nearly everywhere were good luck charms, tiny Nauman's elephant statues, models of the *torii* from the island and other knickknacks which were destined to adorn the display cases (or cardboard storage boxes) of lucky—or unlucky?—recipients of the *omiyage*.

As he walked through the maze of gift covered tables, though, Ken had eyes only for the toy section. He'd been to this store before. He probably could have found his way to the toys blindfolded. He could have smelled his way. Toys have a scent of their own—don't they?

Ken briefly considered one of the toy guns—pop guns, water guns, guns that sparkled and crackled or produced shrieking siren noises when you pulled the trigger. For some reason, a brief memory of the two shadowy figures on yesterday's shore crawled through Ken's mind. Maybe a gun would protect him.

No, he thought, probably not. Those guys wouldn't be afraid of any kind of toy gun. And Ken's attention was immediately drawn away to other toys. He had narrowed his choices down to a few items when he felt an arm circling his shoulder.

"How's it going?" asked Mr. Alexander. Mrs. Alexander was at a nearby table checking out the blueberry jams. She probably would buy something for her parents. *Ojiichan* and *Obaachan* both liked jam on their noon meal bread.

"I think I'll get this one," Ken replied. He pointed to a three-foot long stuffed animal snake coiled on a shelf between two stuffed elephants. The snake had a white belly, a green and white speckled pattern on its upper side, a flicking red tongue protruding from a pink mouth and two googly eyes on its head. Who could be afraid of a creature like this?

"All these rare, exotic, unique things here and you want a snake!?!" Mr. Alexander was perplexed.

"Yeah." Ken was certain.

"OK." Mr. Alexander's response was reluctant but accepting. In the past Ken's parents had tried to persuade him to reconsider some of his shopping choices. More recently, though, they had learned to give up right away. Ken had trained his parents well. Besides, they had come to trust that Ken most often made wise selections.

Ken and his dad took the grinning snake to the cashier. Mrs. Alexander was already there, paying for a multi-pack of blueberry and blackberry jam. That should be a pleasant *omiyage* for the Tanakas. They wouldn't even have to find a vacant space in their glass case to put some unwanted souvenir doll.

Once the snake was paid for, Ken wanted to wear it home wrapped around his neck.

"It might rain again," said his mother. "The snake will get ruined. You'd better get a sack for it.

She was insistent. What's more, she was right. Ken accepted the plastic bag the cashier handed him. He would wait to play with Snakey—that was what his serpent's name would be, Ken had already decided—until he got home. But he got to hold the bag.

As they were on their way out of the souvenir shop, Ken's eyes caught sight of a snack shop in the corner of the building.

I'm hungry," his mouth said. Most likely the message had gone straight from his eyes to his stomach to his mouth. There could not have been time for his brain to have processed those words.

"Already?" asked both his mother and father simultaneously. But they knew that this was very possible. For Ken, seeing special food on display created the appetite, not time or exercise or any of the other normal appetite creators.

A few minutes later Ken followed his parents out of the

store, an "American Dog" in his hand. It was a corn dog on a stick, dipped in mustard and ketchup. Now Ken was content. Now he could go home completely satisfied.

There was one more stop to make before the Alexanders could leave Nojiri village. During the off season the three or four pay phones which were scattered about the NLA were stored inside offices and locked up. If off season visitors required taxi service to the Kurohime station, they needed to come into the village to the taxi office and request a lift in person.

A few blocks away from the restaurant/souvenir store the Alexanders found the taxi dispatchers office. Pushing the door open, Mr. Alexander stepped up to a counter. Behind a glass window, a middle-aged woman was sitting at a cluttered desk, talking on a telephone. The phone was an old device, shiny black with a dial on its face. While Mr. Alexander fidgeted, the lady happily cackled on, scribbling notes on a pad of paper next to the phone. Eventually she finished her conversation, hung up the phone, walked over to the window and peered inquisitively through a round, meshed hole. She turned a smiling face to the Alexander family, giving an especially friendly nod to Ken. She then looked at Mrs. Alexander, even though Ken's mom was standing behind her husband.

"*Hai*?" [Yes?] The query was directed to Mrs. Alexander. It was natural to assume that the Japanese-looking person would be the one who would handle the Japanese business. The big, foreign-looking fellow probably couldn't speak Japanese, and was thus ignored.

Ken's dad, though, apparently feeling confident after a filling meal, plunged in with nearly perfect Japanese and handled the arrangements himself. The woman behind the glass, looking not in the least bit surprised that a foreigner could speak such fluent Japanese, filled out another page on her note pad. The time was set. Sunday at noon exactly, a taxi would be dispatched to the top of the NLA hill to pick up the Alexanders and deliver them to the station. The lady chuckled when Mr. Alexander used the sophisticated version of the Japanese word for "noon." "Shohgo" was not a word one would expect a non-Japanese person to know.

The Alexanders once more stepped into the street, the door swinging shut behind them. Next stop: the cabin. Or not.

As they passed by a small grocery shop, not the one where they had purchased their weekend supply of food, but a tiny local market, Ken's memory was jogged by the sight of some packages hanging near the entryway.

"Can we buy some *hanabi*?" he asked. There had been discussion of doing fireworks here at Nojiri when they were in Annaka a few weeks earlier. Mr. Alexander had suggested the possibility of doing *hanabi* at Lake Nojiri.

"The weather's bad for *hanabi*, isn't it?" Ken's mom mused. A light sprinkle had followed the family ever since they had left the souvenir shop.

"*Soh da na.*" [That's right.] agreed her husband. But I suppose we can get some anyway. We can always save them until tonight—or take them back to Tokyo with us."

And so another pack of fireworks was purchased. This time Ken was allowed to pick out two larger rocket *hanabi* as well. Now he was truly, completely satisfied. Things couldn't possibly get any better than this. Things could only get worse. And they were about to—much worse.

CHAPTER 22

ENCOUNTER AT LAKE NOJIRI

The air seemed heavier and puddles appeared to be larger as the Alexanders worked their way back toward the cabin. Twice along the way they'd been attacked by scattered rain showers.

What a funny name for rain, thought Ken. He pictured a shower falling on a tree on one side of the road with another shower, maybe the size of a garbage can pounding his father's holey umbrella. Perhaps a third downpour, a big one, would be hovering over that resort lodge over there, drenching anybody who tried to get in or out of the building. In between and all around these three showers there would be sunshine. That's what proper "scattered showers" should look like, Ken decided.

The sky had grown darker during the journey home. Occasional splatterings of rain had been replaced by a steady, firm rainfall. The occasional breeze had become an unfriendly wind which occasionally blew sideways blasts of water onto the three Alexanders. Umbrellas were becoming increasingly unhelpful.

By the time they reached the point where the NLA lakeside

road left the main road to wind its way to the left, the rain had become a steady downpour. Clothing and shoes were becoming damp. Only Ken's feet remained dry and warm deep inside his shiny boots.

And then the rain stopped. Completely.

"Strange weather," muttered Mr. Alexander. Conversation had been limited during their walk home. Most of the talk had consisted of comments and complaints about the weather and who was getting wet on which part of their anatomies.

"I think it's cool," said Ken. He was not as chilled as the others: Warm feet equaled warm spirits—or something like that.

Mrs. Alexander was wearing a warm jacket, but her blue jeans were damp. She didn't say anything.

As they proceeded, a huge patch of azure sky appeared above the lake. Waves, still rough and choppy, sparkled brilliantly.

"Maybe the rain's all done," suggested Mr. Alexander hopefully. He truly wanted to believe so. But his wife wasn't so sure. She had heard the weather report on a radio playing in the background at the souvenir shop.

"We're supposed to get more rain tonight," she said. "A storm is headed for Japan."

Mr. Alexander hadn't heard the radio announcement. And Ken had heard nothing but the sound of his own thoughts involving toys in the store. Watching the growing spot of blue in the sky, neither male could believe that the rain wasn't going to leave them for the day.

Soon they reached the fork in the road which offered two routes back to the cabin. The path that led straight ahead would be even muddier than that morning. Mr. and Mrs. Alexander prepared to follow the paved road along the lake. This way would be longer but safer. Besides, Mr. Alexander wanted to walk out on one of the docks again. Only from there would he be able to get a good view of the sky in all directions. He wanted to determine whether or not the rain was truly over.

"I want to go straight home," Ken said.

"You want to walk through the puddles?" his father asked.

"No. I'm just tired. I want to go home the fastest way. I don't mind the puddles."

"It should be OK," said Mrs. Alexander. She had confidence in Ken's ability to find his way home.

"Are you sure you know the way back to the cabin?" asked Mr. Alexander.

"Yeah. I've been this way lots of times."

This was true. Ken knew the way home quite well.

"OK. Here's the key. You know how to open the door?"

"Yeah." Yes, yes, yes. Sometimes his parents worried too much. He wasn't a baby any more.

"OK. See you back at the cabin. Be careful you don't slip in the mud."

(Yeah, yeah, yeah.)

"*Kiotsukete.*" [Be careful.] His mom was at it, too—the parental overprotective routine.

"*Hai! Hai!*" [Yes! Yes!]

Ken walked off along the path, umbrella in one hand, bagged snake in the other. His parents looked briefly after him, then resumed their route along the lake front. Their voices filtered faintly through the trees for a short time, then faded away completely as the two routes grew farther apart.

Ken was enveloped in a green tunnel now. Somehow the path hadn't seemed so dark and gloomy when seen from the paved road. A wall of trees rose from each side of the trail, merging in a dripping, lightless ceiling overhead. Was it the forest, or had the sky gone dark again?

Occasionally Ken caught glimpses of cabins set back in the woods, cold, brown, boarded up. In summer there would be laughter and music from within the homes. Families—safe, warm, happy together. But now the buildings stood there silent and unfeeling.

Suddenly Ken was not so thrilled to be walking alone. The puddles no longer seemed attractive play things. Ken had no interest in playing with Snakey. He just wanted to get home—fast. He wished he'd gone with his parents. Out there on the lakefront road it was brighter—and there was open sky. Here the air was thick and oppressive. It seemed to weigh down on him.

Ken picked up his pace as he moved between and around puddles. Mud was inches deep in places. When he mis-stepped into the muck, the ground seemed to pull at his boots as if to hold him there. Low branches grabbed at Ken's head. The thicket of weeds on either side seemed to spread increasingly farther into the path until it became a mere trail.

Ken came upon an intersection. A stairway of concrete, gravel and dirt dropped off to his left. Here was a chance for escape. He thought that the stairs led down to the lake road. He could take the steps and be reunited with his parents in a matter of minutes. That was what he would do.

But the stairs curved to the left before leading to the shore. There was no clear, straight view to the open lake beyond. The stairs were narrow. They looked muddy, slippery. The forest guarding the way down appeared dense and dangerous—more so than the woods lining the path he was on. Ken wasn't so sure now. Did those stairs really lead to the lake? Or did they dead-end in somebody's dreary back yard? No, he would continue on this path. He had come this far. He knew where this path led. He was not so sure about the steps leading downward. Yes, this was the way to go.

Ken splashed and plodded on. What little light broke through the overhead canopy grew dimmer. There was no sound here save for that of a million leftover raindrops, dripping from leaf to leaf in a constant cascade. That and his own sounds—his nervous breathing and the slipping, sloshing of his boots.

Ken passed another set of concrete stairs, this time leading up the hill to his right. The first cabin on the right was house number four. The number four meant that it was the fourth cabin to have been built on the NLA hill. Ken knew that when his father was a child, the Alexander family had shared this cabin with another family. Each time they visited Nojiri Ken's dad would drag his family to this cabin and describe childhood summers spent there. The cabin had always seemed cold to Ken, lifeless and all boarded up for the winter. And Ken never got to see the swinging porch bench which his dad so lovingly described as having been the location for many a lazy nap. If Grandpa Alexander still owned this cabin, Ken would be safely home by now. But Grandpa had bought another cabin, the one where Ken's family was holed up now. There was still a ways to go, and Ken plodded on, picking up speed.

Suddenly, through the murky depths of green—a sound.

Muffled voices? Had his parents come looking for him? The voices grew louder, clearer—closer.

Realization shattered Ken's thoughts like a thunderbolt. No! Not his parents' voices. But familiar voices. Terrifyingly familiar voices.

All of Ken's fears collided in an explosion of horror. He'd been right. The figures he had seen on the shore the day before—they *had* been the bullies from the airport. There was no mistake. They were here—here at Lake Nojiri. And this time it was no dream.

Ken froze. Every muscle in his body seemed to be shaking. What to do? Where to go? Which way were the voices coming from?

Just ahead of Ken another staircase intersected with his path from the right. The voices seemed to be coming from above, loud and raucous. They must be coming down those stairs.

Ken struggled to think, his mind in a daze. Could he run past the stairs before the boys reached his path? Maybe. But then they would see him. He had his umbrella. He could fight. No. The teens were twice as big as he was. And there were two of them.

Ken turned and stumbled back along the way he had come, as fast as his trembling legs would carry him. Slipping and sliding, he reached the stairs he had passed earlier, the ones leading up to cabin number four. A short distance up the stairs was a huge pile of logs waiting to be burned in someone's fireplace—a stack big enough to hide behind. Ken quickly clambered up the stairs, slipping once and nearly tumbling down the steps. Regaining his footing, he pushed through dense underbrush and threw himself behind the welcoming shelter of the logs.

The two voices continued to grow nearer. Yes, the two youths had turned left from the stairway onto the muddy path. They were coming Ken's way. Had they seen him? Or were they taking the path toward the paved road? Maybe they were headed into the village. Maybe they didn't know that he was there.

Ken huddled behind his stack of logs, shaking furiously. He could clearly make out the words of the two as they approached.

"...do that one tonight," the one was saying.

"I don't know, man." The other sounded hesitant. "It still seems like we're gonna get caught."

"Man!" There was disgust in the first one's voice. "Are you chickening out on me?"

"No, but—"

"Hey, man, I told you—you do it once, you're in it for good. Ain't no backin' out now. And this one's a big one. I think we can find some good stuff in it."

The two boys were nearly below Ken now. Peeking through a crack in the stack of logs, Ken caught a glimpse of two head tops, one bright blond, the other a darker shade of brown, bobbing along behind a curtain of green. The ever present cloud of cigarette smoke trailed behind them. Ken hoped they couldn't hear the sound of his trembling limbs.

"Yeah, but what about those people we saw yesterday," the dark-haired one continued.

"Aw, come on man. They didn't see us. And even if they did, they don't know us. They don't know nothin'."

"I don't know."

"Loosen up, man. Would I mess you up? You had fun last time didn't you?"

"Yeah, but I didn't think we were gonna break so much stuff. If we ever get caught, we're dead."

"So we won't get caught."

Ken was petrified by what he heard. These fellows were more dangerous than he had imagined. Ken moved slightly to hug the pile of logs more tightly. As he eased forward, a sharp splinter from one of the logs dug into Ken's hand. In spite of himself he let out a gasp of pain.

Startled by his own voice, Ken abruptly stepped back. The soft earth of the hillside gave way under his shifted weight. Ken lost his balance and crashed into a dripping bush.

"What the--!" The boys turned in Ken's direction. Ken scrambled to his feet.

"You!" exclaimed the one called Steve.

"I told you I saw him yesterday," howled Phil.

"Shut up!" Steve hissed. He began climbing the stairs towards Ken.

"What did you hear?" he growled at Ken.

Ken managed to take a few steps from behind the logs toward the stairs. He was too terrified to speak.

"Look, kid, we're not gonna hurt you," pleaded Phil. "Come here."

But Steve was furious.

"I'm going to pound you, you punk," he exploded, bounding up the stairs toward Ken.

That was all that Ken needed to hear. Leaving his shopping bag and umbrella in the bushes where he had dropped them,

Ken somehow found the will to run. There was only one way to flee—up.

Wild panic drove Ken as he fled up the stairs, slipping and stumbling. He heard angry words behind him, bad words. The thundering of the two huge bullies sounded close behind. Never turning to look back, Ken raced on, his heart pounding furiously. His breath came in shallow, frightened gasps. But he climbed, on and on.

Ken was thankful for his soccer training. Over many years he had built up stamina and strong legs. Now he reached for every ounce of power he could find within himself.

"I know where you live," taunted a voice—far behind now. "I'm going to get you."

Ken dared not look back. His lungs ached badly, but still he ran upward.

"If you tell your parents, we'll kill you!" came a shout from far below. "And your parents, too!" The threat sent yet another bolt of fear deep into Ken's heart. But the voices seemed much farther now. Had he outrun his tormenters? Or was it a trick and they were right behind him, ready to grab him the moment he slowed down?

Ken couldn't go on. His lungs wouldn't breathe for him anymore. He had to stop. Pausing to swallow a deep breath, he turned to look back down the stairs. Far below, two now tiny figures were bent over, gasping for breath. Their smoking had done them in. As young as they were, their abused lungs were no match for Ken's healthy ones. And Ken had grown up at the nearly mile-high elevation of Fort Collins, where air was thin and running the length of a soccer field required stronger lungs than at sea level. He had the advantage all around.

But this was no time to relax. Even as Ken's breathing began to settle into a normal rhythm, the two figures below began moving again in his direction.

Slightly higher up the hill the stairs met a path to the left. Ken turned onto this horizontal path which passed across the face of the hill. Ken had never been to this part of the NLA. But he guessed that this path would lead towards the safety of home. He began running again. This path was level for a ways and Ken made good time. The side of the hill had been stripped of many of its trees. There was a clear view to the stairs where the two teens continued to plod upwards. Would they never quit chasing him?

And then they did, suddenly turning to lumber down the stairs. Ken paused a moment. It felt good to give his aching lungs and legs a rest. It was over. He had escaped whatever terrible fate the two bullies surely had in store for him.

Suddenly, another terrible thought flashed through Ken's mind. No. They hadn't given up. Eventually Ken would have to find another set of stairs to take him back down to the path to his cabin. They would be waiting for him there, at the bottom of a stairway, ready to grab him, to beat him, to--. Ken didn't want to think further. The thought was too horrible. Would they really kill him?

The two pursuers disappeared from view as they descended through the brush below. There was no way to know which way they would turn when they arrived at the main trail.

The hillside was eerily silent. Far below a blanket of fog was flowing in from the lake, a gray eraser blotting out all the color in its path. Ken slowly continued along the path. Through the clearing Ken could see cabins on both sides. Cold windows, all boarded up, stared blankly at Ken as he passed by. There was nobody home. No warmth, no happy voices—nobody to help him. He was trapped here on the hillside with two hunters between him and his cabin, between him and his parents.

Ken had been too frightened, too physically strained to cry while racing up the stairs. But now tears came freely, cascading down his cheeks in warm torrents. His leg muscles screamed in pain. Heart and lungs worked furiously to return to normal. Pained sobs choked his chest.

Ken wanted so badly to be home—safe, warm, dry. His clothes were wet and globs of mud dangled from his pants. A throbbing on the back of his right hand drew his attention. A short gash left by the splinter on the log was oozing bright, red blood. That pile of logs had been his protector, his safety. And then it had cut him. Was everything against him?

Should he scream for his parents? Would they hear him from far below? Or would his words be lost in the rolling fog? The boys were probably closer than his parents. If anybody heard his calls, it would be them. They'd know exactly where he was. He had to remain quiet. That was his only hope.

Gulping hard, Ken cut off his sobs. He wiped his eyes with a damp shirt sleeve. He had to go on. He was on his own.

Shortly the path was swallowed up by dense forest again. The fog was beginning to sift up through the trees now. It continued to flow uphill from the lake. Paths were like a maze here, leading off in all directions. Ken followed the one he thought would lead him home, even when it nearly disappeared in the undergrowth. Ken walked very slowly now, painfully inching forward. His ears strained to hear any sound that might indicate where the enemy were. But there was nothing to hear but a myriad of drippings and the rustling of leaves as an occasional breeze brushed through the trees.

And then there it was—the way down. Ken stood at an intersection with another stairway. He could turn right and go up, away from the bullies. That would surely confuse them. But that way would take him farther from the safety of the cabin and his parents. How he ached to be held in his parents' arms. Or he could turn left and go down the stairs—toward home.

Another frightening thought crossed his mind. Weren't these the stairs that the two boys had come down? They must be. That increased the chance that they would be coming back this way. Or waiting below for him. Maybe he should go on and find another way down. The possibilities played a brutal game of tag in Ken's mind. What should he do?

The choice was difficult but necessary. He would go down. If the bullies were waiting for him, he could run back up the stairs again. They would be rested, but so was he. He had outrun them before. He could do it again.

One cautious step followed another as Ken descended the stairs. Soon, through layers of drifting fog, Ken could see the bottom of the steps. The way down seemed so much slower than when he'd sprinted up the other set of stairs, terror in hot pursuit. Ken came to a complete standstill. He stood there, silent, for what seemed like a never-ending eternity. No sound.

Ken gingerly took a few more steps, carefully avoiding mud and puddles which might turn his boots into betraying noise makers. He waited for another eternity, ears reading the silence for any sign of hidden foes. Again there was nothing.

Barely daring to breathe, his heart thumping furiously,

Ken took the final few steps into the path. Quick glances left and right revealed only fog-filled tunnels in each direction. Could it be? Were they gone? Had the bullies given up? Or were they hiding behind some big trees or a stack of firewood as Ken had done only moments earlier?

Ken turned right, in the direction of home and safety. Only a few steps away was another staircase. This one was wide and familiar. It was the stairway leading down to the auditorium—and the lakefront. Ken crept to the top of the stairs. Still no sign of the teenagers.

Another dilemma attacked Ken's brain. Should he run directly to the cabin in hopes that his parents would already be there? Or should he dash to the lakefront, hoping that his parents would still be down below somewhere along the paved road, still enjoying a leisurely walk? But would they still be down there in this cotton-thick fog? Would they have hurried home to get warm and dry? Or were they out somewhere looking for him, worried, missing him?

His parents had made most of the big decisions for Ken all his life. But they had also given him a wide range of freedom and responsibility in making many of his own decisions. Right now Ken didn't want to have to think. He didn't want to take any responsibility. He wanted his mother and father.

As if in response to Ken's desire for guidance, a harsh blast of lake air washed over him, sending chills through his dampened clothes and causing him to shudder. But the sinister breeze carried with it something else—a sound.

Riding on the wind came the stifled sound of two voices. One was that of a woman—Ken's mother!

Running as fast as he could with numb muscles and

flopping boots, Ken dashed down the stairs and across the stepping stones past the stark auditorium. He raced down the stairs past the splashing spring. As he tore across the muddied parking lot, Ken could see two veiled, ghostly figures at the upper left end of the H of the dock. Nobody could stop him now. He was safe.

Ken's screaming voice flew ahead of him as he ran.

"*Okaasan*! [Mother!] Papa!"

Ken's parents turned through the mist to see their terrified, muddy, frantic son racing towards them, screaming desperately. Dropping umbrellas, they hurried toward him.

They met at the end of the dock. Bodies crashed as Ken hurled himself into his parents' arms. Sobs poured.

"What happened? Did you get lost?" Mr. Alexander's understanding of the situation was as thick as the fog.

"*Dohshitano*?" [What's wrong?] Mrs. Alexander's voice was soothing ointment for emotional scars. She looked at Ken's muddy clothes. "Did you fall down?"

Ken couldn't remember having ever been so afraid. He tried to speak but his words would only come out in broken gasps. His mother held him tighter. She could tell that this was no ordinary terror her son was feeling. Even Mr. Alexander seemed on the point of tears as he watched his son struggling to talk through his fear.

"It's OK, Ken," comforted his dad. "Everything's OK. We're here. Take your time."

Little by little Ken blurted out his story—of hearing the bullies, hiding, seeing them, being discovered, then being chased. As he recounted his tale, Ken sensed his father growing quieter, stiffer. Mr. Alexander's questioning voice was becoming harsher. He was becoming angry—very angry.

Ken knew that the anger was directed at the two teenage boys who had dared to threaten his son. But Ken didn't want anger. There had been enough of that. All he wanted was love and warmth and peace.

"I want to go home now," Ken croaked hoarsely.

"Let's go home," agreed his mother.

The three crossed the paved road, and sidestepped the puddles in the parking lot. Ken walked in the middle, a parent on each side. Both parents had an arm around Ken, but he leaned towards his mother. His father kept asking questions, digging for details of the incident.

At one point Ken interrupted.

"Would they really kill me? They said they'd kill me and you and Mama if I told you about them."

"No, no, no, Ken. There's no way they would kill anybody. They were just trying to scare you."

That's what Ken had thought. His parents had always told him to never be afraid to tell them anything, no matter what anybody said. But those boys had been so terrifying. They had sounded so convincing.

"You were right to tell us, Ken. You did the right thing."

This was what Ken wanted to hear. He needed reassurance.

"*Daijobu.* [It's all right.] Nobody's going to hurt you." Ken's mom was calm, firm. Ken guessed that she was boiling mad inside, too. But she covered up her anger better than Mr. Alexander.

Ken was beginning to get angry, too. His legs had stopped quivering. His breathing was back to normal. And his heart had fallen into an easy, steady rhythm. Tears still stained his cheeks, but his eyes were dry now.

"I should have fought them," Ken said. Images of the taunting faces clouded his vision. He wanted to smash the two bullies, pound them—kill them. How dare they chase him and scare him and threaten him and his family? How dare they be so evil?

"Do you really think you could have?" asked Mr. Alexander. "What would have happened if you hadn't run away?"

And there it was, the truth of the matter. There was absolutely nothing Ken could have done—except run. And he hated himself for that. A fresh flood of tears poised ready to flow at the brink of Ken's eyes.

"But I was a chicken. I always just run away."

"No." Ken firmly told himself. "They would have beaten me up or killed me no matter what."

Ken had learned—at home and at school—all the things you were supposed to say to bullies:

"I don't like it when you do that." "Leave me alone." "Stop it. I don't like that."

All the messages that were supposed to protect you from bullies. But he had never had to use any of those words. Ken had never had enemies in school. And he was tall so bullies never picked on him. Ken had never been in a fight. Sure, he'd played rough with his friends, wrestling. Sometimes he or one of his friends had even gotten hurt. But it had never been on purpose. And Ken had never hit anyone in anger.

But those boys had been different. Ever since that time at the airport Ken had sensed that they were especially evil, that no words could ever change their minds. If they wanted to beat you up, they would do that—just because they could.

A new flow of tears streamed down Ken's face. He couldn't help himself. He was so angry, so frustrated, so scared.

The Alexanders were past the auditorium now, half way up the stairs. They had been forced to walk separately across the stepping stones in front of the auditorium, single file. Now on the wider stairs Ken once more took his place between his parents.

Strangely, the fog had lifted, as if a curtain had gone up on a new act of a play. But Ken wanted only to see the curtains in his bedroom being drawn together to close out an unbelievable day.

Mr. Alexander had a sudden thought.

"Where's your snake and umbrella?"

Ken struggled a moment to remember, then recalled the hiding place behind the pile of logs.

"I don't want to get them now," Ken said. "I just want to go home."

"It won't take long to get them," said Mr. Alexander. "If we leave them there and it rains tonight, the snake will be ruined by morning."

"We'll both go with you," assured Mrs. Alexander. "*Iko.*" [Lets' go.]

Ken hated the thought of returning to the scene of his ordeal. What if the bullies were hiding there? What if they really did plan to kill the Alexander family?

Ken voiced his concerns.

"I promise you, Ken, nobody is going to hurt you," replied his father. "I'm sure those guys are long gone. And even if they are there, there are three of us. Besides, I know *karate*, and *judo* and *aikido*—and a whole bunch of other Japanese words."

Mr. Alexander was trying to cheer him up with some of his poor humor, Ken knew. But what good could a lame joke like that possibly do to make him feel better at a time like this? The absurdity of the whole idea actually brought a minor smile to Ken's face. Yeah, his dad was pretty weird at times. But right now it felt good to have him by his side.

Reluctantly, Ken led his parents to the stairway he had gone up to hide. It took only a brief search for Ken to find his umbrella and the plastic bag with Snakey in the bushes. Both the outside of the bag and the umbrella were wet, but were none the worse for having been abandoned during Ken's flight. Apparently the bullies had not seen the items. Ken was glad for that.

Ken carefully peeked inside the plastic bag. There was Snakey, still coiled comfortably in the bottom, snug and sound. Ken was glad that his parents had insisted that he bundle Snakey up in the bag when they left the souvenir shop. He felt much better than he had for quite some time now. Umbrella and snake safely in Ken's hands, the Alexanders returned to the main path and headed in the direction of the cabin.

"Ken?" said his father.

"Yeah?"

"Can you show me which stairway it was that those guys came down?"

"Yeah. It was that one." The stairs from which he had first heard those terrible voices was just ahead.

"I would guess that they were coming from their cabin," mused Mr. Alexander. "They must be staying somewhere up that way."

"So?" asked Mrs. Alexander.

"If I come here tonight, I should be able to find their cabin. I'll just look for a cabin with its lights on."

"What are you going to do?" worried Mrs. Alexander. "It might be dangerous."

She didn't like the thought of her husband wandering around in the dark, muddy night, especially with a couple of potentially violent teenagers lurking out there somewhere.

Mr. Alexander answered in Japanese. "I just want to find out where they're staying. Then tomorrow we can go into the Shinano Town and tell the police. It sounds as though these might be the people who are breaking into cabins and trashing them."

Ken had told his parents as much as he could remember of the two boys' conversation. It seemed very likely that they were the mysterious vandals who had been destroying NLA cabins.

"But won't they ruin another cabin tonight?" Ken asked. He recalled what the boys had said about doing another one tonight.

"I doubt it," replied Mr. Alexander. "They know that you know about them. And they probably figure that you've told us about them, despite their threats. They're probably worried. So I don't think they're going to take any chances by doing something stupid tonight. In fact, I wouldn't be surprised if they've already left Nojiri now that they've been discovered. I'm guessing that they're pretty big chickens themselves, actually.'

"What do you mean?" Ken wanted to know.

"Well as far as Grandpa Alexander tells me, all they've done so far is trash empty cabins. They've never hurt anyone.

And you're the only one I've even heard of being threatened. I doubt they'd have the guts to really hurt anyone."

"But what if they hurt somebody but we just didn't hear about it?" Ken still had doubts.

"Believe me, if anybody at Nojiri hurt anybody else like that, everybody would know about it—and fast. Including Grandpa. And he would have told me. So I really think we have nothing to worry about."

The Alexanders were nearing their cabin. The sky had grown increasingly dark, both from ominous clouds and the onset of dusk.

"Maybe we should go to the village tonight," Mrs. Alexander suggested.

"That would probably be a good idea," responded her husband. "But if we don't know where the boys are staying, the police can't do anything. Besides, it's almost dark, and the weather looks like it's getting worse."

A fresh wave of fog had begun billowing its way in from the lake, buffeted about by increasingly strong gusts of wind. All three Alexanders were shivering now, as the chill penetrated damp clothes and goose fleshed skin.

Mrs. Alexander agreed. Soon the Alexander family turned off the main path onto the welcoming private path leading up to their cabin. Tree branches sagged especially low here. All three Alexanders squealed as dive bombing leaf drops scored back-of-the-neck bulls-eyes.

"Pop?" asked Ken.

"Yeah?"

"Why were you out on the dock? You couldn't see anything, could you? I mean it was all foggy."

"Good question, Ken. And one that Mama kept asking me. But it was cool to be standing out there in the fog. We wanted to see how far we could see—or how far we couldn't see because of the fog."

"And--?"

"Just before you came, the fog was so thick that from the end of the dock we couldn't even see the shore. It was really spooky. I've never seen fog that thick at Nojiri. Or anywhere, I don't think."

Ken couldn't help but smile at the picture. There he'd been running for his life, up and down the crazy hill. And there had been his parents, standing at the end of a pier in the fog just to see how far they could see—or couldn't see. Or maybe they were kissing, Ken thought, hidden from view by the fog. Yuck.

"Darn!" Mr. Alexander's exclamation interrupted Ken's thoughts.

"We left our umbrellas on the dock," Ken's dad grumbled.

"*Ah, soh ne*" [Oh,that's right], said Mrs. Alexander. "But we can get them tomorrow. Nobody will take them."

"Yeah," agreed Mr. Alexander as he stepped onto the cabin porch. "If anybody wanted those umbrellas, they'd have to be pretty desperate."

The Alexanders slipped out of muddy footwear, then hurried into the cabin as fast as they could. There were kerosene heaters in the cabin for warmth, but the Alexanders never used them. Instead, they closed the door quickly and pulled curtains tight to keep in warmth and shut out the evening air. Sweatshirts were enough to keep everybody comfortable indoors. And maybe an extra pair of socks if it became particularly damp and chilly. Of course, once they were in bed, their bodies heating up the cotton *futon,* and covered under a mountain of blankets, no summertime chill could ever reach the insides of their cozy nests.

Lights were turned on. The old radio on the counter was turned on to NHK, the Japanese National Broadcast Corporation station, about the only station that could be picked up on that old set up here in the mountains. Sweet classical music bathed the room in soothing tones. A feeling of security filled the living area.

Wet clothes were replaced with fresh ones and draped over chairs. (Ken had insisted that both parents accompany him into the dark upstairs to fetch dry clothes. They understood and went along without protest.)

Mrs. Alexander turned on both burners of the tiny kitchen stove to prepare dinner. As small as they were, the flames added their warmth to the growing atmosphere of coziness.

`Ken felt his body—and his heart—beginning to thaw. Carefully, so as not to get it wet, Ken pulled Snakey out of its damp plastic bag. He found that Snakey was long enough to wrap around his neck two times. Snakey was still cold from being outdoors, but he warmed up quickly next to Ken's skin.

Mr. Alexander went into the kitchen to help his wife with dinner while Ken played with Snakey. Things were much better now. Yummy dinner scents began to waft in from the kitchen. His parents were here. And he had Snakey.

Occasionally, Ken looked up from his play to check the windows. The curtains were pulled tight, but they were thin. If there had been a face at a window, peeking in, you'd be able to make it out through the wispy fabric. Ken couldn't help but expect to see two sinister faces glaring at him from out of the black. But tonight there were no shadowy figures.

After a number of nervous glances at the windows, Ken realized something peculiar. There was *nothing* at the windows. Ordinarily, once the evening lights were blazing in the cabin, there would be a million moths batting their wings against the panes. The lights glowing through the curtains called to the creatures in unknown ways.

There would be your average, everyday moths—whatever those were. There would be a seemingly infinite swarm of minute moths flitting about in dizzying dances of mass hysteria. These were the ones, some of which managed to find a way through cracks and holes into the cabin. It was their tiny bodies, sacrificed to the gods of the lights, which littered the tables each morning.

And then there was the occasional Luna moth, clinging patiently to a screen, large, majestic—the pale green queen of the night. But where were these night aviators tonight? Why was there no cloud of insects enveloping the Alexander cabin, struggling to reach the lights?

The explanation was simple. It was the same reason that Ken's father had been correct in predicting that there would be no vandalism that night. But Mr. Alexander had been wrong about why the NLA cabins would remain safe and untouched. No, the reason was an entirely different one. And it was about to arrive. Had Ken been aware of its approach, he would have been concerned. Very concerned.

CHAPTER 23

OFURO

The comforting combination of clattering in the kitchen and the scrumptious aromas floating from that room assured Ken that dinner would soon be ready. Shortly his mother's voice confirmed his expectations.

"*Gohan yo.*" [It's dinner. (Literally: "It's rice.")

Welcome words on most evenings, but especially so tonight. Ken didn't even need to be told to wash his hands. He could have done so in the tiny wash room next to the stairs leading to the second floor. There was a faucet in that room and a small wash basin, as well as the bath tub.

But Ken preferred to wash at the kitchen sink. His parents were in this room. And it seemed warmer and brighter—and safer—in here. The water from the faucet was cold. No hot water heater here. The water flowed straight through the underground pipe from the huge Alexander tank sitting above the cabin on the hill. Fortunately, the tank had been filled recently. Ken would have died if his parents had asked him to go out tonight to fill up the tank.

On his way back to the dining area, Ken was asked to carry his own bowl of *miso* soup. His father had already wiped the table. The entire family traipsed back and forth between the kitchen and the dining room carrying dishes, silverware and food.

Dinner was simple. Each person had a bowl of instant *miso* soup. A packet of *miso* had been squeezed into each bowl, followed by a tumbling cupful of boiling water from a teakettle. One kettle was used for boiling hot water for tea, coffee and soup. The other one contained the drinking water. A brief bit of stirring and tada!—there the soup was, all set to warm the coldest soul.

In addition, there were fresh tomato, cucumber and carrot slices. Vegetables bought at the market near Kurohime Station always seemed so much fresher and flavorful than ones bought back home in Fort Collins. And there was spaghetti. Spaghetti and *miso* soup were not ordinary companions at the dinner table. It was like having pretzels with a turkey dinner. Or pancakes topped with peanut butter with a steak dinner. Not that either of those combinations would have bothered Ken. Food was food. And good food was good food. The more of it, the better, never mind the combinations. (Which was perhaps why Ken liked to scoop chocolate-mint ice cream onto frozen blueberry pancakes before warming up the concoction in the toaster oven back home. It was so much fun to see the expressions on his parents' faces when he created such culinary delights. But that was another story entirely—delightful to a kid, gross to a parent.)

Ken's mom had not lost her mind. She appreciated good, well-organized proper meals as much as any adult. But the last night or two at Nojiri were times to clear out the cabinets and refrigerator. It was leftover time. It was time for chaotic, jumbled dining. What fun! Ken half expected leftover cookies to be sitting atop the spaghetti in sweet little toppings. But alas, such was not the case. The cookies were safely tucked away in their packages on the shelves, waiting for an invitation to become dessert. Instead of cookies topping the spaghetti there was tomato sauce with mushrooms from a can. Fancy cooking had been left behind in Tokyo.

And there were assorted odds and ends. Ken battled his dad for the last few bites of the sacred *miso pea*. Surprisingly, each managed to grab an approximately equal share for himself. To steal this much of the prized snack away from his dad—now that was a major victory for Ken. Or had his dad held back? On his good days, Mr. Alexander could be very generous!

There was also a bag of sliced white bread. Old bread. Stale bread. Unappetizing bread. No longer soft bread.

"Why don't you have some of this delicious bread," Mr. Alexander urged his family. "It'll go really well with spaghetti."

As happened every year, Mr. Alexander had bought too much bread on his visit to the market when he first arrived at Nojiri. Ken knew and his mother knew—and Mr. Alexander knew that they knew—that he would have to finish the bread himself. Otherwise, he could always use the final cardboard slices as toast the next morning or use them to make sandwiches for the trip back to Tokyo. But then he wouldn't be able to eat an *obento* on the train. Or buy fresh, fragrant bread of a thousand varieties at a Japanese bakery shop. Mr. Alexander would suffer through ancient bread while his family feasted on fresh, scrmptious Japanese food. That would be agony! Unfair!

So Mr. Alexander pleaded and begged and cajoled and

finally his wife and son split one slice of bread between the two of them. Drowned in spaghetti sauce, the bread wasn't all that bad.

"Oh, thank you, thank you, thank you," thanked Mr. Alexander, falling to his knees and bowing deeply to his family in mock gratitude.

"Oh darn," he muttered, slinking back into his seat. "I got my knees dirty."

Ken chuckled. The evening was progressing quite well. The afternoon—had those terrible events really happened only a few hours earlier?—had been hideous. But that seemed so long ago. The entire day seemed a cobwebbed, distant memory. There had been the snake in the rice paddy (the real snake), the floppy boat ride, lunch at the restaurant, the shopping for souvenirs—and starting the day off, the breakfast.

Suddenly an evil, fiendish grin crossed Ken's mouth, as another memory mischievously plopped itself into his head. Yeah, there had been breakfast and the conversation, and--.

"*Okaa-san*?"

"*Hai*?"

"I want anteater pie for dessert."

The expression that crossed Mrs. Alexander's face was exactly what Ken had been fishing for. He laughed.

"Ken, I think we're out of anteater pie," said his dad. "Maybe we can have some cockroach cookies instead."

Mrs. Alexander quickly left the room. The two Alexander men—boys?—grinned at each other.

"I guess we got her," Ken gloated.

"I hope we didn't gross her out too much," worried Mr. Alexander.

There was a brief moment of silence, half awkward, half stifling of laughter. But there was no need for concern. A minute later Mrs. Alexander returned, a freshly opened tin can in her hand. She held out her hand, offering the contents to her family.

"How about some pickled slugs?" she asked sweetly.

Mr. Alexander nearly choked on a mouthful of cardboard bread. Ken blew a stream of milk out of his nose. Mr. Alexander gulped and gagged. Ken grabbed a napkin and attempted to wipe up the fresh little puddles of milk on the table between spasms of laughter. Mr. Alexander swallowed vigorously and blurted out to Ken,

"That's gross."

Mrs. Alexander nonchalantly sat at her place at the table. Ignoring the chaos around her, she proceeded to spoon some of the contents of the tin onto her plate. The can actually contained sardines in a sweet soy sauce.

Ken managed to grab a brief moment of composure.

"I lose to you, Mother," he giggled admiringly before collapsing into another fit of laughter.

"*Sugoi*!" [Wow! Great!] added Mr. Alexander. "You surprised me!"

Mrs. Alexander smiled vaguely at her family and continued eating. Ken and his dad eventually settled down to eating. The meal continued, accompanied by pleasant conversation and often interrupted by blasts of laughter. Eventually, everything was eaten—except for the bread which remained in a woeful stack inside its wrapper. Cookies—not the cockroach variety—were fetched from the kitchen and happily disposed of.

"Well, Ken, ready for a bath?" asked Mr. Alexander. The

one luxury—actually a necessity to Japanese people—that the cabin had was a bathtub. No, not a bathtub—an *ofuro*. There was a world of difference—or at least an ocean of difference—between the Japanese *ofuro* and the American bathtub. In America baths, you sat in the tub and washed and rinsed. And there you were, sitting in all your scummy suds. That was no way to get clean.

Now a Japanese *ofuro*—there was a bathing experience of ecstasy. The tub was filled with water. A furnace—fueled by wood in the old days, almost always gas-fed nowadays—was lit. An hour or so later, the water would be ready. Sometimes hot spring minerals were added to the water. Either way, the water would be hot—steaming, toasty hot.

Japanese bathroom floors were either tiled or had wooden frames resting on concrete surfaces. A floor drain was part of the furnishings. There would be a basin or two and a tiny stool made of wood or plastic.

You went into the bathroom, removed the cover from the bath and stirred the water with a basin. If the water was too hot, you could add cold water from a faucet. Once the temperature was right—meaning almost bearably hot, you'd rinse the stool with a basinful of hot water from the tub and sit down.

A selection of soaps and shampoos would usually be handy. You would pour another basinful or two of water from the tub over your body. Then using the soap and shampoo, you would wash, brush, scrub and shampoo yourself to a state of perfect cleanliness. Then, being careful not to get any soap or shampoo in the bath itself, you would scoop up basinful after basinful of water and pour it over yourself, rinsing yourself thoroughly. Once all dirt and suds and muck had been carefully washed away—and only then—would you enter the *ofuro*.

Seldom could Westerners plunge right in. If the water was the desired temperature, you would test it first with a toe or two. Then slowly you would lower yourself into the cauldron, warming your feet, legs and torso as you eased yourself in, until you were up to your chin in the water. As each inch of body yielded to the steaming water, another inch of tension would fade. By the time you were immersed up to the neck, the warmth of the water would have penetrated to the deepest part of every tired, aching muscle. And then you would just soak, happy and content.

If you were a kid, of course, you could play with bath toys. There might be rubber duckies or other squeeze toys and windup boats galore.

But if you were an adult, chances were you'd drift off into a state of mental and physical well being that nothing could penetrate. Eyes closed, listening to the sound of bath waves gently lapping at the sides of the *ofuro*, breathing deeply the steam—pure or with added fragrance—you would drift away into a liquid universe of peace and warmth. The ecstasy was beyond description.

Japanese *ofuro* were traditionally larger than American baths. Often, families would bathe together. Many a Japanese child has grown up with fond memories of warm, happy times in the *ofuro* with one of his or her parents. Giggling, splashing, toasting together—what a delight for a young Japanese child! And you could even spill water on the floor without being scolded!

Ofuro made you mellow. *Ofuro* made you relaxed. A wise

man once said that if all the leaders of the world would take off their clothes and get into an *ofuro* together for an hour, there would be no more wars. How could you soak in a Japanese bath without having all your hatred and hostility drained out of you. It wasn't possible.

The Nojiri bath, located in the washroom, had been cleaned out by Mr. Alexander. Despite the cover on it, several creepy type things had managed to find their way into it over the winter, leaving little carcasses all over the bottom. Mr. Alexander had painstakingly removed the debris and filled the tub with water. He always liked to shave and bathe the day before his family arrived.

Mr. Alexander had left the water in the *ofuro* after his bath the night before Ken and his mother arrived at Nojiri. This was another advantage of the Japanese system of bathing. Since the water was clean—no soap or scum in it—the water could be used by several people and even for two or more nights if everybody bathed carefully before getting in. The water was simply reheated each evening at bath time.

The gas burner had been turned on before dinner. By now the water was hot and ready for a plunge. Oh, sure, there was a stray hair or two floating around in the water. Probably from that barren spot growing on the back of Mr. Alexander's head. But the tightly fitting lid had kept dust, dirt and critters out of the tub. No *benjo mushi* in there. Ken was more than eager for a bath.

"Can I leave the door open?" he asked. The fears of the day had largely faded, but he still wanted his parents to be within hearing range.

"Let's leave it open a little," Mr. Alexander suggested. He

didn't want bath water splashing onto the wooden floor outside the bathroom. Ken understood. The compromise was acceptable.

The bath water was unpleasantly hot. Ken added some cold water from the tap, filled a small blue-green basin with water from the tub and began to wash. Steam poured from the *ofuro*, keeping the room toasty despite the chill outdoors. Soon all the dirt and tear stains from the day had been scrubbed away. Doing a quick job on his hair—why waste shampoo? Ken often thought—he rinsed. Now he was ready for the sweet reward that followed the less-than-enjoyable washing.

Holding firmly onto two sides of the *ofuro*, Ken lifted his right leg over the side and dipped it in the water.

"Yeoww!" he exclaimed, yanking his foot out immediately. "That's too hot."

But Ken had experience with *ofuro*. He knew his first impression could be misleading. Gingerly he lowered his foot again, allowing just the toes to break the surface of the water. No problem.

Slowly the foot descended. So far, so good. Taking it slowly—that was the way. After what seemed like an eternity, the foot reached the bottom of the tub. This was good. This much heat he could take.

The process was repeated with the other leg, faster this time. Already tongues of warmth were shooting up Ken's entire body, all the way to his head. Soon, Ken was kneeling on the bottom, his chin just barely bobbing above the surface of the water. The water was a little too deep for him to sit on his bottom, but he didn't mind.

The Alexander cabin *ofuro* was not as large as some. It was of a smaller size often found in apartments and smaller houses. But for Ken, it was amply big.

Muscles began to turn to Jello. Ken's face grew as red as the spaghetti sauce he had had for dinner. His breath came slow and easy. He hadn't felt this relaxed in days.

Ken looked around for something to play with. Nothing. But then a delicious idea bubbled into his mind. He grabbed the wash basin and pulled it into the bath. Tipping it upside down, he dragged it under the water, trapping some air inside. Ken tipped the basin sideways, allowing some air to escape. A huge bubble exploded on the surface of the water. Ken found that by tipping the basin more or less, he could control the size of the rising bubbles. Soon he was sending bubble Morse code messages to the surface. Bloop, bloop, bloop...bwopp, bwopp, bwopp...bloop, bloop, bloop. He wasn't sure, but he thought that that was SOS. That was all Ken knew of Morse code.

Mr. Alexander's head appeared in the doorway.

"Yes?" he asked.

"What?" asked Ken.

"You called?"

"What?" repeated Ken.

"Well, I thought I heard an SOS."

Ken was pleased. His bloops and bwopps had actually made sense.

"I'm just playing," he explained.

"I know," said Mr. Alexander. "Sorry we don't have any bath toys here."

"That's OK. I'm having fun."

"Good. Enjoy yourself."

And Ken was left alone. When he was little, he had taken

many baths with his dad. That had been fun. His dad had shown him various ways to squirt water with his bare hands. Sometimes Mr. Alexander could hit the ceiling with his hand water guns. Ken still hadn't figured out how his dad did that.

As Ken grew older, though, he preferred to bathe by himself. But he still liked it when his father sat outside the tub while he took a bath or shower. Those were times for good conversation. Sometimes his father told him original stories. Other times they exchanged jokes.

Now that he was bigger, Ken enjoyed being completely by himself. Sometimes back in Fort Collins, he would listen to the radio while he bathed. His parents had taught him that the radio should be on the far side of the bathroom, out of reach of the tub. They didn't want their son to get electrocuted. Ken understood this and was very careful. His parents trusted him in this way. Ken appreciated that.

After awhile, bubble-making became boring. It was time for a new adventure. It was time to explore. Ken reached out of the *ofuro* to where the folded bath cover rested against the near wall. Placing the accordion-like piece of plastic on top of the bath, Ken unrolled it lengthwise until all but a few feet of water were covered. Between the surface of the water and the lid there was now a dark, mysterious cavern.

Ken knew not to completely close the cover over his head. The steam and heat would quickly suffocate a boy—or even an adult. Leaving a safe breathing space, Ken turned his attention to the beckoning grotto. If he had had a boat, the passengers on the craft would have done the exploring. But there was nothing but that old blue-green basin. And that wouldn't quite do the trick. So Ken himself became the adventurer.

Ken slid under the lid and was engulfed in partial darkness. The lid was white, but the tub itself was a light blue. Ken was in a misty blue semi-darkness. His head just fit between the water and the plastic overhead. Steam swirled around him, sometimes doing a little exploration of its own—up Ken's nostrils. Ken's nose tickled. He sneezed, banging his head on the cover as he jerked from the nasal explosion.

"Ow," he thought. But he wasn't hurt. And the steam had given him an idea. Ken snorted. Then he growled. He was the mighty underwater dragon. Not the fire-breathing kind, mind you. Fire-making nostrils wouldn't last very long deep here in the mysterious Lake *Ofuro*. No, he was a vicious steam-breathing dragon.

"Hmm," Ken thought. "How can you have steam without fire? And how can you have fire under water? And why is that hideous giant staring at me?"

Mr. "hideous giant" Alexander had entered the bathroom, unnoticed over the sound of the dragon's snorts and growls. His face was dangling over the edge of the bathtub. Fogged up eyes were attempting to peer through the steam under the ceiling of the cave.

"Anybody home?" thundered the giant, his voice echoing in the blue cavern.

"What do you want?" Ken echoed back. He really didn't want to be bothered just now. Steam-breathing dragons should have the right to snort and growl in peace.

"Just checking to see if you're OK," answered Mr. Alexander. He had raised his head so his voice didn't resonate in Ken's water world this time.

"Yeah, I'm fine," snorted Ken. He was about to let loose

with a deadly blast of steam to turn the giant into stewed Papa.

"OK," said the huge beast, turning toward the door. "We'll give you another five minutes. But then it's time for bed."

Ken didn't answer. He was already gone. In his place a monstrous reptile prowled the depths of the lake, hunting for prey. Maybe it could find an elephant to lunch on. Now that would be a fine meal, worthy of the ruler of this underwater kingdom. But what about the hair? Weren't Nauman's elephants hairy? Suddenly, the ravenous appetite was gone. A mouthful of hair did not sound appealing. Maybe there was such a thing as a hairless mammoth—a bald Nauman's elephant...?

The scaly monster turned its attention elsewhere. There—on the bottom of the lake—a shiny black fish. An appetizer! With lightning speed a razor-tipped claw knifed downward. The hapless fish was no match. Triumphantly, King Dragon held the prize in a firm grasp. He was undefeatable in speed, matchless in cunning, number one in skill and—cold on his shoulders? And what was that terrible gurgling sound that seemed to threaten the very existence of his world?

OOPS!

The mighty ruler of the lake had just pulled the rubber *ofuro* plug.

Ken quickly reached down into the bottom of the tub, and after a little fumbling, managed to slip the plug back into the drain hole. Not too much water lost. Fresh water could be added, the gas burner could be fired up again, and there would be plenty of hot water for the rest of the family. No problem. He hoped.

It was very definitely time to end his bath. Ken climbed out of the tub, replaced the *ofuro* cover and began drying off. He noticed that he had turned a delightful shade of scarlet, from shoulders to feet. Ken could not see his face, but he imagined it was similarly hued. And his fingers! What had happened to his fingers? The skin on them looked like purple prunes. Like the wrinkles on a ten thousand-year-old elephant. Had he really been in the *ofuro* that long? Or had the exceptional heat of the water pickled his fingers in record time?

Never mind. By the next day Ken's skin would be back to normal. Or at least he hoped so. He didn't want to go back to Tokyo looking like a shriveled peach. What would his friends say?

"Oh, look! It's a giant raisin. No wait, it has a face! It's a small elephant. But what happened to its trunk? And why is it wearing clothes? Oh, no—it's Ken." Or something like that.

Ken slipped on his *Doraemon* pajamas. They were covered with pictures of the cartoon robot cat lazing peacefully on marshmallow clouds. What a great idea, Ken thought. He was more than ready for bed.

What a day it had been—a wonderful, terrible, crazy mixed up day. An entire lifetime worth of ups and downs in just one twelve-hour time span. But now there was rest. Nothing could relax a person into a ready-for-sleep mode better than an *ofuro*.

Ken brushed teeth in a warm haze. Then he snuggled up on his father's lap for a final hug. Somewhere in a foggy distance his mother was huddled in front of the television. Through layers of gauze, muffled voices were describing a storm. Ken easily shut out the sound. He'd had enough of storms today. His mind was now enveloped in the soft cotton of pre-sleep. He wanted to get upstairs to his *futon* before he was completely asleep.

Mrs. Alexander joined the two at the dining table. Ken gladly accepted a ride upstairs on his father's broad back. He hadn't done this in months. Mr. Alexander lumbered up the stairs, his wife close behind him. Had Ken been only a little more awake, the thought of being carried up those precariously steep dark stairs might have jolted him into full wakefulness. But tonight the ride was welcome. Ken rested his head on his father's shoulder, full of feelings of trust and warmth and security.

Ken barely felt his parents tucking him into his *futon*, one on each side. Soft words of "Sleep well" and "Good night" were merely sweet whispers somewhere at the fringe of his consciousness. And then Ken was asleep.

A few times, later in the dark hours of early morning, Ken dreamed horrid dreams. Later on he would toss and turn as restless visions of the previous day returned to haunt him. But for now he slept on, peaceful dreams filling his mind. Right now, any fear that existed in the cabin—a pained concern over terrible, uncontrollable things to come—was in Mrs. Alexander's mind. The tempest was coming.

CHAPTER 24

TAIFUU

The Atlantic Ocean gives birth to hurricanes. The warm waters of the western Pacific Ocean also generate tropical storms. The Asian storms are called typhoons. The Japanese word for typhoon is "*taifuu.*"

Each year a number of destructive *taifuus* reach Japan causing flooding, landslides and occasional deaths from their turbulent winds and heavy rains. Usually they arrive in late summer. And normally the storms strike Kyuushu, the southernmost of Japan's four main islands. Or they attack other coastal areas of the island nation.

Once in awhile, however, *taifuu* arrive as early as June. And sometimes a *taifuu* makes its way inland. The year that Ken Alexander suffered his ordeal with the Nojiri bullies was an extraordinary year. Not only was Japan in the path of its second *taifuu* of the season, an unusual set of atmospheric conditions had aimed this monstrous tempest directly inland at Nagano Prefecture. Lake Nojiri was in Nagano Prefecture.

This was what had concerned Mrs. Alexander as she sat enveloped in the television news. The *taifuu* was on a course to pass directly over Lake Nojiri. The winds and rains of the day had been a preview of worse things to come. Ken's mom was especially concerned about the cabin.

The ancient Alexander cabin was built on the side of the NLA hill, precariously close to the edge. Only a few yards separated the front porch from a cliff which overlooked the lake front area. A landslide had long ago closed a stairway which passed in front of the cabin between it and the cliff. Ken's mom was certain that one day the entire cabin would follow the suit of the steps and slide off the hill, crashing below in a pile of shattered timbers and tin roofing. And even if that would not occur this year, there would certainly be damage to the frail cabin. So she stayed up most of the night, following the storm's progress on the television and hoping for the best.

Mr. Alexander, who did not share his wife's concern, went to bed at his usual time. After all, he reasoned, the cabin had stood the test of time—many years of heavy rains and storms. And according to his father—Grandpa Alexander—the cabin was built on solid ground, firmly held together by the roots of huge trees on the hillside.

The wind did howl and torrents of rain did pelt the cabin, sometimes blowing sideways, rattling against the windows. But the building stood firm, and by morning the danger had passed with no damage to the cabin.

Only when she was convinced that the cabin had survived the ordeal did Mrs. Alexander wearily slide into her bed, wrapping herself in the cozy warmth of the *futon* and its coverings. Needless to say, she was the last one to rise the next morning.

The next morning the sun broke through the curtains of the bedroom in glowing rays. Ken happily descended the stairs to find his father at the breakfast table, toasting elderly, stale bread and working on another crossword puzzle. He had happily finished one of the "challenger" puzzles—with frequent glances at the answers—and begun the adventure of challenging another one.

Ken enjoyed the daily hug on his dad's lap, then procured a bowl, spoon, cereal and milk to begin his breakfast. After eating he brushed his teeth and then played contentedly with Snakey and his robot toy. Memories of the previous day were shut out of his mind.

Mrs. Alexander joined the family an hour later, still groggy-eyed. Over breakfast she described in great detail the happenings of the previous night—the updated reports on the progress of the *taifuu* broadcast on the television, the pounding of the storm on the cabin, and the relief when the tempest had passed beyond Lake Nojiri. Mr. Alexander and his son listened attentively. They appreciated that Mrs. Alexander had been genuinely petrified at the thought of disaster hitting the cabin.

Eventually Mr. Alexander rose and headed for the front door.

"Where are you going?" asked Ken.

"I'm going to head into Shinano Town and talk with the police. I know there's a police station there."

"What are you going to tell them?" Ken wanted to know.

"Well, this morning I woke up early and went for a walk up those stairs you showed me yesterday. And I found a cabin where there was loud music playing and a motorbike in the yard. I heard talking and laughing from inside. I heard enough to know that the guys staying in that cabin were the bullies who threatened you yesterday. So I'm going to tell the cops that I know who's been damaging the cabins up here."

"Can I go with you?" asked Ken.

"No, you stay here and keep Mama company. Oh, by the way, we forgot our umbrellas on the dock when you came to us yesterday. Maybe you can go down there and get them for us—if they didn't get blown away by the storm."

Ken wasn't sure he wanted to leave the house alone, but the sun was so bright and the lake so blue he felt comfortable. So the two Alexander males shoed up and left Mrs. Alexander to clean up the breakfast dishes. Ken had cleared his items from the table, but it was his mother who would wash them with hot water boiled in one of the teakettles.

When they reached the end of the private pathway leading from the cabin, the two parted company. Ken turned right to head down the main path toward the auditorium, parking lot and docks. Mr. Alexander turned left to climb the steep stairs that led past the faucet where the family obtained their drinking water. Mr. Alexander was going to challenge the more difficult route to the top of the hill from where he would take another narrow road into Shinano Town. Nojiri village was too small to have its own police presence.

Ken felt lighthearted as he traipsed along the rain-soaked trail. Surely the worst was over now and he and his family could enjoy another fun-filled, final day at the lake. He had no idea how wrong he was.

CHAPTER 25

INTERMISSION

We interrupt this story to bring you
Two Legends of Lake Nojiri, One Dark and One Light.

TWO LEGENDS OF LAKE NOJIRI, ONE DARK AND ONE LIGHT

LEGEND 1: THE TALE OF KUROHIME (DARK)

In a remote region of Japan there once stood a huge, elegant castle by the name of Nakane Castle. The castle, surrounded by stately mountains and emerald hills, was home to the Takanashi family. Masayori, the lord of the castle, was known both in Shinshu (now Nagano Prefecture) and the neighboring Echigo area (now called Niigata Prefecture) as a brave and powerful warrior.

As is true in so many ancient legends, Masayori had been blessed with a most beautiful treasure—a daughter. Her name was Kurohime—Black Princess. She was Masayori's only child and he cherished her as the flowers do the sun. She was like the sun and the moon and the stars to him, lighting up his days and nights with her charm, beauty and cheerful laughter. As she grew older, her beauty and sweetness only increased.

One day the princess, for she had indeed become a princess, having reached the age of marriage, held a huge, flower-viewing banquet by the side of a lake. The shore of the lake, a turquoise-blue gem sparkling among pristine hills, was the ideal location to celebrate the arrival of spring's flowery heralds. (Perhaps this was the very lake known as Lake Nojiri—the legend does not say.)

Japanese people have always loved nature, especially flowers of every sort. Even today picnics are arranged in the spring when cherry blossoms begin to bloom. It is not unusual for thousands of people to gather in parks where they spread blankets under pink canopies to eat, drink, sing and enjoy the first floral visitors of spring.

As the maiden, her attendants and the many invited guests enjoyed themselves, a serpent raised his scaly head from the depths of the lake to observe the festivities. It was only natural that his eyes should be immediately drawn to the princess. Her beauty attracted eyes like an exotic orchid among a field of daisies. The serpent was immediately smitten with love for the princess and vowed to himself to make her his wife.

Early the next morning there came a knock upon the enormous wooden gate of the castle. A sentry fetched Masayori to the portal, where he found before him a most noble and elegant looking *samurai* warrior.

"How may I be of service to you?" inquired Masayori in his most noble and kind voice.

"I beheld your daughter at the banquet by the lake yesterday," answered the young man. "I have fallen deeply in love with her and wish for her hand in marriage."

"And from whence do you come?" asked the lord of the castle. "I have not seen you before in these parts."

"I am the lord of Oike," replied the stranger.

A deep chill slithered through Masayori's body. Oike meant "large pond" and was the name of the lake where his daughter had picnicked the day before. There was no human lord of the lake. Masayori knew immediately that this could be no human standing before him. It must certainly be the serpent of the lake disguised in human form.

"I am sorry," stammered Masayori, shaken but still retaining his outward dignity. "I cannot allow my daughter to marry a non-human."

The *samurai's* coal-black eyes began to glow ruby-red.

"What are you saying?" he demanded. "What are you calling me?"

"There is no human lord of Oike. I believe you are the serpent who resides in the water kingdom."

A remarkable change took place before Masayori's eyes. All blackness was lost from the *samurai's* eyes as they burned with fire. The skin on the handsome face crystallized into harsh scales, and a long, split tongue darted from the suddenly lip-less mouth.

"I came to you as a man," snarled the creature. "I could have borne your daughter away on a wind or in a storm any time I wished. Yet I was courteous enough to ask your permission to marry her. But you have insulted me and rejected my offer."

"I am sorry," repeated Masayori. "I do not believe that Kurohime could find happiness with someone such as yourself. Please forgive us. I am certain that you will be able to find another bride, perhaps a lovely serpent." He wished the half-creature standing before him would leave. But he strove to remain polite. He did not wish to upset the serpent who was rumored to have fantastic powers. The serpent would not relent, however.

"If I am permitted to marry Kurohime, I will cherish her forever. I can give her eternal life. And I shall also protect you and your family and your castle and all the land for all time. However, if you deny me, I shall bring disaster to the land. Think upon my words. I shall return tomorrow."

And the creature, shaping itself completely back into the form of a snake, slipped silently away into the forest.

True to his word, the serpent, once again disguised as the young *samurai*, appeared at the gate the following morning, repeating his demand for the princess's hand. Once more his request was declined. And so it went, the lord of the lake visiting the castle daily and as often being denied his heart's desire.

Then there came a day when the serpent could no longer tolerate his rejection. Storming into a rage and completely shedding his disguise, he screamed at Masayori,

"I shall wait no longer! You have had your chance. Now you will be sorry!"

"Do as you must," said the father, sadly turning from the gate. "But you shall not have my daughter."

Shortly thereafter, the clouds darkened in a way they never had been known to. Though it was mid-day, an evil night fell upon the land. So dark was it that only fierce flashes of lightning allowed any visibility in the black nightmare. As the people quivered in their homes, the very earth began to tremble with a mighty rumble. Mountains crumbled as the land, so calm and safe since all time, began to shake with its first ever earthquake. Gentle hills split, spewing forth crimson rivers of fiery lava and billowing clouds of poisonous smoke. It was as if hell itself had opened up and invaded the peaceful land of Shinshu.

Overcome by the horrible cries of the residents of the castle and the terrified peasants of the countryside, Kurohime stumbled from the castle. Staggering, she made her way through the storm to the edge of the roiling waters of Lake Oike. She raised her head and screamed to the sky,

"Lord of Oike, end the storm! Take me, but have pity on us and end this tempest!"

Princess Kurohime instantly disappeared and the storm faded as quickly as it had arisen. The hills swallowed the lava they had spit out and once more became green havens. The clouds vanished, as though sucked away by a gigantic breath. And the earthquake lay down and ceased its shaking. All was as it had been. But the castle was never more blessed with the laughter or bright smile of Masayori's daughter.

Some time later, the serpent moved to the peak of a majestic mountain where it was said he lived in royal grandeur with his bride, the princess Kurohime. Today Mount Kurohime remains, a velvet green marking the border between the prefectures of Nagano and Niigata. To this day a festival is held on July 17 to console the soul of Lord Masayori's daughter. And it is believed that every year on this day rain falls from sad skies, brought by dark clouds swirling downwards from the peak of Mount Kurohime. The clouds carry upon them, people say, Princess Kurohime, who is allowed once a year to visit her home, the land of Shinshu, beside the mystical waters of Lake Oike.

LEGEND 2: THE CRAB AND THE SNAKES (LIGHT—SORT OF)

This story takes place once upon a time, long, long ago, in the olden days, way back in time—even before Mr. Alexander was born. (And according to Ken, that's really old!)

Near the shore of Lake Nojiri, close to where Nojiri Village is located today, there is a small island. Benten was the goddess of this island, which today is known as Biwa Island. Biwa Island probably gets its name from its shape which is similar to that of a Japanese musical instrument called a biwa, a 4-stringed lute. It is said that the island was nicknamed after Benten, who used to live on this island, which is why they nicknamed the island after her. Back in the old days, the island was also known as Biwa Island, though I don't know why, because it would have made sense to name the island Benten Island after the goddess of the island who was named Benten. Well, for some reason, which who knows, the island was and is called Biwa Island.

And when are we going to get started with the story? Good question. OK. Here we go.

Benten—the god, not the island—had two messengers or servants serving under her or for her, as the case may be. They were a certain Mr. and Mrs. Snake. Well, actually they were a snake couple, but who really knew their names? One thing that was known about them was that each year they had ten baby snakes. That's a lot of little wriggling snakies, and you can be certain that Mr. Alexander, as much as he loved babies, would never have wanted to meet ten baby snakes—or ten snakes of any age, for that matter.

It so happened (and there would be no story if it hadn't so happened) that in the area there also lived a couple of crabs—not crabby people, but real, live crabs, the ones with eight legs—or however many legs crabs have. They lived at the foot of a waterfall which was where the Seki River (no, I never heard of that river, either) dropped out of the hills into Lake Nojiri.

These crabs also gave birth to ten babies each year, though in their case it was ten baby crabs. That meant something like eighty baby crab feet in all. Mr. and Mrs. Crab—if those were indeed their names—were extremely protective of their babies. But they never bought shoes or socks for their kiddos. Who would want to try putting shoes and socks on eighty little crab feet?

Well, the baby crabs grew up to be kiddy crabs, as most baby crabs do. When they could walk on their own eight legs, mama and papa crab took them on a long expedition to Lake Nojiri. Now along the way, the parent crabs came upon that year's ten snake babies. The story does not tell what the baby snakes were doing. They probably weren't wrestling, because baby snakes tend to get all tangled up when they wrestle, especially if there are ten of them. Anyway, apparently the parent snakes were not with them. In other words, the snake parents were not apparent. Or something like that.

(Skip this next paragraph if you are easily grossed out.) The crab mommy and daddy snatched up the baby snakes and fed them to their kiddy crabs. (Even Mr. Alexander, despite his relationship with snakes in general, does not appreciate this story. No matter how scary critters are to him, he respects their lives and does not wish death on any one of them. Not even snakes. Just mosquitoes, which you already know about.)

As any good parents would if their babies got eaten by kiddy crabs, when they found out what had happened to their offspring (or should we say "offslither," since snakes can't "spring"), the parent snakes became furious. And so began the great Battle of The Snakes Vs. The Crabs. Now apparently, each parent crab was approximately five hundred meters in size, about half the size of Benten—oops, I mean Biwa—Island. That's pretty large for a crab, and as you can very well imagine, their claws were humongous. The legend does not tell us how big the snakes were. However, we do know that each crab was capable of instantly cutting down a 300-year-old tree with one swipe of its razor-sharp claws.

Ma and Pa Snake soon saw that they were up against overwhelming odds—you can see that, too, can't you?—and tried to surrender. However, it is hard to kneel, grovel or fall flat on the ground in surrender when you're already crawling around on the ground. The snakes needed only a few vain attempts at kneeling—impossible to do without knees, they discovered—before coming to the realization that words might serve the purpose better than posture.

"Please stop," the serpents bellowed—or perhaps "hissed" would have been more likely. "We surrender. We give up."

The crabs, being reasonable creatures—as reasonable as a creature can be that will feed your babies to its own young ones—ceased hostilities, and a truce was drawn up. The snakes vowed that from then on they would be servants to the crab family. This was the only time Mama and Papa Crab considered buying shoes and socks for their children. They had servants now who could do the putting on of footwear for them. Only when the parent crabs were reminded by their kiddy crabs that snakes have no fingers or hands (Duh!) did they give up on this idea.

And thus the god of Benten Island (remember her?—this story started out to be about her) lost her two servants, but the Crab family gained two. And they all lived happily ever after—except for the ten baby snakes who got eaten, of course. And for their continued good service, the snake couple were allowed to keep their future annual ten babies without fear of the little ones becoming crab chow.

Today it is said that if you should encounter a snake in the Lake Nojiri area, simply say,

"I'm going to tell a crab on you," and most likely the snake will slither away with utmost haste and not bother you.

It is also said that it was after this fantastic, true (?) historical event that snakes became strong and evil—except for the snakes in this tale, of course. And it is also said that since this major confrontation, every lake and pond in Japan has come to have one snake as its lord and master. If you don't believe that, just read the previous story.

CHAPTER 26

THE FINAL ENCOUNTER

The umbrellas were exactly where Ken's parents said they would be. Surprisingly, they were still there, their handles caught on the metal bars that made up the skeleton frame of the absent diving board.

Ken disentangled the umbrellas. His family would be happy to get them back. Good thing they hadn't blown into the lake. Would umbrellas sink or float on the water, Ken wondered. He walked to the edge of the dock, umbrellas in hand. The water was clear as an autumn morning. Ken knelt down and peered into the inviting depths. He couldn't quite see to the bottom, but he spied a school of small fish flitting about in the sun's scattered rays.

Looks like they're having fun, Ken thought. Had the little, silver swimmers even known that there was a storm last night? Or had they been safe and snug far below the surface in their cozy water world? Maybe they'd seen all sorts of objects falling into the lake and guessed that something horrendous was occurring above them: leaves, branches, trees? And various bits and pieces of trash. And umbrellas? What would the fish think of an umbrella floating about in their homeland? Would they think it was some sort of new net intent on catching them for somebody's dinner? Or would they see it as a strange new fish, with great big fancy, flappy blue fins and the most peculiar, long black curved nose they'd ever seen?

Ken wished he could be with the fish, dancing serenely below the waves. But then he would sure have to hold his breath for a long time!

Suddenly a shadow fell across the dock beside Ken. Not a cloud, but something far, far worse. Ken turned to see two large figures blocking his way back to the shore. The bullies!

"Well, well, well. If it isn't our nosy little friend," the one called Steve snickered. Ken could barely find the strength to struggle to his feet.

Phil chuckled. "Maybe he wants to go swimming." Ken glanced into the lake. The water didn't look so inviting now. It was deep here, over his head, and coldly dark in its depths.

"Do you think he'd drown if we pushed him in with his clothes on?" Steve wondered out loud. Ken's heart froze. He pictured himself splashing frantically in the water, soaked clothes tugging him downwards, huge hands pushing him under every time he tried to climb back on the dock.

"How about it, kid? How well can you swim?" Phil's voice dripped with cruelty.

Steve moved an ominous step closer to Ken. Phil inched frightfully closer as well.

An image flashed through the dark fear spreading through Ken's brain. The two umbrellas being jabbed handle first into Steve's stomach. Steve doubling over in pain. A quick shove by Ken and the big boy sprawling backward into the lake. A quick duck as Phil's fist flailed over Ken's head. Another swing with the umbrellas catching Phil in the back of the head, sending him flying into the glistening waters. And Ken running as fast as he could, back to the cabin, to the safety of his mother's arms.

The image faded into black nothingness. And there stood Ken, clutching the umbrellas in his hand, frozen. The darkness in his mind had spread throughout his body, paralyzing every muscle. The boys were now inches from Ken, their reeking cigarette breaths hot on his face.

Ken's eyes raced landward, seeking help. But there was nobody about on this peaceful Sunday morning. Maybe his mom would be looking at the lake from the cabin porch and see him? No—this dock was not visible from the cabin.

There was nothing but the radiant sun sparkling on the topaz water, a few marshmallow clouds drifting lazily in the crystal blue sky, and an occasional bird happily trilling its Sunday morning serenade. And the two dreadful, towering figures closing in on Ken. And now they were reaching out to grab him.

"STOP!"

The clear morning was shattered by a thundering shout. The two bullies moved back in surprise as the words echoed across the silent lake and up the emerald green hillside. Ken flinched, startled. He struggled to understand where the voice had come from. It had come from—him! And there were more words, erupting forth from his deep inner volcano of fear and anger.

"LEAVE ME ALONE!" Ken screamed.

Phil retreated another step, but Steve held his ground.

Again, but not so loud this time, but equally forceful,

"Leave me alone! I never did anything to you!"

"Well," snorted Steve, recovering from his initial shock. "Looks like the little punk knows how to talk. Are you going to call your mommy and daddy now?" He chuckled. "Go ahead. Nobody can hear you out here."

Phil managed a difficult grin, but his face took on a slight touch of uncertainty. Steve's voice oozed renewed evil as he moved toward Ken again.

"So you can talk? You can yell for help when we throw you in."

But Ken wasn't finished. Every muscle had turned to jelly except for the knot in his stomach and his vocal cords.

"My mom and dad know what you did. I told them."

Steve swore at Ken. "I told you we'd kill you if you told them. Now we have to kill your mom and dad, too." His face was painted with rage and his right hand gripped powerfully on Ken's shoulder.

"It's too late. My dad's gone to the police to tell them. Let go of me." Ken pulled away from Steve's suddenly weakened grasp.

"You're lying!" hissed Steve, but the glare in his eyes was as much from fear as anger now.

"Hey man, we're finished," choked Phil. "Let's get out of here."

"I don't care, man. This kid's screwed us. He's going to pay." Steve reached once more for Ken. Ken stepped back.

"If you hurt me, you'll be in even more trouble." Ken's words were clear and firm. Despite the trembling in every muscle of his body, his thoughts and voice were steady, as if some unknown being had taken over from inside.

"He's right. Leave him alone," pleaded Phil. "Come on, let's go."

"I'm going home," stated Ken. Summoning every cubic inch of strength he could find, Ken took a step forward. Amazingly, his tormentors stepped back.

Ken forced himself to continue to walk away, one shaky leg in front of the other. He tried to hold his head as high and straight as he could. He expected any moment for vicious hands to fall upon him and fling him into the chilly water. But there was no sound behind him except for the nervous click of a cigarette lighter. Ken didn't turn, but he sensed that a cloud of smoke was rising above the two boys. Ken's dad had told him that when smokers became nervous or stressed out, they reached for the comfort of a cigarette to suck on. How sad for them, Ken had thought.

Then, just as Ken was about to step to the safety of the shore, a harsh voice grabbed out at him from behind.

"Hey kid!" This time Ken couldn't help himself from turning. He expected to see the bullies lumbering down the dock in a final attempt to stop him. But the boys were still where they had been, heads low, lost in their smoky cloud of worry.

It was Phil who had called him. Much more softly now: "You're OK kid." And once more, almost inaudibly, "You're OK kid. You win."

Ken said nothing but turned homeward. A smile almost crossed his face. Something inside felt like hollering out in relief: "I won! I WON!!"

But it hadn't been a contest. And it hadn't been a fight or a battle. It had been fear and terror and nightmares and his body was still shaking. And his breath, which had been so under control and firm only moments ago, now struggled in and out in ragged gasps and sobs. No, he hadn't won anything. He had survived. That was all.

Once out of sight of the dock, Ken began to run. He wanted nothing more than to be home in his mothers' arms. And he didn't want to take any chances on the boys changing their minds and coming after him.

As Ken reached the top of the stairs past the auditorium and turned onto the muddy path, he slowed down. There was no sound of pursuit. He felt fairly safe now. Besides, his body refused to run anymore. It had been drained of energy by the trauma of the encounter with the bullies.

As Ken plodded on, his mind began reliving the events of the morning. From deep down inside, perhaps from where the brave voice had come, a new thought arose. Perhaps he *had* won. Ken had just been more terrified than he had ever been in his entire life. He had felt fear in every molecule of his body, from the top of his head to the tips of his toes.

But he had overcome his fears. He'd beaten that ugly, jumbled jelly mess of panic that had captured him. Yes, he thought—he had won! HE *HAD* WON! And this time—through the shaking and the tears and the sobs and the gasps—Ken *did* smile.

EPIGLOGUE

SUNDAY AFTERNOON

"What's going to happen to those guys?" Ken wanted to know.

The Alexanders were seated around the dining table, trying to concentrate on a late lunch. Because of the excitement and confusion of the morning, they had decided to remain at the cabin an extra night. A chance to relax, settle tense nerves—to recover together from the tensions of the past two days. The taxi company had been notified of the new departure time after a quick hike into Nojiri Village. A visit to the grocery store to replenish supplies was planned for later in the afternoon.

"I asked the policemen the same thing," answered Mr. Alexander between bites of a now very stale piece of toast covered with margarine and cinnamon and sugar. "Of course the two guys are minors."

"Miners? They dig in the dirt for gold and stuff?"

"No, minors. Not adults yet."

"I know," said Ken. "Just kidding."

Ken was slowly recovering his sense of humor. He had been going through wild mood changes since the two teens had been taken away by the police. Relieved and ecstatic one moment. Then overcome with horrible images and leftover fear the next. He suddenly felt an overwhelming need for a hug and crowded onto his mother's lap. Soft, warm arms enclosed him.

"*Daijobu yo.*" [It's OK.] Mrs. Alexander's words were firm, confident. Ken felt an additional hand on his shoulder.

"It's OK, Ken." Mr. Alexander said, stroking Ken's shoulders and patting his head. "It's all over. This time it's really all over." His words were gently reassuring.

The policemen had questioned Ken thoroughly, prodding for all the details of his experience, and especially for Ken's memories of what he had overheard the two boys talking about. Mr. Alexander recounted his clandestine hike up the hill to the cabin where the boys were staying. The officers had found the two inside the building, attempting to hide.

Ken turned to look at his father. Mr. Alexander sat down again.

"So what's going to happen to those boys?" Ken repeated the question.

"Well, they'll probably be held by the police until their parents can be contacted. I understand that their parents are back in the States. The older boy is a student at the American School In Japan in Tokyo. The other guy, Phil I guess his name is, used to be, but his family moved back to the U.S. a year ago. He came to Japan for the summer to stay with Steve. Both of them got out of school in May, so they could come up here in the off season. Steve's parents own the cabin where the boys were staying."

"So Steve was meeting Phil at the airport when I saw them first?" Ken interrupted.

"Right. I guess Steve has been coming up here every summer off season. He brings a different friend each time and they find a cabin to rob and trash."

"But why would they do something like that?" Ken wondered.

"Boredom. Parents who are too busy to care about their kids. Something like that. And some natural nastiness I guess. Anyway, the boys always come up here at night so no one can see them. You can ride a motorcycle when you're sixteen in Japan, so they both came up on Steve's motorcycle. They didn't expect us to be up here this summer, and they sure didn't expect to run into you, Ken. You know, you helped to solve the mystery of the damaged cabins. You're kind of a hero."

Ken smiled at this. He didn't think of himself as a hero. But it felt good to know that he had helped to solve a mystery.

"Will the boys go to jail?" Ken had one more question.

"They might for awhile. But probably not too long because they're young and they confessed to the police and said they're sorry. But they and their parents will have to pay for all the damage. And the boys will probably be banned from Nojiri forever. No more trashing cabins."

Ken was pleased with this answer. The two bullies deserved to be punished. He smiled again at the thought of the two in jail. He slid out of his mother's arms and ambled out onto the porch. Plopping into one of the wicker chairs that sat there, he gazed out at the azure blue of the lake and sky. Leftover raindrops still fell from overhead trees, plip plopping on the cabin's tin roof. Ken felt serene. Yes, the past two days had been full of turmoil. But it was now over and he had bravely beaten the two bullies. Around him, nature seemed to be heaving a sigh of relief. Ken was content and happy. All was well.

Inside the cabin Mrs. Alexander hummed a happy tune as she cleared some of the lunch dishes. The family had survived two tempests—the *taifuu* and the ordeal her son had gone through. She also was content and full of joy. All was well.

As for Mr. Alexander, he was smiling broadly as he finished his crusty toast. He was relieved that the interrogation by the policemen was over. And, best of all, he now knew—finally knew!—what he would write his book about. He, too, was content and happy. All was well.

AUTHOR'S NOTE

I first started writing this novel in 1999. For some reason, not even known to me, I put this work away for 20 years and only finished it in 2019. Much has changed in Japan since 1999, so please keep that in mind when reading this book.

Non-smokers' rights have increased dramatically in Japan. And the Shinkansen ("bullet train") has replaced many of the *tokkyuu* trains. Shadowy figures do not sell telephone cards in Ueno any more. Also, nowadays all passengers at Narita Airport are able to deplane from their airplanes directly into the terminals. And foreigners are no longer directed to gates labeled "ALIENS" when passing through immigration. In addition, ticket punchers in stations have been replaced by automated ticket reading machines in most stations.

Most of the other details are based on real occurrences, other than the main character's encounters (and other than the legends, of course!).

CPSIA information can be obtained
at www.ICGtesting.com
Printed in the USA
LVHW080511150420
653530LV00018B/1574

9 781977 222824